THIEF

OF

FATE

Also by Jude Deveraux and Tara Sheets

CHANCE OF A LIFETIME
AN IMPOSSIBLE PROMISE

For additional books by
New York Times bestselling author Jude Deveraux,
visit her website, www.judedeveraux.com.

For additional books by Tara Sheets,
visit her website, www.tarasheets.com.

JUDE DEVERAUX

AND TARA SHEETS

THIEF
OF
FATE

mira

ISBN-13: 978-0-7783-3358-6

Thief of Fate

For questions and comments about the quality of this book, please contact us at CustomerService@Harlequin.com.

Mira
22 Adelaide St. West, 41st Floor
Toronto, Ontario M5H 4E3, Canada
BookClubbish.com

Printed in U.S.A.

Recycling programs
for this product may
not exist in your area.

For everyone who believes in the power of true love

THIEF
OF
FATE

PROLOGUE

"YOU'RE BROODING." SAMAEL STRETCHED HIS snowy wings, frowning down at his associate. He couldn't remember the last time—if ever—he'd seen Agon so pensive.

"Am I?" The dark-haired angel was slumped in an overstuffed recliner with his chin in his hand. He swiveled back and forth, the tips of his wings displacing wisps of fog as they trailed against the wall of mist.

Agon's gloomy countenance was a sharp contrast to the bright area rug spread across the floor. Heedless of Samael's grumbled protests, Agon had taken a keen interest in decorating the Chamber of Judgment, evidenced not only by the rug and recliner, but also his newest acquisition: a pair of ridiculous, lumpy seats Agon called "bags of beans," or some such nonsense. The place was beginning to look less like an ethereal portal between worlds and more like an odd clubhouse in the sky.

Samael plucked a fluffy bit of down clinging to his blond hair. "You're shedding feathers, too. This is not like you."

Agon tried to give him a reassuring smile. The failed attempt was even more alarming than his uncharacteristic melancholy.

In the centuries Samael had known him, Agon always had a sunny disposition. He remained ever the optimist about human nature, full of lighthearted hope and the infinite conviction that mankind was redeemable, and love would prevail.

"It seems I've become quite attached to our wayward rogue," Agon said with a sigh. "Liam's heartache is beginning to take its toll on me." He twitched a wing, sending several more feathers sifting to the floor.

"The rogue's journey has always been a gamble," Samael reminded him as he paced the chamber. "You knew it from the moment he sailed through the fog and landed at our feet. Liam O'Connor's propensity to fall back into old patterns and resort to selfish behavior should come as no surprise. It's nothing we haven't seen before."

"I know," Agon said glumly. "It's just hard to watch him fail."

Samael suddenly felt an odd tingle along the curve of his upper wing and watched in consternation as one of his own feathers floated to the floor. Now him, too? This wouldn't do at all. For hundreds of years Samael had worked at the Department of Destiny, and he'd always prided himself on his unaffected, steadfast disposition, and his ability to pass judgment with somber, dignified grace. Emotions were tricky things, and not at all useful in his line of work.

"Enough of this." Samael slapped his hands together and drew a clipboard from a pocket of mist. "We shall seek solace in the bracing rigor of a good day's work. Now, it says here—"

A small hatch in the mist swung open, and a white cat sauntered in from the fog.

Samael gave Agon a stern look of disapproval. "Must you invite that thing here?"

"He only visits on occasion." Agon grinned as the cat, Angel, jumped into his lap. "They think he's prowling the neighbor-hood, so he won't be missed."

"The celestial Department of Destiny is no place for such creatures."

"Nonsense. Cats have always straddled the line between this world and that." Agon's face regained some of his usual cheer as he smoothed the purring cat's fur. "It's common knowledge. Even humans suspect it."

Samael opened his mouth to argue, but the cat seemed to lift Agon's spirits, so he refrained. Muttering to himself that he was going soft, he waved a hand as a window to Liam's current life appeared in the wall of mist.

Liam was lounging in the passenger seat of Cora McLeod's car, a soft smile playing about his lips. Cora spoke with ani-mated hand gestures as she drove, her blond curls blowing in the breeze. It was impossible not to notice the soul-deep admi-ration Liam held for her, and the pure masculine desire brew-ing in his dark eyes. He was drinking her in—the gentle curve of her mouth, the delicate line of her slender neck, the feathery crescents of her eyelashes—like he was a man dying of thirst, and she was a shimmering oasis just out of reach.

"Even a blind person could see how much he loves her," Agon said wistfully. "If only he could learn what it is to be utterly selfless to atone for his past. I wish there was more we could do to help him restore the balance. Perhaps—"

"We've already done too much," Samael interrupted. "You saw the orders from on high this morning. We weren't supposed to show him the future, and now we can no longer interfere. There's nothing left to do but watch and wait. This could be the end of the line for him…and countless others."

"But humans are wonderfully unpredictable." Agon snuggled

the cat closer, resting his chin atop its furry head. "He may surprise us yet. If Liam truly loves her, then he will not fail."

"From your lips to the boss's ears," Samael said, ignoring the twinge in his wing as another feather floated to the floor. "Godspeed, Liam O'Connor."

1

LOVE WAS PATIENT. LOVE WAS KIND. IT WAS A GREAT many things, Liam knew. But he wasn't convinced the heart-shaped, vibrating bed with the coin slot on the motel nightstand that read Love Machine: 25 Cents for Three Minutes fell into any of those categories. Still, he found the concept intriguing enough to search his pockets for a quarter, just to be sure.

"Liam," Cora said in exasperation. "A little help over here?" She was crouched on the motel floor, kneeling on a hefty man who was flailing under her knee like a beached octopus. The man was almost twice her size, but the stench of whiskey and marijuana wafting through the dingy room, not to mention the lines of white powder on a hand mirror beside the bed, explained why he was such a mess. Wally Jensen was good and bolloxed.

"We need to get him over there so I can question him." Cora pointed to a red velvet chair with cigarette burns on the arm-rests. Like everything else in the place, it had seen better days.

The Fantasy Palace, a seedy establishment just north of down-town Providence Falls, was little more than a roadside motel. It had been there since the early seventies, and from the looks of the shag carpet, geometric wallpaper, and stained popcorn ceiling, it hadn't changed much. From the outside, it looked like a cartoon castle, complete with two turrets and a faded banner waving in the wind.

Each "luxury" motel room was designed in a different theme, like Kingdom of Camelot, Space Odyssey, Tropical Escape, and Wild West. But according to the brochure on the TV stand, this honeymoon suite, the Lover's Dream, was the ultimate upgrade. It was steeped in shades of crimson, from the lacquered headboard and ruffled pillows to the sparkly curtains and feather boa lampshades. The overkill of blood reds on every surface gave the room an almost sinister vibe, and while it did seem like someplace from a dream, Liam wasn't sure it was a very good one.

"You ruined my vacation," Wally grumbled. He was somewhere in his early forties, but the sagging jowls, nicotine-stained teeth, and bloodshot eyes made him appear much older. "Scared off my girlfriend, and now she's gone."

"Come, man. We're not that scary." Liam gripped Wally under the arms and hauled him off the floor. "I'm sure any woman of yours would have to be made of far sterner stuff than that." He tried to sound encouraging, but he'd seen Wally's girlfriend peeking through the window when they'd first arrived. She'd bolted from the room, jumped into a Camaro with a dented fender, and peeled off down the street without looking back. They'd called in her license plate, so she wouldn't get far, but it was clear Wally's vacation was officially over.

Once Wally was seated, Cora placed her hands on her hips and gave him a hard stare. Today she'd pulled her blond curls into a high ponytail, which only served to accentuate her delicate features and guileless blue eyes. Liam wondered how often people underestimated her as a police officer. She looked neither formidable nor intimidating, but maybe that was her greatest weapon. No one ever expected the steely core of determination hidden beneath Cora's sweet demeanor until it was too late.

Pride swelled in Liam's chest for this woman who'd captured his heart. He'd loved her across lifetimes and would go on loving her, even after he was gone. *Which will be soon*, he reminded himself. He had only one month left to help Cora fall in love with her intended soul mate, Finley Walsh, and by God, he would succeed. After what the angels had shown him, he could not—no, he *would* not—fail.

"Mr. Jensen, a lot of people are looking for you," Cora said. "The Booze Dogs know you spray-painted over their security cameras the night their money was stolen. They're hunting you down, as we speak."

Wally tried to lurch to his feet, but Liam stopped him.

"Don't bother denying it," Cora continued. "After you went missing from the compound, they searched your room and found paint on your clothes that matched the paint on the cameras. Now you're on their radar, but we've found you first. It must be your lucky day."

"Luck?" Wally snorted. "My girlfriend took off, and now you pigs are breathing down my neck."

"Aye, *luck*." Liam pierced him with a glare. "What do you think those bikers would've done to you if they'd found you first?" The motorcycle club's president, Eli Shelton, was not what anyone would call a merciful man. Rumor had it that the Booze Dogs took care of their own problems with a twisted sense of rough justice. Ever since Eli discovered someone had stolen almost two hundred thousand dollars from his compound, he'd been out for blood.

This seemed to sober Wally, and he sagged in the chair. "How'd you know where to find me, anyway?"

"We didn't," Cora said. "We were answering a domestic disturbance call. You and your girlfriend were partying a little too loudly in here and one of the maids saw your drug paraphernalia through the window. Guess it's our lucky day, too."

Wally dropped his face into his hands with a garbled curse.

"Tell us about the night you took the money," Liam demanded. "Who were you working with?"

"No one," Wally said. "Somebody paid me to take out the cameras. That's it. That's all I did."

Cora raised her brows. "Good luck convincing our captain of that."

The city of Providence Falls had suffered two murders in as many months: the first was John Brady, a prominent businessman, and the second was Lindsey Albright, a young college girl who'd been dating a boy from the motorcycle club. So far, the police had no strong evidence to connect the two deaths, but Captain Boyd Thompson was convinced the bikers were behind everything. Cora and Liam had a different theory, but they agreed to keep their suspicions to themselves for now.

"Two people may have been killed over this money, and we're looking right at the Booze Dogs." Cora paused to let that sink in, then shrugged. "Maybe we won't have to look very far. Maybe it was you."

"No way! I'm not a killer." Wally's face grew red enough to match the decor. "And I didn't steal no money from the club, either. Only an idiot would steal from Eli Shelton. Do I look stupid to you?"

She refrained from commenting. "Who paid you to paint over those cameras, Mr. Jensen?"

"I don't know."

Liam scoffed. "You expect us to believe—"

"I got a text," Wally wailed. "Said if I blocked the security cameras that night, I'd make a quick two grand, no questions asked."

"So, you took a bribe to betray your own club," Cora said. "Without even knowing why."

"It wasn't like that," Wally said in frustration. "I figured one of the guys wanted the cameras out so he could sneak around with someone's old lady. No harm, no foul. It wasn't supposed to be a big deal. Look, my girlfriend and I have been on the rocks for a while. I thought if I spent some money on her and took her someplace nice like this, she'd stick around. I just wanted to show her a good time." He looked at Liam. "You get that. Right, bro?"

Liam glanced at the mirrored ceiling above the heart-shaped bed. The Fantasy Palace had some interesting amenities, to be sure, but it wouldn't have been his first choice to impress a woman.

"How did this anonymous person pay you, Mr. Jensen?" Cora asked.

"They left an envelope of money on my windshield the next morning. I thought that'd be the end of it, but then Eli found out all that money was stolen, and all hell broke loose at the compound. People started fighting and pointing fingers. I got spooked. So, I told my girl we'd go on a little vacation, and I took off."

"And you came to the Fantasy Palace." Cora looked skeptical. "This isn't much of a hideout, Mr. Jensen. It's not even outside the city."

"I know, but my girlfriend always wanted to come here," Wally said. "And I wanted to prove I'd do anything for her."

Liam frowned. "Even risk your own neck?"

"My neck's never been worth much." Wally slouched in the chair, looking more miserable by the second. "Anyway, I love her. What good is my life if she ain't in it?"

Liam had no answer. How many times had he asked himself the same thing about Cora? Poor man. Wally Jensen was on the wrong side of the law, his life was in danger, and he was in love with a woman he couldn't keep. He'd made his bed and had to lie in it, but Liam couldn't help feeling a stab of pity for the man. Fate was a fickle bedfellow, and every soul was just one twist away from either happiness or heartache.

"I was hoping everything would blow over, and they'd forget about me," Wally said, rubbing his chin. "I was going to lie low here for a while, then take my girlfriend to California, where my cousin is. But I don't know. I haven't figured it all out yet."

"Well, there's no need," Cora said briskly. "You're coming to the station with us."

To Liam's surprise, Wally sagged in relief. "You're locking me up?"

"That's correct, Mr. Jensen." Cora snapped handcuffs on his wrists while reading his rights.

They escorted Wally to the car without a struggle. Sloshed as he was, he still seemed to have enough self-preservation to recognize jail was the lesser of two evils. Better safe with them than facing the Booze Dogs' method of justice. Maybe if his luck held, the law would shield him long enough for Eli Shelton to forget all about his betrayal. Not likely. Liam knew that would take a miracle, but he hoped, for Wally's sake, he had one coming.

On the way back to the station, Liam contemplated his own poor luck. Given his lack of success over the past couple of months, and the fact that Cora was still no closer to loving Finn, the future was looking dimmer with every passing hour. Still...

If there was even just a *sliver* of a miracle out there for him—he didn't need much, just a leftover scrap or a crumb from the celestial table—Liam would snatch it and run like the thief that he was.

―――――――――――――――
―――――――――――――――

2

"I CAN'T BELIEVE THEY LET THAT SLIMEBALL WALK free," Cora muttered under her breath late Thursday afternoon. She stormed out of the police station alone, barely able to contain her anger. Captain Thompson had just announced Magnus Blackwell was released without charges.

Marching across the parking lot, Cora kicked a rock in frustration, sending it skidding under the dumpster. Then she kicked another, pretending it was Magnus's backside. She'd only dated the crooked attorney a couple of times before she'd discovered the stolen money under his bed. After he'd tried to bribe her to keep silent, they'd fought, and in the struggle, Cora had almost drowned. If it hadn't been for Liam and Finn arriving at Magnus's lake house just in time… She shuddered to think what could've happened.

After he was arrested, Magnus told the police he'd been framed and had no clue about the money. Cora knew it was a flat-out lie, but Magnus had the power of his law firm, Johnston & Knight, behind him. Since there was no clear evidence connecting him to the theft—not even his fingerprints on the stolen cash—he'd somehow managed to evade justice, and now he was out there walking around as if nothing had ever happened.

It irked her. No, it *infuriated* her. The fact that Captain Thompson ordered her to forget Magnus and focus the investigation on the Booze Dogs was like a kick to the kidneys after she was already down. Cora had always respected the captain's expertise and deferred to his better judgment, but not this time. How could a creep like Magnus Blackwell get away with theft and maybe even the murder of two innocent people? Where was the justice in that?

With a growl of frustration, she stomped out of the police station parking lot to speed-walk down the street. Cars whooshed past, the swirling scents of warm asphalt and exhaust fumes mingling with the sharp, crisp scent of freshly mowed grass from the nearby baseball field. For a midsummer afternoon in Providence Falls, it was unseasonably mild, with a light breeze rustling through the maple and poplar trees, but Cora was too annoyed to appreciate the gorgeous weather. With no destination in mind, she strode past storefronts and offices, determined to blow off steam.

Ten minutes later, she was turning down a side street when Liam pulled up beside her in his car. His glossy dark hair was disheveled, and there was a shadow of stubble on his jaw. In a rumpled black shirt and jeans, driving an ancient beige sedan, he really had no business looking hotter than Hades, but the man couldn't seem to help it.

Rolling the passenger window down, Liam eyed her like she was a grenade sans pin. "There you are."

"I'm fine," she insisted, even though he hadn't asked. That was what she was supposed to be, right? Fine, fine, fine. She continued marching down the sidewalk, staring straight ahead.

"I'm inclined to believe you," Liam called, keeping pace with her in his car. "It's only you have a bit of a bloodthirsty gleam in your eye, and I saw a fox with that same look once when I was a wee lad. She was defending her den and almost took my arm off."

Cora gave him the side-eye but kept walking. "No doubt you deserved it."

"Not at all. I was only trying to steal one of her cubs to take home and raise as my hunting hound. She had several, so I didn't think she'd mind, but for some reason, the greedy vixen wasn't feeling charitable." He gave her a crooked grin that somehow managed to puncture the bubble of anger encasing her. Liam could always do that. Her best friend, Suzette, called it "lethal charm," and Cora couldn't deny it.

When she'd first met Liam, she'd done a pretty decent job of ignoring the initial jolt of attraction she'd felt, convincing herself she was immune to men like him. Sure, he was witty and gorgeous, with flashing dark eyes and a body that seemed sculpted from hard hours at the gym, but he wasn't anything special. At least, that was what she told herself. Often. But somehow over the course of the summer, Liam had slipped seamlessly into her life, and now she couldn't imagine living without him. Lord knew the man wasn't a stellar roommate. He was overprotective and stubborn, and he didn't know the first thing about working the dishwasher or folding laundry or paying bills online. But he was perfect in the ways that really mattered. He was kind and trustworthy and surprisingly intuitive. He always seemed to know what she needed, whether it was quiet companionship at the end of a long day, or some lively distraction to lift her spirits.

"Cora, it's going to be okay," Liam said in a melting-honey voice that soothed all her raw edges. "Do you want to get in, so we can talk about it?"

Her shoulders slumped, and she stopped on the sidewalk to face him. "You know that feeling where you just *know* deep down in your bones how things should be, but everything spins out of control, and all you can do is sit back and watch it all go to hell?"

A strong emotion flashed across his face, too fast for her to catch. "I do. Come, and let's go home."

Cora sighed and got in the car, grateful that Liam had brought her purse and jacket from the station. The last thing she wanted was to see the captain right now.

"Talk to me," Liam said, slamming on the accelerator to speed through an intersection on a yellow light.

Cora pressed her hand against the glove compartment, not bothering to comment on his aggressive driving. She'd grown used to it over the past couple of months, and besides, asking him to slow down was as futile as asking the wind not to blow. Liam was a speed demon, but after his expert driving skills had helped save her life, she couldn't fault him for it.

"It's just so disheartening that Captain Thompson isn't on my side about Magnus," Cora said. "We've never been at odds like this before. And now what am I supposed to do if I run into the creep?" Her voice began to rise in frustration. "Act like nothing happened? Like he never hit me? Like I didn't almost die in that lake? Something's going on because none of this sits right with me. He shouldn't be exempt from the law just because he's a hotshot attorney."

Liam punched the accelerator again, weaving through traffic with breakneck precision. He hissed something under his breath that sounded like "swiving" and "pig."

Cora glanced sideways at him. "Now who's got the blood-thirsty gleam in their eye?"

"I can't help it." He scowled at the road. "Every time I think of that night, Cora… You struggling in the water, your head disappearing below the surface—" He broke off as if he couldn't bring himself to speak of it.

Cora stared out the window, willing the bright sky and billowy clouds to dim the memory of that terrible ordeal. She'd been having recurring nightmares about it. The freezing cold water closing in around her. The curling tendrils of dread squeezing her lungs as she started to lose consciousness. It was all too terrible to talk about.

"That rat bastard will get what he deserves," Liam said flatly. "Boyd can dictate what he wants us to do when we're on the clock, but he can't tell us what to do on our own time. Magnus will pay for his crimes, especially when we prove he's connected to the murders."

"That's the million-dollar question, though," Cora said after a long pause. "*Is* he a killer? I just don't know."

Liam stopped at a red light, his face incredulous. "You almost died at his hand."

"But when I set aside my emotions and try to think objectively about that night, I can't be certain he was trying to kill me. Yes, we fought, and I was afraid. Our altercation on the boat dock happened so fast. We both fell into the water by accident. But maybe he would've eventually hauled me to shore, offered me a towel, and tried to reason with me again."

"Or maybe he'd have dragged your dead body into the woods like Lindsey Albright," Liam pointed out. He was cool and controlled behind the wheel, but Cora could see anger riding him hard. It was there in the little things—the hard line of his mouth, the muscle ticking in his jaw, and his white-knuckle grip on the steering wheel as he pulled onto the highway.

She laid her head back on the seat. "All we know for certain is Magnus lied about the stolen money, he's a brilliant attorney, and he's used to manipulating people and situations to get what he wants. If he could do those things without a conscience, then could he be involved in the deaths of two innocent people? I don't know, but I intend to find out."

They slipped into silence as they drove home, the downtown bustle of shops and businesses giving way to quaint, residential neighborhoods. It wasn't until they were turning onto the quiet street where they shared a rental house that Liam said, "We have an ally."

Cora glanced sharply at him. "What are you talking about?"

"There's someone who wants to help us bring Magnus down."

"No, Liam," she said in alarm. "Our plan is a secret. If Captain Thompson finds out, he could take us off the case and bury us in enough paperwork to keep us at our desks for the rest of the year. I've seen him do it before. He's merciless when crossed."

Liam scoffed. "I don't doubt it. Boyd never did like being undermined or outsmarted."

It reminded Cora that Liam and Boyd had been childhood friends in Ireland before life led them in different directions. She couldn't quite imagine them as friends because Liam, for all his fierce protectiveness and occasional bouts of melancholy, was easygoing and quick to laugh. He had an eager curiosity about everything, and a lightness of spirit that made him shine from within. Even though some part of his past still haunted him, he knew how to revel in life's simple pleasures. Captain Thompson, on the other hand, was jaded and stoic and barely ever cracked a smile. Cora couldn't even imagine the captain as a boy. He seemed much older than his years, weighed down by responsibility and perhaps disillusionment. Even his relationship with his wife seemed joyless.

"Our ally won't breathe a word to anyone," Liam assured her

as he drove toward their house. "I spoke with him on the phone before I left the station today, and he's all in."

Cora bristled. "I can't believe you would do that without my—"

"We can trust him," Liam insisted.

"Who?" She couldn't think of a single person she'd trust as much as Liam. The only other person who even came close was—

"Finn." Liam pointed to the man standing in front of their house. "I invited him for dinner so we could discuss it and come up with a plan."

Finn Walsh was leaning against the side of his Porsche, his arms crossed casually as if he had all the time in the world. Cora would bet a million dollars he'd been wearing a suit that day, but the jacket was gone and so was the tie. His white shirt was unbuttoned, leaving the base of his throat bare, and the sleeves were rolled to reveal tanned, sinewy forearms. Now that she knew what he looked like in almost no clothes, she wondered how she'd ever missed how physically fit he was. He was tall and lean with broad shoulders, built like someone who rowed crew or did triathlons in his spare time. Ever since she'd seen him in the cage fight, she hadn't been able to think of him as a stuffed shirt anymore. Yes, he wore designer suits like most of the successful attorneys at Johnston & Knight, but Cora now knew there was another side to Finn—a gritty, rugged, masculine side—she'd never imagined and wouldn't soon forget.

When they were all seated around the kitchen table, Liam passed out beers, idly chatting with Finn about sports cars. It seemed like they'd bonded since the night of her rescue. A month ago, Cora would have sworn the two men were different as night and day, but now she wasn't so sure. Both men had a steely resolve, a propensity to take immediate action when needed, and mysterious pasts they preferred not to talk about. They might seem different on the outside, but in essentials, Cora suspected they were quite similar. Her best friend, Suzette, would never believe it.

"Liam tells me you want to help us bring down Magnus Blackwell." Cora set plates and napkins beside the two large pizzas they'd ordered.

"He can't evade the law this time," Finn said in that clipped tone he usually reserved for the courtroom. Cora was beginning to realize he slipped into attorney mode when he felt the need for control. "I recognize you can't talk about all the details of your investigations, and I respect that, but I want to help in any way I can. This time Magnus has gone too far."

"He swears he's innocent, and there wasn't enough to hold him." Cora bit into a slice of margherita pizza, momentarily distracted by the tangy burst of marinara sauce and fresh herbs.

"It's not just about the money, Cora. He *hurt* you." A muscle clenched in Finn's jaw.

"Which is why the bastard will pay," Liam said. "I don't care how we gather the information. I'll do whatever it takes."

"So will I," Finn said. "I'm moving away at the end of this month, but it won't sit right with me if that man isn't brought to justice before I go. Not if I can help it."

"You shouldn't be leaving at all," Liam said in irritation. "You're needed here more than you realize. Neither of us wants you to go. Isn't that right, Cora?"

"Sure. We don't want you to go, Finn. But I do understand if you have a better job lined up—"

"Hang the bloody job," Liam said with a scowl. "Some things are far more important. Like saving people's lives."

Finn looked surprised and a little confused. "Are you talking about my pro bono work?"

Liam didn't answer. He seemed deeply disturbed. Almost... desperate. He picked at the label on his beer bottle, his troubled gaze a million miles away. What was going on with him?

"I'll keep doing it," Finn assured him. "My new contract in New York still allows me to donate a percentage of my time to the underprivileged who can't afford representation. But for now, if I can help you put him behind bars where he belongs, then I'll consider that paying it forward tenfold." He leaned back in his chair and crossed his arms. "I'm here, and there's still time. A lot can happen in a month."

Liam dipped his head in acknowledgment, then took a healthy swig of beer.

"And after what he did to you, Cora?" Finn's face grew cold and emotionless, reminding her of the night he'd fought as the Jackrabbit. "I'm making this my sole focus."

She suddenly felt a wave of gratitude for both the men sitting at her kitchen table. They were like two sides of the same coin, both warriors at heart, and both so willing to champion her cause.

"There's nothing I'd like more than to jump that man in a dark alley when he least expects it," Liam said fiercely. His pepperoni pizza remained untouched on his plate, which was proof he wasn't kidding around. "I say we rough him up and threaten him at gunpoint. Or we can tie a rope around his ankles and dangle him from a bridge for a few hours. That should get the blood flowing to his brain, so he'll talk. There's this man on TV called the Punisher who—"

"Whoa there, vigilante," Cora said, patting Liam on the shoulder. "As much as I'd like to see Magnus go down, we can't get physical, and we can't threaten him with a loaded weapon."

Liam cocked a brow as if to say, *Watch me.*

"We'll have to be careful how we get our information," Cora

continued. "Magnus isn't stupid, and he's probably going to be more diligent than ever covering his tracks."

"What would you have us do?" Liam asked. "Send him a polite text message with a request for damning information? Men like him never talk unless their lives are threatened, or they stand to lose something they value."

"If he's working with someone, we'll need hard proof," Cora said. "Emails. Phone calls. Pictures."

"I thought about 'creatively procuring' his laptop, but he hasn't come back to Johnston & Knight since his arrest," Finn said. "Apparently, he's taking time off to recuperate from his undeserved hardship."

Cora rolled her eyes. "The only hardship that man suffered was the lack of designer sheets and gourmet meals during his brief stint in lockup."

"I can try to get his laptop when he returns to the office," Finn offered.

Cora shook her head. "We can't wait that long."

"Then we spy on him now," Liam said, thumping the table with his fist. "We can do that thing where you sit in a car and drink coffee and eat food from bags while you watch someone's house."

"A stakeout." Finn gave Liam a strange look. "It's not the worst idea. I have a friend who used to do consulting work. Private investigations. He might have some equipment we can borrow."

Cora paused with her pizza halfway to her mouth. "Surveillance equipment?"

Finn nodded like it was no big thing.

She blinked. "For *spying*."

"Yes."

Cora studied him like she'd never seen him before. First, he was a former underground cage fighting legend, and now he had access to secret surveillance devices? The more she got to know Finn, the more she realized she never really knew him at all. "Who even *are* you?"

His mouth kicked up at the corner. "Just your friendly neighborhood—"

"Don't." Cora pointed her pizza crust at him. "You and I need to have words. I've got a lot of questions for you. But more to the point, we can't just rush out and go all MI6 on Magnus's house. Someone in the neighborhood could see us—or worse, he could catch us. Can you imagine the backlash? We could lose our jobs."

"We won't get caught," Finn assured her. "Anyway, I'm not suggesting we rappel from the ceiling to plant bugs in the bookshelves or anything like that."

Cora folded her arms. "Then what exactly are you suggesting?"

"Nothing too crazy," he said with a shrug. "Some jet packs. Exploding chewing gum. An amphibious car. That sort of thing."

"Uh-huh. Nothing too crazy."

"Just the basics," Finn deadpanned.

She tried not to smile but failed. This teasing, mischievous side of Finn surprised her. He was full of surprises lately.

"Well, that's settled." Liam slapped the table. "Let's drink to it." He rose and walked to the fridge for more beers. "Tomorrow night, then?"

"Works for me," Finn said.

They both looked expectantly at Cora.

She pushed her plate away and finished her drink in one nervous gulp. It was all happening so fast. She'd never participated in a half-baked, harebrained scheme like this. At least, not as a full-grown adult whose professional career was to uphold justice. All it would take was one mistake, and they'd be so screwed. But neither of her partners in crime seemed to have a problem with the plan, and she was out of ideas. Maybe she was over-thinking it, and everything would be great. Maybe they'd actually learn something useful.

"Fine," she said in a rush, before she could change her mind. "But I'm driving."

Finn flashed her a grin and called, "Shotgun."

Liam pulled his head from the fridge and shut the door. "You can't." He gave Finn a look of pure commiseration as he plunked three beers, a half-eaten pie tin of strawberry cheesecake, and a package of Oreos on the table. "She said no weapons, remember?"

Cora closed her eyes, dropped her face into her hands, and began massaging her forehead. Yup. Everything was going to be great.

3

THE WORLD WAS ON FIRE. THE SCENTS OF BURNING GAS AND *gun smoke and decay hung thick in the air, choking Liam until he couldn't breathe. Soldiers marched through a war-torn village in the desert, their boots kicking up dust and shattered glass as they gunned down civilians. Planes bombed oil rigs in the ocean, the fiery explosions silencing hundreds of lives. Protesters dodged bullets and tear gas, rioting as armed tanks rolled down abandoned city streets. Nations were at war. Newspapers and television stations spoke of the great energy crisis. Civil upheaval. Social collapse. Global warming. Image after image shuffled through Liam's mind like a deck of morbid playing cards in a game that was inescapable, and everybody lost. Each scene the angels showed him was startling in its violence, more shocking than anything he'd ever witnessed.*

"No more." Liam tried to shield his eyes, but his hands wouldn't cooperate. His body felt mired in tar, his lungs stinging with acrid soot. "Please, I've seen enough. Make it stop."

"There is no stopping," thousands of voices cried in unison. The noise punched through Liam's bones like cannon blasts. "This is the future, and it's all your fault."

★ ★ ★

Liam awoke gasping, legs tangled in the bedsheets, and heart beating out of his chest. A fine sheen of sweat covered his shaking limbs as he slowly sat up and leaned against the headboard. Through bleary eyes, he checked the clock on his nightstand. It was just past midnight. How unfortunate. He'd never get back to sleep now.

Cursing under his breath, he kicked off the covers, swinging his legs over the side of the bed.

Cora's cat, Angel, made a grumbling meow, poking its head from beneath the pile of blankets near the foot of the bed. He gave Liam one of those lofty stares of disapproval that all cats had perfected since birth.

"Sorry," Liam said in a hoarse whisper. "It's the nightmare again."

Ever since the evening of Finn's house party, Liam had been plagued with images of what the angels had revealed. Before, he'd roiled with jealousy over Finn, secretly hoping to outwit fate and keep Cora for himself. But now he carried this crushing burden of unwanted responsibility overshadowed by an inescapable sense of doom. This wasn't just about him anymore. No matter how much he hated the idea of Cora loving another man for the rest of her life, Liam had to see it through.

"It breaks protocol for us to show you the future," Agon had explained. "But you need to understand the magnitude of the task we've given you, and the dire consequences should you fail. Cora is going to have a child who will someday bring much-needed peace to the world. She and Finn will teach their child the meaning of kindness and compassion. Honesty and integrity. Love. All these things will nurture the young one's brilliant mind, fostering a deep-seated passion for helping humanity and the earth. The child is destined to unravel the mystery of cold fusion. Unlimited energy would become available to all. Tensions

between nations would ease, and the earth would begin to heal. This was meant to happen back in your time, rogue. Had you not taken Cora from her intended fiancé in 1844, war and countless tragedies might've been avoided."

Liam bowed his head, crushed by guilt as the memory of Agon's words washed over him. He had no knowledge of modern science, but he could still imagine a world with unlimited energy. Everything would change for the better. Back in his old life, horses and carriages, oil lamps and candles, even coal-burning stoves, were luxuries he could not afford. He'd never forget the bone-deep chill of winter in Ireland, huddling with his brother's family in their tiny cottage. The dying fire in the hearth was often their only source of light after nightfall, and the cold was so invasive, spidery fingers of frost would creep through cracks in the thatched roof until their breaths misted in the air.

Unwilling to dwell on such dark thoughts, Liam rose from the bed and went to the kitchen in search of a drink. Sometimes, a shot of good Irish whiskey was the only thing that could ease his spirits. Either that, or—

"I didn't expect to see you awake." Cora's soft voice was sweeter and far more comforting than anything he'd get from a bottle. She was curled on the living room sofa with a mug of hot tea. The crisp, herbal scents of bergamot and lemon permeated the air around her. Wrapped in a faded quilt with her hair a tumble of ringlets around her delicate face, she looked younger and more vulnerable than usual.

It reminded him of the first time he'd ever seen her. She'd been reading a book in bed, surrounded by a mountain of ruffled pillows, when he'd climbed through her bedroom window like the lowly thief he was. From the moment he saw her, she'd been like a beacon of light in his dark life, smiling at him like an angel as she chattered away and helped bind his wounded foot. He'd been speechless, at first, wondering if he'd accidentally stumbled through some back door into heaven.

Cora was never for him; he knew that. A poor thief who had nothing but the ragged shirt on his back wasn't meant for someone like her, but somehow, they'd become friends, anyway. The day she admitted she loved him, the day they decided to run away together… He'd known it was wrong, but she'd stolen his heart and he couldn't give her up. A starving man doesn't turn down a feast fit for a king, no more than a pauper would walk away from a cavern full of riches, and Cora's love was better than any of that. She was every dream he'd never dared hope for. If only he'd known how that dream would end.

The fateful night they'd tried to flee on horseback brought with it another crushing wave of guilt. It had been raining, and her horse had slipped. One moment, they'd been racing toward their shining future together, and the next… Liam swallowed hard. He'd held her for hours after she fell. He'd begged her not to leave him. Pleading with God, and every saint he could remember. He'd bargained with the only things he had—his life, his soul—promising to give her up, to take her back home and never see her again. But his prayers went unanswered. She'd died in his arms, taking his heart with her. What happened afterward barely had any meaning. He'd been too stricken with grief to defend himself, and too numb to realize the danger he was in until it was too late.

"Insomnia?" Cora asked, drawing him from his dark thoughts.

Liam blinked as the memories faded. The past was over, and she was here now. Strong and healthy and gloriously alive. "Something like that."

"Join the club," she said with a weary sigh. "I've spent the last few hours staring at the ceiling and finally gave up. My mind just keeps spinning with everything going on at work, and when I do manage to fall asleep..." She trailed off and took a sip of tea.

Liam walked into the living room and took the other side of the sofa. "What is it?"

She tugged at a loose string on the edge of the quilt. "Let's just say, my dreams aren't the best company lately. I'm told it's common in situations like mine. I guess my brain wants to replay the whole 'submerged underwater and struggling to breathe' thing."

"Christ, Cora." He'd been so wrapped up in his own problems he hadn't even stopped to think she could've been plagued by nightmares after what happened at the lake. As a dedicated police officer, Cora always acted so strong and focused, but of course she'd be struggling on the inside. People didn't just bounce back from near-death experiences like nothing happened. What the hell was wrong with him? He should've known. He suddenly wanted to reach out and gather her into his arms. The urge to do it was so strong he clenched his hands into fists and reminded himself of all the reasons he couldn't get too close.

"I'll be fine," she said with a shrug. "It's just one of those things. I'm sure it'll fade soon enough."

Liam noted the shadows beneath her eyes and the slight strain around her mouth. He hated that she felt the need to pretend with him. If he hadn't been watching so closely, he'd have missed the slight tremble in her hand when she set down her mug of tea. How many other signs had he missed?

On impulse, he reached for her. "Come here, *macushla*." To hell with the past and the future, this was *now*, and she needed comforting. He'd almost lost her that night at the lake house, and he had to reassure himself she was okay.

Cora squeaked in surprise as Liam reached across the sofa and dragged her toward him, blanket and all. He slung his arm around her shoulders and pulled her beside him, reveling in the delighted laughter that escaped her. When she snuggled deeper into the quilt and relaxed against him with a contented sigh, he wanted to freeze the moment and live in it forever. It felt so *right*, holding her close like this.

"I'm sorry I didn't think to ask how you were feeling," he said quietly. "I've been too focused on my own problems. Forgive me for being such a selfish jackass."

"You're not," she said, nudging his shoulder with hers. "Don't say that. You're the one who saved me, remember?"

"And Finn," he reminded her. "If it hadn't been for him and his fast car, we wouldn't have arrived when we did."

"Yes, you both showed up just in time."

And thank all that was holy for that. Liam gave her shoulders a tight squeeze, as though to reassure himself she was alive and well. Finn had helped save her. He'd fought Magnus in the lake while Liam dragged Cora out of the water. It was the first time Liam had seen Finn fight, and the man was no slouch. He'd fought to protect Cora, and Liam couldn't help but be grateful to him. Who knew his opinion of Finn would change so drastically over just a few months?

"But today, when I found out they let Magnus go?" Cora made a frustrated, kitten-like growl in the back of her throat that made Liam smile. "I was *so* mad."

"Aye, you had steam coming out of your ears. That's how I found you in my car when you stormed out of the station. I just followed the trail of smoke."

She pursed her lips. "I'm still mad, you know. If I wasn't certain Magnus was lying, I'd never agree to go behind the captain's back. I mean, come on. A secret stakeout with shady surveillance equipment?" She shook her head. "We're going off the rails."

"We're taking matters into our own hands," Liam said. "Don't let Boyd's opinion get to you. The man is dead wrong, and we're going to prove it."

"It's not just that." She rested her head on his shoulder. "I was also mad at myself today. When I heard they let Magnus walk, the first thing I felt was fear. And I *hated* that. Logically, I recognize he'd be too stupid to live if he tried to approach me or do anything, and we all know he's not an idiot. But for some reason, my subconscious mind hasn't gotten the memo, because after I fall asleep…the nightmare comes, and his face is front and center."

Anger snaked through Liam's gut, coiling to strike at the man who'd caused her so much fear. Someone as brave and strong as Cora should never have to be afraid of a low-life brute like Magnus Blackwell. "That scum of the earth will never come near you again," Liam said fiercely. "If he even so much as looks in your direction, I'll knock that blackguard's block off and toss it to the crows. Then I'll throw the rest of his worthless carcass into a bog and dance a bloody jig around it."

Cora's lips twitched, and her eyes sparkled with mirth. "That sounds fearsome indeed."

"You mock me?"

"Never." The sweet sound of her laughter chased away the darkness until the sadness of the past and uncertainty of the future disappeared, and for a moment, it was just the two of them—no souls at risk, no destinies hanging in the balance— just a man and a woman in a cozy home sharing a quiet evening together. Liam wanted to stop time and stay in this moment for as long as he could, but time had never been on his side. It marched relentlessly onward, deaf and blind to the wishes of mere mortals, and heedless of the broken hearts scattered in its wake. Still, he was grateful for every stolen hour. Moments like this were etched into his memory with diamond-sharp clarity, so he could take them out later and remember.

"Can you really dance a jig?" she asked with an impish grin.

"Of course, woman. I'm Irish."

"Prove it."

His forehead creased. "That I'm Irish?"

"No, the jig. I know you're Irish. Your accent gets stronger whenever you get worked up or say violent things."

"Well, that's no surprise," Liam said, propping his feet on the coffee table. "We can be a right bloodthirsty lot, especially when our kinfolk are threatened."

"Kinfolk." Cora repeated the word as if it amused her. "We crazy Americans just say 'family.'"

"Aye, our people." Liam absently smoothed a curl from her forehead, the tip of his finger sliding featherlight across her temple. "Loved ones."

Cora slowly tilted her face toward his. Her smile was incandescent, glowing with warmth and more precious to him than sunlight. Sitting this close to her was intoxicating. Liam could feel the soft exhalation of her breath against his cheek, and the silken brush of her hair where it trailed over his arm. Her eyes were the summer sky from his childhood, a bright, endless blue that made him want to spread wings and fly. She reminded him of what it felt like to hope, and she made him yearn for home—not the one he'd left behind, but the one they'd both imagined together.

"Liam," she whispered, shifting to face him. The blanket suddenly slipped off her shoulders to reveal part of a silky black chemise. Edged in delicate lace, it skimmed over the upper swell of her breasts, the thin straps clinging to her shoulders with nothing but a hope and a prayer.

Liam sucked in a breath, firing off a silent prayer of his own for strength to resist her. What in the name of Jesus, Mary, and Joseph was she wearing, and why the hell couldn't he see the rest of it? He eyed the offending quilt, willing it to disappear.

"I know it's only been a few months," she began shyly. "But sometimes I feel like I've known you forever. I never expected to feel this way when we met. But then I got to know you and trust you, and now I'm just so glad we have each other." Her soft voice brushed across his senses in pleasurable waves, the cadence like a siren's song to a desperate sailor lost at sea. "You and I, we're good together. Don't you think?"

He nodded like a dumbstruck fool. So, *so* very good.

Cora's gaze slid to his mouth, the line of his neck, and the hollow at the base of his throat. She sucked her bottom lip, gently tugging the plump softness between her teeth until it slipped free.

Liam's mind blanked. Heat rushed through his veins until every muscle in his body ached with the need to touch her. He wanted so badly to kiss her. To taste her. To hold her close and sip the soft sighs of pleasure from her lips. It had been so long, and she was so warm and sweet and *his*. He knew it. She felt it. Would it be so bad to steal just this one moment?

Somewhere down the hall, Cora's cat, Angel, let out a loud, forlorn meow.

Warning bells suddenly clanged inside Liam's head. With Herculean effort, he slammed his eyes shut and called forth every harrowing scene the angels had shown him—the explosions and the chaos and the people in despair. He yanked the images around him like armor, shielding himself from temptation so he would remember why this couldn't happen. Not with her. Not like this.

Cora leaned closer and whispered, "Maybe we should—"

"Get some rest," Liam blurted. He stood up so fast she almost toppled into the spot he'd been sitting. In three strides, he was across the room, his chest heaving with unsteady breaths as he pretended to check the clock on the mantel. "It's late. We're going to need our wits about us tomorrow if we're to spy on Magnus." He tossed the man's name into the air like a bomb to kill the mood. "I'm going to sleep now. You should go, too."

Cora lowered her gaze, but not before he caught the flash of disappointment in her eyes.

Liam cursed under his breath. What he would give to trade places with Finn so he could spend the rest of his life making her happy! Then he'd never have to see that look on her face again.

"All right." Cora shrugged off the quilt and stood, revealing a pair of black silk pajamas that were flimsy scraps of nothing— just a whisper of a top with lace cutouts and matching shorts that emphasized her lush curves and long, toned legs.

Liam froze, unable to tear his gaze from the exquisite vision standing before him. He'd seen Cora in revealing clothes before, but never in something so intimately sensual, and never in the middle of the night when they were alone like this.

She tossed her hair from her shoulder, lifted her chin, and glided from the room like a queen. "Sweet dreams."

He waited until he heard her door shut down the hall. Then he collapsed onto the sofa with a groan, dragging the discarded quilt over his head. Cora's subtle scent of warm vanilla and lavender enveloped him like a cloud, tormenting him for the rest of his sleepless night.

4

"AND THAT'S IT," CORA SAID WITH A SIGH. "HE BA-sically ran screaming like I'd suddenly grown horns and a tail." She stole a french fry off her friend Suzette's plate and dragged it through her chocolate milkshake before popping it in her mouth.

"Okay, first of all, that's disgusting." Suzette wrinkled her nose at Cora's choice of comfort food. They were seated at Shakey's Burgers for lunch on Friday. It was an old-fashioned diner with pleather seats, laminated menus, and an ancient juke-box in the corner. The eighties song "Love Is a Battlefield" mingled with the sounds of boisterous chatter, the clink of pans from the back kitchen, and the occasional jangle of bells hang-ing above the entry door. The place wasn't chic or hip by any stretch of the imagination, but Cora had gone there with her father ever since she was a kid, and it was still one of her favor-ite restaurants.

"Second of all," Suzette said. "A man like Liam O'Connor does not run screaming from anything, so I know you're ex-aggerating."

"Fine, but he did jump off the couch right when things started getting interesting," Cora said. "We were sitting so close, and when I leaned forward and the quilt slipped from my shoulders, I swear I thought he was going to kiss me."

"He didn't even try?"

Cora shook her head glumly and planted her chin in her hand. That morning on the commute to work, Liam had been quiet and withdrawn. Cora didn't want to make small talk, so she'd pretended to read the news on her phone. By the time they arrived at the station, they hit the ground running, and within a couple of hours, it was business as usual. Any awkwardness had melted away, but Cora still couldn't shake her disappointment. She knew Liam had feelings for her. When she'd impulsively kissed him that night at the lake, he'd returned the kiss with an eager, demanding heat that scorched her from the inside out. There was no mistaking his ardor. Cora had hoped it was the start of something great between them, something they could build on, but so far, nothing.

"Maybe Liam misread the situation," Suzette said, smoothing her shiny red hair. She'd flat-ironed it today, and with her sultry eye shadow and Hollywood-red lips, she looked like a modern-day Jessica Rabbit. Suzette said looking chic was part of her job requirement since she worked at an upscale medical spa, but Cora knew it was just coded into her best friend's DNA. If all Suzette had to wear was a burlap sack, she'd still find a way to doll it up with a trendy hairstyle, flawless makeup, and matching heels. "Maybe he didn't realize you were coming on to him."

Cora rolled her eyes. "Suze, I couldn't have been more obvious if I'd hung a blinking sign around my neck that screamed Open for Business."

"Then none of this makes sense. You must have done something to spook him, or— Oh, hold up." Suzette pursed her lips and gave Cora a warning look. "Tell me you weren't wearing that Ballbreaker AC/DC shirt with the hole in the armpit? I told you to toss that thing before it sprouted legs and crawled into the sewer on its own."

"I was wearing those new silk pajamas," Cora said indignantly.

Suzette gaped in disbelief. "He walked away from you in *that*? What, exactly, did he say?"

"Just that we should go to bed," Cora said with a shrug.

"Uh-huh. See? Right there." Suzette pointed a red manicured nail at her. "That was your cue, and you missed it. He probably meant you should go to bed *together*."

"Not even," Cora said in exasperation. "He told me to get some sleep. Then he ruined the vibe by mentioning work-related stuff involving Magnus."

Suzette's auburn brows snapped together, and she slumped in defeat. "What the heck is going on with men these days? They're acting so out of character. How are brilliant, beautiful women like us supposed to rule the world if we can't count on men to be predictable?" She folded and refolded her napkin. "Take Rob Hopper, for example."

Cora's eyes widened in surprise. "You're talking to him again?" Rob was a police officer who worked alongside Cora. He was a ridiculous flirt with a reputation for being a ladies' man, and he'd been trying to woo Suzette for years. She always turned him down, but one night a few weeks ago Rob convinced her to go to dinner. One thing led to another, and just when they started kissing, Suzette saw a text message on Rob's phone from a girl he planned to hook up with later that night. As far as Suzette was concerned, it was game over.

"I'm only barely talking, and not by choice," Suzette said. "After that dinner fiasco, I told Rob to give up because I wasn't going to be one of his booty calls. He said he didn't want to lose me, and if all I offered him was friendship, he'd gladly take it.

But whatever, right? That's probably just the stock line he throws out whenever things with a woman start to go south. Anyway, I figured that was the end of it. So, I carried on with my summer and ignored him." She waved a hand in irritation, like she was shooing flies. "But he's been hovering in the background all along. And he's bugging the hell out of me."

"What's he doing now?" Cora had no idea Rob was bothering Suzette. When she got back to the station, she was going to hunt him down, and they were going to have words.

"He texts me every day to say *good morning,*" Suzette said, wrinkling her nose. "And he sent flowers to my work. Three times." She leaned forward like she was about to impart something outrageous. "Just. Because."

Cora blinked in surprise. "That's...bad?"

"Of course it is!" Suzette looked at Cora like she was crazy. "Think about it. We've known him for years. Rob Hopper is a total player. He flits from one relationship to the next without blinking. Common knowledge, right?"

Cora nodded, because it was kind of true. Rob went through women like they were delectable morsels of chocolate in a box of Godiva. He plucked them up, savored them for a short time, then moved on to choose another.

"So, if Rob was texting me every night to ask what I was wearing," Suzette continued, "that would be typical. If he sent me red roses with sexy notes, or those flowers made from lace panties you can buy at the Gas n' Go cash register? That would all make sense. I'd expect something like that from him, and I could easily ignore it. He's always been over the top, laying on the charm and the innuendos. No subterfuge with that one." She glared into her diet soda, stabbing the ice cubes with her straw. "But instead, he sends me these cheerful bouquets of peonies and lilies—very tasteful and sweet, like something I'd choose for myself—with notes saying he hopes I'm having a good day. I mean, what the hell?"

Cora opened her mouth to speak, but Suzette cut her off, adding, "Oh, and last Thursday, I ran into him at the grocery store. It started pouring down rain outside, and he walked me all the way to my car with his umbrella so I wouldn't get wet. It's like he's been body snatched, and some well-mannered gentleman alien took his place."

Cora began to smile. "It sounds like he's actually trying to be friends."

"Well, it's weirding me out," Suzette said grumpily. "The flowers. The kind messages. And then he pulls that umbrella stunt? I'm telling you, Cora, it's not normal. Rob Hopper does not do 'sweet and thoughtful.'" She poked at her half-eaten turkey burger, then pushed the plate away. "All I can figure is he's trying to play the long con. But it won't work. I'm not falling for any of his shenanigans. Fool me once, and all that."

"What if he's not playing?" Cora asked. "He seemed pretty remorseful when he talked to me at the station after your failed date. I think he might really like you, Suze. That's a first for Rob. I've never seen him so worked up about someone."

Suzette looked surprised and a little vulnerable, but she quickly shrugged it off. "The important thing here is, these men are acting shifty. We need to arm ourselves, so we don't get played." She opened her purse and began digging around until she pulled out a compact mirror and lipstick. She expertly applied her signature shade of Candy Apple Red to her lips, before blotting with a napkin. After checking the results, she dropped the items back in her purse with a satisfied nod. "There. Now I'm ready for anything."

"That's your armor?" Cora grinned around her milkshake straw. "Makeup?"

"Flawless war paint is a woman's first line of defense," Suzette said, batting her sooty lashes. "Same goes for a killer outfit and accessories. It's like our secret ammunition. That's not to say there's anything wrong with a bare-faced girl who can kick back with a beer in jeans and a T-shirt. That's all fine and good, and guys love that natural vibe. But when a woman really needs to *slay*? It helps to bring out the big guns." She gave her best megawatt smile and held her palms out like a showgirl.

Cora chuckled, suddenly regretting her hastily applied lip balm and mascara this morning. Maybe Suzette had a point. "So, what should I do about Liam?"

"Absolutely nothing. Last night was a fluke. You and Liam will be spending almost all your waking hours together, and he's a hot-blooded male who looks at you like he's starving and you're a triple deluxe cheeseburger with all the fixings. I've seen it. He can say whatever he wants, but it's clear he wants you."

"I wouldn't go that—"

"Trust me," Suzette insisted. "I'm not sure what's going on in his head right now, but it doesn't matter. He's a guy, and you, my dearest friend, are a complete goddess. You're brilliant, beautiful, kind. The whole package— No, don't roll your eyes at me. I'm totally serious. He won't be able to resist you for long. I'd give him another week—ten days, tops—before he caves. Just you watch."

Cora hoped her friend was right, but the thing between her and Liam was a lot more complicated than just physical attraction or casual affection. Ever since they'd met, there was an undeniable pull between them that she couldn't deny, no matter how hard she'd tried. He was like a cyclone that came spinning into her life, stirring up all sorts of emotions, and she'd given up trying to fight against it. She'd always been levelheaded and logical, especially when it came to her dating relationships, but the way she felt about Liam was different. There was no explanation for the mysterious dreams she had about him, the strange moments of déjà vu she experienced sometimes when they were together, or the way he often spoke to her as if he'd known her forever. She felt like every path she chose from here on out was destined to lead toward him. It was almost as if the universe was trying to tell her something, and she finally wanted to listen. The question was, did he?

5

MAGNUS BLACKWELL'S HOUSE WAS TUCKED AT THE end of a quiet street with trees so lush and tall their branches formed cathedral-like arches overhead. In the daylight, Liam could imagine the neighborhood's custom homes, meticulously manicured lawns, and fancy European cars sparkling like jewels in the dappled sunlight, but on a night like tonight, the place seemed shrouded in gloom. Most of the houses were modestly sized for their exorbitant prices, but according to Cora, their close proximity to fine restaurants, a bustling bar district, and high-end shopping boutiques made it a prime spot for the wealthy and "respectable" members of society.

"Except for Magnus, of course," Cora said dryly from the driver's seat of her car. They were parked across the street from his house, hidden beneath low-hanging branches and a burned-out streetlight. "Nothing respectable about him."

Liam yanked a red licorice rope from the bag of snacks on the center console. "A low-life reprobate like Magnus doesn't deserve to live in a mud pit, let alone a place like this." But he wasn't surprised. In his limited experience, wealth didn't always equate to respectability and integrity. Aside from Squire McLeod, most of the wealthy men Liam had encountered were too enamored with their own sense of entitlement to bother with pesky things like that.

"He's still not moving," Liam said in growing aggravation. For the third time in as many minutes, he lifted the pair of binoculars Finn had acquired, peering through the large window at the front of the house. The curtains were wide open, leaving a clear view of the open floor plan. There was a dining area to the left, a kitchen beyond that, and a hallway leading toward the back of the house. The largest space was the living room, where Magnus was now stretched on his sofa, talking on the phone and occasionally flipping through TV channels. "He's just lying there like a lazy, flea-bitten mongrel."

"Patience." Cora calmly snapped open a can of soda and took a sip.

"I've none left to spare," Liam said with a growl. If they didn't find some action soon, he was going to go mad. "We've been sitting here for almost three hours watching him do nothing."

"Exactly," Cora said in amusement. "Most stakeouts are long, drawn-out exercises in boredom. What did you expect, an action-packed adventure like they show on TV?"

"No, of course not." Yes. A bit. He loved those action shows. There were always stakeouts and gunfights and important clues to be found. The best usually ended in an epic car chase, followed by someone walking away from an explosion in slow motion. While he hadn't expected they'd be lucky enough for one of those scenarios, he'd certainly expected more than this. "Magnus could at least walk around and give us *some* sort of action," Liam grumbled. "A slow shamble toward the kitchen would be thrilling at this point."

He lowered the binoculars and bit forcefully into his licorice stick, grinding the waxy, strawberry-flavored candy between his teeth. He'd brought two grocery bags filled with snacks, and even stocked a small cooler in the back with cans of soda. If Cora hadn't put her foot down, he would've added beer, but she said they needed to stay sharp and couldn't risk falling asleep. Not that it mattered, Liam thought in annoyance. He was about to pass out from boredom, anyway.

"Maybe Magnus is making plans to meet with his accomplice right now," Finn offered from the back seat. "He's been on that phone for a while." Of course Finn would say something hopeful. Liam had been champing at the bit for the past two hours, but Finn was just sitting quietly back there, watching Magnus's house with calm, intense focus. As much as Liam had grown to respect Finn over the past few months, sometimes the man's unending well of patience got on his nerves. Liam was a man of action. He needed to *do* something already.

"He's moving," Cora said suddenly.

Liam jerked the binoculars up to see. Magnus was still talking on the phone, but he was sitting up. Now he was standing and even stretching, thank all that was holy. Maybe the night was about to get more interesting. Liam watched in hopeful anticipation as Magnus checked his wristwatch, glanced at the front door...and flopped back onto the sofa.

"Oh, for the love of—" He shoved the binoculars at Finn. "Enough of this. I'm going to go see if I can hear what he is saying through the window."

"What? *No*," Cora said in alarm. "Liam, you promised you wouldn't do anything crazy. It's the only reason I agreed to be here."

"And I won't. There's nothing wrong with taking a quiet stroll down the sidewalk like a normal passerby," he said innocently.

"Liam." Cora narrowed her eyes and drew out the syllables

of his name in a warning tone. She was far too smart for him, God love her. It was true, he had no intention of staying on the sidewalk, but he couldn't very well say he planned to hide in the bushes, lurking underneath Magnus's window. Cora would handcuff him to the steering wheel. Best not to mention it. Besides, forgiveness was easier to get than permission. Another bit of wisdom he'd learned in life that still applied, no matter the century.

"You won't be able to hear anything if you're passing by on the sidewalk," Finn pointed out, helpful as ever. "Even if the window's open."

"Huh." Liam pretended to consider that for a moment. Then he shoved open his door to make a quick escape. "I suppose I'll just have to improvise."

"Oh, no, you don't." Cora grabbed his sleeve. "You—"

"Wait," Finn said in a hushed voice. "Look." He was pointing to a red car that was just pulling into Magnus's driveway.

A young woman in a fitted dress slid from the driver's seat and walked toward the front door. Before she even had a chance to knock, the door flew open to reveal Magnus with a thunderous look on his face. He grabbed her roughly, yanking her inside and slamming the door. A high-pitched shriek came from within the house, followed by a loud thump.

"What the—" Cora sat bolt upright. Loud jazz music began to blare from within the house. A muffled cry could just be heard over the music. She glanced worriedly at Liam. "Maybe we should call this in. We already know Magnus is dangerous, and if he's hurting her—"

"He's not," Finn said in an odd, strained tone. "I'm pretty sure she's okay."

"How do you know— *Oh*." Cora's face turned pink.

Liam followed her gaze to the smaller window on the left

side of the house. Magnus and the woman were silhouetted behind a sheer white curtain, and they were lip-locked in a frenzied embrace. His hands were bunched in the woman's hair. She broke the kiss to rip his shirt over his head. He hoisted her onto a table, then lowered his head until he was out of sight. The woman threw her head back in apparent ecstasy.

Cora dropped her forehead to the steering wheel. "Next time you wish for action, Liam, can you please be more specific?"

He nodded absently as he watched a high-heeled shoe sail past the living room window. Then another. "Jesus, they're going at it like a pair of spring rabbits."

Suddenly Magnus hauled the woman up and strode past the living room. Her legs were wrapped around his waist, and her dress was hiked up to reveal a pair of skimpy purple underwear. Still kissing, they disappeared down the hall toward the back of the house.

For one long, tense moment, nobody said anything. The only sound was the muffled jazz music coming from the living room.

"Well, that was fun." Cora broke the silence with false cheer. "Good stakeout, guys. I think I'll leave now and go look for some brain bleach."

"I'm going in," Finn announced.

Liam and Cora both twisted in their seats to gape at him.

Finn was riffling through his leather messenger bag. "Magnus left his phone on the coffee table, and he's clearly occupied right now. This may be the only chance we have. If I can get to that phone, I can clone it." He pulled out two wires, a small laptop, and a device that looked like a cell phone. "It should only take a couple of minutes. Then we'll be able to track his incoming calls, texts, everything."

Liam began to smile, deeply impressed. "That's brilliant."

"No, that's breaking and entering," Cora said sternly. "And

it's illegal. If Magnus catches you—if anyone in the neighborhood even sees you, they could call the police."

"It won't come to that, I promise." Finn opened his door and slid from the car, glancing back to add, "But just in case, keep an eye out for any police officers, okay?" Then he gave Cora a wink and melted into the shadows.

"You know," Liam said in bemusement, "I'm really beginning to like that man."

"Right now, that makes one of us." Cora smacked the steering wheel. "I can't believe Finn, of all people, would just rush off and—"

Liam bolted from the car before she could stop him. He could practically feel her shooting daggers at the back of his head as he crossed the street, so he didn't dare look back. It was his idea to do the stakeout in the first place, and by God, if anything actually happened tonight, he wasn't going to miss it.

The night air was balmy and warm, with a gentle breeze rustling the leaves in the massive oak trees. Liam made his way toward the foundation shrubs along Magnus's house until he reached Finn's hiding spot underneath the living room windowsill.

Finn was in the process of trying to slide the window open. He glanced sharply at Liam, then exhaled a sigh of relief.

"Any luck?" Liam whispered.

Finn shook his head, then pointed to the dining area window a few yards away. The sheer curtains floated inward on the night breeze. They moved carefully along the wall, slinking behind the bushes until they reached the window. The glass was open a hand's width from the bottom, which explained why they could easily hear the music and sounds coming from inside the house.

"I'll go," Liam whispered, buzzing with newfound energy. This type of thing always made his blood rush with excitement.

It had been a long time since he'd done anything so clandestine, and he was good at it.

Finn looked doubtfully at Liam, then back at the window. "No, it should be me. I know how to work the cloning device."

"But I can go fetch his phone and bring it out to you. It's much simpler than hauling your things in there." Liam was already gripping both sides of the window frame. He looked at Finn's worried face. "I've done this a thousand times, and I'm good at it. Trust me."

Finn looked like he wanted to argue, but Liam didn't give him a chance. Running his fingers along the frame, he quickly removed the screen and slid the window panel higher until there was enough space to climb through. Then he pulled himself over the window ledge and slid into the house in one fluid motion. Within seconds, Liam was standing inside Magnus's dining room. Without hesitating, he flew to the living room, where Magnus's phone still lay on the coffee table. Moments later, he was climbing back out the window with Magnus's phone. The whole operation took him less than a minute.

Finn blinked at him in astonishment.

"What?" Liam asked, handing him Magnus's phone.

Finn shook his head and crouched under the windowsill. Balancing the laptop on his knee, he hooked in the phones and began typing out commands, his fingers flying over the keyboard in a blur.

Liam watched, impressed at Finn's ability to stay so calm and focused under pressure. He was proving to be quite resourceful, and a hell of a lot stealthier than Liam would've given him credit for. If Finn weren't such a successful attorney, he might've even made a fairly good thief. Liam almost chuckled at the irony. Who knew the stuffy Finley Walsh could throw a decent punch, lurk in the shadows, and perform illegal activities like the best of them? Liam had been so wrong about the man. Any humor he was feeling suddenly morphed into stinging guilt. All this time, Liam thought he knew better than the angels, but Finn was clearly a man of hidden talents and surprising loyalty. Back in his old life, Liam had been so quick to judge Finn, believing he was just a lecherous solicitor with no honor, using his connection to Cora's father to prey on her innocence. Liam had been convinced Finn wasn't worthy of her, but he now realized he'd been wrong. Finn was a good person, and Liam was the unworthy one.

"Done," Finn said, pulling Liam from his dark thoughts. "Now we wait. Should take around five minutes."

The jazz song came to an end, and another one started. In the short silence between songs, they could hear a woman's escalating moans and a rhythmic thumping that sounded like a bed frame knocking against a wall.

"Let's hope there are five minutes to spare," Liam said wryly, sliding to the ground beside Finn. The scent of damp earth and green things growing surrounded them as they crouched against the side of the house, and Liam felt oddly nostalgic. He could almost imagine he was back in 1844 carrying out some shady plan with his band of thieves.

"So, you've had a lot of practice breaking into houses," Finn said thoughtfully. "How exactly does a man on the right side of the law acquire that skill?"

Liam studied the laptop screen, feigning interest in the progress meter. "Standard police officer training. It's part of our annual skills test. We have to be lithe and nimble on our feet."

Finn grunted in amusement. "If that were true, Providence Falls would be missing half their police force. I've seen some of those officers at the station."

Liam considered spinning up another story, but for some reason, he didn't want to lie to Finn anymore. After a long pause in which he debated how to frame his answer in the best possible light, he finally shrugged. "When I was a lad in Ireland, I was young and reckless and did a lot of things I'm not proud of. Things were different for me and my family back then. We didn't have the easy life a lot of people have here. It was a constant struggle just to put food on the table. Let's just say, I got in with the wrong crowd and learned some painful lessons the hard way."

"I hear that," Finn said, staring into the shadows. There was a bleak look on his face that Liam recognized because he'd worn it many times himself. "I had a similar situation after my dad died. My mom couldn't support us, so I did what I had to do."

Liam waited for Finn to elaborate, but he said nothing further. It seemed neither of them wanted to dwell on the past, so they slipped into silence, watching the progress meter inch its way across the screen until it finally reached one hundred percent.

"Done." Finn pressed a few keys and disconnected Magnus's phone. "Better hurry. No telling how much longer they'll be occupied."

Without a word, Liam took the phone and climbed back into the house. He crept to the living room and was just about to place Magnus's phone back on the coffee table when he heard heavy footsteps approaching from down the hall.

Liam ducked behind the armchair just as someone lumbered into the room. He could tell it was Magnus by his muttering voice. Liam squeezed himself closer to the floor between the chair and the stereo system.

With a curse, Magnus skirted the sofa and came thundering to a stop right next to the chair.

Liam flinched, knowing he was only seconds away from being caught. A hundred excuses began spinning up in his head, but nothing that would appease Magnus. A solid punch to the face was all Liam was going to get. Clenching his fists, he barely resisted the urge to jump up swinging, but adding assault charges to breaking and entering would only make things worse for himself. He could just imagine Cora's disappointed face. She was already annoyed at him for running after Finn. After this, she'd be downright livid.

Focus! He tried to think of a plan. If he couldn't fight, he could always flee. He was fast on his feet. It would be so easy to just bolt across the room and sail out the window, but even if he got away, Magnus would still recognize him. *Damn.* Why hadn't he thought to wear a ski mask like the people on TV? Cora could say what she wanted about those shows being unrealistic, but clearly there were valuable lessons to be learned there.

"Where are you?" Magnus snarled under his breath.

Liam swore silently. There was no imaginable scenario where he'd get out of this unscathed, but maybe he could divert Magnus's attention, giving Cora and Finn a chance to get away. He braced himself to stand.

"Hey, Tammy," Magnus shouted. "Is my phone back there?"

Liam froze as Magnus leaned forward to turn off the stereo, his arm just inches from Liam's face. The sudden silence was deafening. He clutched Magnus's phone in his hand, not daring to breathe.

"I don't see it," she called from down the hall. "It might be. I'm not sure, though. Hey, can you bring me a drink?"

Magnus muttered something about "brainless" and "good for only one thing." He stomped around the living room, presumably searching for the phone. Liam heard the coffee table scrape over the floor. When the armchair began to slide away from him, Liam clenched his jaw and prepared to face the music.

Suddenly, something hard smashed against the front door from outside.

"What the—" Magnus paused, abandoning the armchair to stride across the living room. He swung the door open, cursing under his breath.

Liam peeked around the edge of the chair.

In nothing but a pair of boxer shorts, Magnus rose from grabbing something off the doormat. It was a smashed, fizzing can of Dr Pepper. "Damn neighborhood kids," he hissed, stepping outside to look for the culprits.

Liam wasted no time. He lurched from the floor, tossing Magnus's phone to the sofa before darting across the living room to dive through the open window. He clipped his shin on the ledge as he sailed over, then landed on the hard-packed dirt, barely managing to stifle a groan as he rolled to a stop underneath a shrub. Clenching his teeth through the pain, he caught sight of Finn crouched a few feet away, blinking at him like a wide-eyed owl.

They remained silent until they heard Magnus slamming the front door again, his heavy footsteps fading down the hall.

Finn crawled silently over to Liam. "Are you all right?"

Liam nodded, then hauled himself up, leaning against the side of the house to catch his breath. "I thought you'd be at the car by now."

"And miss all the fun?" Finn whispered, clutching the equipment to his chest.

A huff of amusement escaped Liam. For a moment, they just grinned at each other like fools, and he felt a sudden camaraderie with Finn that surprised him. He'd been in situations like this a thousand times as a thief, either by himself or with Boyd and the Bricks. But if anyone had ever told him he'd someday do this with the holier-than-thou Finley Walsh, Liam would've laughed himself sick.

"Let's go." Liam pushed off the wall. "Cora's already mad at us. The longer we make her wait, the worse it's going to be."

"Right." Finn's smile faded. He fell into step beside Liam, both of them keeping to the shadows at the edge of Magnus's yard. "Maybe she won't be too mad when she finds out we were successful."

Rounding the edge of the lawn, they crossed the street and came to a halt by the spot where they'd parked. There was no sign of Cora or her car.

"Where...?" Finn trailed off, glancing up and down the street. "Did she leave us?"

"No. She'd never do that unless she had a good reason." Sure, she was mad at them for being reckless tonight, but Cora wasn't the type to drive off in a sulk just to teach them a lesson. "Keep walking. We can't be caught out here like this."

They rounded the corner and walked another block. Liam took his cell phone from his pocket just as Cora's car pulled up beside them. She looked simultaneously annoyed and relieved.

"What happened?" Liam asked as they jumped into the car.

"I saved your butt is what happened," Cora said with storm clouds brewing in her eyes. She gunned the engine until they were heading toward the main road. "I was watching through the window, and I saw you duck behind that chair. I knew I had to create a diversion, so I nailed the front door with that can of soda."

"Nice," Liam said with an admiring grin. Once again, Cora's resourcefulness saved his hide.

She wasn't smiling. In fact, she looked downright livid. "I had to drive away right afterward because I couldn't take the chance Magnus would see me."

"Good thinking," Finn said from the back seat. "Thank you for doing that."

"Don't bother," Cora said, staring him down in the rearview mirror. "I almost didn't come back for you guys. It would've served you right for going rogue on me like that. I can't believe you took that kind of a risk. What the heck were you both thinking?"

"Look, before you get too upset," Liam began.

"Oh, I'm way past that. I'm—"

"We did it, Cora," Liam said quickly. "Mission accomplished. Finn successfully cloned Magnus's phone, and now we can track everything he does."

Her eyes sparked with interest, but there was still a stubborn tilt to her chin. "That's great, but I'm not done being mad at you guys."

"And you have every right to be," Finn said earnestly. "We shouldn't have been so reckless, and I'm grateful you were there watching out for us. If you hadn't intervened, Liam would be in serious trouble right now, and probably me, too. There's no way we could've done this without you. I'm sorry, Cora."

To Liam's surprise, her expression began to soften. Finn was actually defusing the situation. Who knew he had such wisdom when it came to women? Or maybe he was just flexing his attorney skills. They were wizards when it came to analyzing a situation and spinning pretty words to gain a desired outcome. Either way, Finn was doing a cracking good job, and Liam didn't dare interrupt.

"My place isn't far from here," Finn continued. "If you guys want to come over, we can take a look at this device and see what that snake in the grass has been up to. Maybe there's enough evidence here to put him away for good."

"All right," Cora said with reluctance. "But just so you vigilantes know, I'm never going on a stakeout with either of you again. *Ever.*"

"Fine by me," Liam said, digging through the grocery bag near his feet. "I'd rather till an acre of rocky soil with my bare hands than sit around like that again, anyway. Hey, where's the tin of sugar biscuits?"

"In Magnus's yard. Along with the last two cans of soda." Cora took the exit ramp into Finn's neighborhood, catching sight of Liam's forlorn expression. She gave an indignant shrug. "What? It took me a few tries to hit the door."

6

AN HOUR LATER, CORA FLOPPED BACK ON FINN'S couch and handed him Magnus's cloned phone. "Take it. The ick factor is strong with that guy, and I'm too tired to read any more tonight."

"If you want, I'll keep monitoring it over the next few days," Finn said. "I've taken time off work to pack for my upcoming move, so it won't be hard for me to check it throughout the day."

"That's good, because I can't risk taking it to the station. Captain Thompson would blow a gasket if he caught wind of what we were up to." She yawned and checked the clock. It was well past midnight, and Liam had quit almost an hour ago to get some fresh air on the patio. Cora could see him through the sliding glass door stretched on a lawn chair fast asleep, and she couldn't blame him. They'd all taken turns scrolling through Magnus's text messages, email threads, and calendar—anything that could give them some insight into the stolen money or murder cases. So far, they'd found nothing.

"Magnus is bound to make contact with his accomplice at some point," Finn said, setting the phone on the coffee table.

He picked up the half-empty bottle of Pinot Grigio he'd opened for her earlier. "All we need is one small slipup, and we've got him. I don't think we'll have to wait long."

"I hope you're right," Cora said with a sigh. "So far, I see no proof of questionable behavior. Not unless you count all the women he seems to be juggling." It was a wonder he could keep them all straight. If she had to sift through one more text thread where Magnus and various women planned casual hookups, she was going to be ill. She tried not to remember how close she'd come to being one of them.

Finn held up the bottle of wine. "Cleanse the palate?"

"Please," Cora said, holding out her glass. Granted, they'd been drinking for a few hours, and she was feeling a little blurry around the edges, but she welcomed the floaty sense of detachment. It was one thing to know Magnus was a creep and a womanizer, but to have to read through all those conversations that toed the line—and sometimes blew right past the line—between flirting and sexting? Well, there wasn't enough wine in the entire state to make that go down easy.

"He's just such a sleazeball," she said after a generous sip.

Finn laughed wearily and propped his feet on the coffee table. "The understatement of the century." He ran a hand over the stubble on his jaw, then reached for his beer. Tonight, he looked scruffier than usual, but still handsome in the dark jeans and the faded black hoodie he'd worn for the stakeout. There was something strangely intimate about seeing him so casual and relaxed, so at ease in his own home like this. Outside in the real world, Finn never seemed to let his guard down. Even when he'd fought that mountain of a man named Meat in the Booze Dogs' illegal cage fight, he'd been calculating and focused, every action precisely measured. She knew him as Finley Walsh, the razor-sharp lawyer who battled in courtrooms and sipped cognac with state officials. She'd also seen him as the Jackrabbit, an underground cage fighting legend in a screaming crowd of bloodthirsty bikers. But right now, Cora felt like she was witnessing a secret side of Finn he rarely showed other people. Maybe this was the real man underneath everything else. Just a simple guy who liked to have beer and watch TV with a girl on a Friday night.

"Exactly how did you become mixed up with the Booze Dogs?" she asked. It was nosy, sure, but the drinks and exhaustion from the day's events seemed to loosen her inhibitions. On any normal day, she'd probably approach the subject with more tact, but "normal" flew out the window the moment they'd skirted the law with that stakeout operation tonight. The two of them shared secrets now. In fact, she'd been keeping Finn's secret ever since she'd discovered his involvement with the motorcycle club, so he owed her an explanation.

"My father," Finn admitted after a pause. "He loved motorcycles, and he had this old chopper he was always tinkering with on the weekends in our garage. He and his buddy made a hobby out of helping each other with their bikes, and they started buying and selling parts as a side hustle from time to time. My dad would buy three bike parts, sell two, and use one on his own bike, that sort of thing. It wasn't anything big, but he got a reputation for doing good work, and that's how he got in with the Booze Dogs. Anyway, he did this for a few years, and it turned out one of his suppliers got busted for dealing in stolen parts. My dad was implicated because he was a regular buyer. We couldn't afford a lawyer, so my dad ended up getting a public defender who suggested he make a plea deal."

"But your dad wasn't an accomplice," Cora said, astonished. "He had no knowledge of the supplier's crime."

"No, he didn't," Finn said. "If I knew then what I know now,

I could've helped him, but I was young, with no idea how the system worked. None of us knew, so my dad just took his attorney's advice."

"Well, it was crap advice." Cora scowled. "They should've thrown *him* in jail for being a disgrace to the profession."

Finn's mouth twitched at her outburst. "He believed my dad would just serve minimal time—maybe even get out early—and go on to live his life and put the past behind him. He thought it was my dad's best option." He paused for a few moments as if lost in thought, then added in a more somber tone, "Unfortunately, it didn't work out that way. Shortly after he went to jail, my dad got killed trying to break up a fight between two inmates. With a shaved-down toothbrush, of all things. I couldn't believe it when I first found out. My dad… He was this huge guy with a booming voice and the kind of larger-than-life personality that filled a room. He always seemed so strong to me. It was crazy to think that something so small and trivial could end his life."

Cora's heart ached with sadness. "I'm so sorry, Finn." She hated the bleak look in his eyes, and she could barely imagine how horrible and helpless he must've felt as a young adult, powerless to save his father.

"It was a long time ago." He finished off his beer and set it on the coffee table.

Cora could tell he wanted to change the subject, and she was happy to move on. "Did you meet the Booze Dogs because of your dad's chopper hobby?"

"No." He leaned over and poured the last of the Pinot Grigio into her glass.

She let him, even though she knew she was heading deep into tipsy territory. But it was so nice just to be able to unwind after such a long, stressful workweek, and Liam was right outside, so she didn't have to drive. Besides, Finn's couch was almost as comfortable as her bed back home. Yawning, she dragged a fuzzy throw blanket over her lap and snuggled deeper into the leather sofa cushions.

"After my dad died, my mom was really struggling to hold it together," Finn said. "She tried to put on a brave face for me and my little sister, but things began to fall apart. She couldn't make ends meet, and the bills began piling up. We couldn't make rent. The fridge was bare more often than not. I remember being so angry all the time. I started hanging out with this rough group of kids, buying booze with our fake IDs, drinking and getting into fights. One night we ended up at the Rolling Log bar, and one of my friends dragged me into a fight. He started arguing with this huge tank of a guy. You've met him, actually." Finn glanced at her in amusement. "Bear."

Cora gaped. She'd met Bear at the gates of the motorcycle compound. He was yoked like an ox, with huge beefy arms and tree trunks for legs. Cora had never met anyone with a more appropriate name. The guy looked like he could fell a tree with a single swipe of his paw. "You tried to fight *Bear*?"

"*Tried* being the operative word," Finn said with a grimace. "My friend was a pretty scrawny guy, so he pulled me into the argument as backup. Next thing we knew, we were in a full-on brawl. It was Bear and three other bikers against just the two of us. My friend went down right away, and he stayed down, but—"

"Not you," Cora guessed. "I've seen you fight." She'd been shocked how fast and dexterous Finn had been on the night of the cage fight. He'd had to fight a man who was almost double his weight, but Finn had a way of dodging and leaping that seemed to defy gravity. It was no wonder they called him the Jackrabbit.

"Oh, I got knocked down, too," Finn assured her. "Over and

over. I didn't know how to fight smart back then, but I was big enough that I could take a hit. I just kept getting back up. That surprised them. I held my own a lot longer than Eli expected me to, and that's how it all started."

"Figures Eli was there watching it all go down," Cora said with distaste. Eli Shelton was the motorcycle club president, and a misogynistic creep. The last time Cora had been alone with him, he'd made a pass at her with his wife in the next room. "Was he as bad then as he is now?"

"Worse," Finn said with a chuckle. "I think he's mellowed a lot with age."

"That's a disturbing thought. So, what did he do?"

"He watched me fight until I'd worn myself out and taken a couple of his guys down with me. I remember I was on the floor with a black eye and a bloody mouth, laughing. Back then, I welcomed any fight. It drowned out everything else I was feeling. It sounds crazy, but it gave me something to focus on, something that was immediate, rather than just the anger that always simmered in the back of my mind. So, there I was, lying on the floor and laughing like a lunatic, and Eli came up to me and said, 'Boy, it's clear you don't have two brain cells to rub together. But you're full of fire, and you've got potential. Now, the way I see it, you have two choices. You can let my guys keep knocking you around until you're unconscious, and they dump your body in the creek. Or you can come work for me and make more money than you've ever seen. What'll it be?'"

"So, you chose the money." It made sense, considering how young and desperate Finn must've been at that age. With his mom struggling to make ends meet, the lure of making fast money would've been irresistible.

"Not quite," Finn said with a pained grin. "I chose to punch him in the face."

Cora gave a delighted gasp that ended on a hiccup. She slapped a hand over her mouth. "You punched Eli Shelton?" She'd have paid good money to see that.

"I did, and it's the only time I ever got the chance. He knocked my lights out right afterward, but instead of waking up in the creek, I woke up on a lounge chair at the Doghouse. That's when Eli offered to train me, and he told me how much money I could make if I joined the circuit."

"So that's how Finley Walsh became the legendary Jackrabbit."

"It wasn't easy, but I learned fast. Eventually, I made enough to help out my mom and sister while putting myself through college. Halfway through, I'd earned enough money to quit fighting, and after graduation, I went on to study law."

"And the rest is history." She stared into her now-empty wineglass. "Talk about landing on your feet. I bet your mom is really proud."

"She'll say that now, but back then I drove her crazy. Before my dad died, I was a model student with big plans for my future. I wanted to do photojournalism and travel the world. Maybe do an internship abroad. But things didn't work out that way, and I ended up making a few detours." He gave her a boyish smile that was contagious. "My mom says I didn't just go off the deep end, I did a running swan dive into a pool of angst and never came up for air until years later."

"Is that when you got that big tattoo on your back?" Cora teased. "During your angsty phase?" She'd been shocked the night of the barn fight when she'd witnessed Finn walking through the screaming crowd toward the cage. He'd been wearing shorts and gloves and not much else, and it was the first time she'd seen the large tattoo across his back. It had never occurred to Cora to wonder what Finn looked like underneath all his designer clothes and starched shirts, but if she had, she certainly wouldn't have imagined the inked, sleekly muscled athlete she'd seen that night.

Finn's cheeks flushed at her gentle teasing. He seemed suddenly younger and even a little self-conscious, and for a moment, she caught a glimpse of the carefree boy he must've been before things fell apart. The boy his mom must've missed.

"It was definitely a result of my rebellious phase," he said. "My mom still gives me hell for it, even after all this time."

"Let's see it," Cora said impulsively. She twirled her finger at him. "Turn around and show me."

Finn looked surprised, then hesitant.

"Oh, come on. It's not like I haven't seen it before." The barely-there blush across his cheeks deepened, and this time Cora couldn't help giggling. "Besides, it's the least you can do for all the trouble you gave me earlier at the stakeout."

With an exaggerated sigh, he turned and reached over his shoulders, dragging his T-shirt up over the broad expanse of his back. In slow increments, the fabric lifted to reveal inch by inch of tanned skin until the dark, swirling tattoo appeared across his shoulder blades.

FIAT JUSTITIA RUAT CAELUM.

"Wow," Cora said with admiration. "It's...stunning." If she was staring a bit too long, it was only because the tattoo was exquisitely detailed, with darkly looping script and intricate, wicked-edged lettering. It was clearly a work of art. Her prolonged perusal had nothing at all to do with the fact that Finn's broad shoulders and back rippled with lean, honed muscles that shifted intriguingly as he twisted to glance back at her. Somewhere in her alcohol-induced fog, Cora managed to tear her gaze away and say, "What does it mean?"

"'Let justice be done, though the heavens fall.'" Finn dropped his shirt and turned back to face her.

A slow smile stretched across Cora's face. Of course it did. How fitting. He was all about upholding justice, no matter the cost. "It suits you."

"Tell that to my mom," Finn said with a laugh. "It's what I tried to explain back then, but she was thoroughly horrified that her teenager did something so permanent. She said I'd live to regret it someday."

"And do you?" She highly doubted it.

"Not at all." He settled back into the sofa cushions. "I first saw the phrase in a book I found in the library shortly after my dad passed away. I was trying to understand how the legal system worked, and how it could've failed him so spectacularly. When I saw the translation, I read it over and over again, and it really resonated with me. It still does. Probably even more now than it did then. I don't know. It's just..." He trailed off and shrugged, his face warming again as she stared at him.

"You," Cora said simply. "It's just so perfectly *you*."

Finn blinked at her in surprise. His soft brown eyes filled with so much warmth and appreciation, and for a split second, Cora got the feeling she was catching a glimpse of him at his most vulnerable. There was gratitude that he could share his feelings with her, yes, but there was something else in the way he looked at her. Some stronger emotion she didn't want to analyze.

She glanced away and began folding the blanket in her lap. "Anyway, you're lucky you chose a tattoo that's stood the test of time. My friend Suzette once dated a guy who inked an image of her face and the words *Suzette 4EVR* on his forearm."

"And how'd that work out?" Finn asked in amusement.

"Not well. She broke up with him a week later. A *week*. She said any guy dumb enough to tattoo a girl's face on his body after only two dates wasn't exactly 'forever' material. The tattoo, however, was in it for the long haul," Cora said with a helpless giggle.

Finn laughed as the patio door slid open. Liam stepped through with his hair mussed into a dark halo and a shadow of stubble across his jaw. Even rumpled and bleary-eyed, he looked ridiculously, sinfully gorgeous.

Cora laid the folded blanket on the arm of the couch. "Good, you're awake. I've had one too many glasses of wine, so you get to be the designated driver. Ready to go?"

Liam shoved a hand through his hair, eyeing her and Finn on the sofa with an odd expression on his face. "Not…just yet. I came in for some water, so carry on with whatever—" he waved his hand in the air "—you're doing." He strode past them into the kitchen, grabbed a bottle of water from the fridge, and made a beeline for the patio again.

"Liam," Cora called out. He stopped without turning around, but she could see his face reflected in the sliding glass door and he didn't look happy. "Come and join us."

"No, I'm well enough out there." He glanced over his shoulder with a casual smile, but she wasn't fooled. Something was up with him, and whatever it was, he was conflicted about it. "Don't let me interrupt."

"Wait." A sudden thought occurred to her. God, did he think there was something romantic going on between her and Finn? That wasn't good. She needed to nip this in the bud immediately. "You're not interrupting. We were just shooting the breeze. Anyway, I want to go home with *you*." Okay, that didn't come out quite right. "I mean, I need to go to bed, and I want you to take me." Worse. Much worse. *Thanks, alcohol.*

When it looked like Liam was about to argue, Cora added more firmly, "Please. It's been a long day, and I'm exhausted.

I'm also way past the age where it's cool to crash on someone's couch—even though this one is ridiculously comfortable." She bounced a couple of times on the springy cushions, then jumped to her feet, stumbling a little.

"Whoa there." Finn shot off the sofa to steady her, but Liam beat him to it. He wrapped a strong arm around Cora's side and gave Finn a reproving look. "How much wine did you give her?"

"Don't ask him that," Cora said, digging her elbow into Liam's ribs. "It's not up to him. *I* choose. And for the record, it was only two glasses."

Finn glanced sideways at her.

"Or three," Cora amended. "Two or three."

Finn pressed his lips together like he was trying not to laugh.

Did she drink more than that? She eyed the empty Pinot Grigio bottle on the coffee table. No wonder she felt like her head was stuffed with cotton balls. She was going to be in hangover hell tomorrow. "Come on, Liam. Take me home."

She spun to leave, and Liam kept his arm clamped around her side to steady her. Somewhere in the back of Cora's mind, she realized she should be self-conscious about her slight lack of coordination, but she wasn't sober enough to care.

They said their goodbyes, Finn promising to call them as soon as anything important popped up on Magnus's phone. Liam led Cora toward the bank of elevators down the hall.

When the elevator doors closed, she leaned her head against Liam's biceps, blinking up at him as she swayed on her feet. With his sun-bronzed skin and thick, dark lashes, he was even more handsome up close. How was that possible? Nobody looked better in HD. Not in the real world, anyway. She reached up to swipe a lock of hair from his forehead, but she ended up poking him in the eye. "Whoops. Sorry."

He rubbed his eye with a crooked grin. "It's all right. I have another."

"Okay, here's the thing," Cora said in a conspiratorial whisper. She held her hand up, pinching her thumb and forefinger together. "I'm a little bit tipsy."

Liam's deep, rumbling chuckle sank under her skin, spiraling outward through her limbs until she felt warm and languid and blissfully content. "I think you're well past that."

Cora shrugged. Maybe she was, but at the moment, she didn't care. Resting her head on his shoulder, she hummed happily. "This is nice. I like this."

"Good," he said, wrapping both arms around her. "You'd best enjoy it now while you can, because tomorrow you're going to have the devil beating a war drum inside your skull. Believe me, I'd know."

"Worth it." Cora tipped her head back and blinked lazily up at him. He peered down at her with amusement and a spark of mischievous fire that licked along her nerve endings and sucked all the gravity from the room. If she weren't tethered by the smoldering look in his half-lidded eyes, she could float off into the atmosphere, too mesmerized to care. Why did he have to be so irresistible? He was just so... Cora drew in a breath and exhaled, "So handsome."

Liam lifted a brow in amusement.

Wait, did she say that out loud? She lifted her chin, owning it. "Well, you are. As a police detective, I am compelled to state the facts. You are, objectively speaking, ridiculously attractive."

"I'm very glad you think so," he said with a grin. "Though you are deep in your cups tonight. In my experience, strong drinks and good judgment make poor bedfellows. But I'll take your compliments any way I can get them. Tomorrow, you may regret telling me." Cora considered this with a small frown, but he reached up to smooth the crease between her brows with his thumb. Then he cupped her face gently with his palm and said, "As a police detective myself, I feel compelled to state this unshakable fact: every day, every night, and every single moment, you are adorably, intoxicatingly, unbearably beautiful to me."

Pleasure flared so hot and bright inside her chest she felt incandescent. "I am?"

"Always," he said solemnly.

Their faces were so close Cora could feel his breath stir the fine strands of hair at her temples. He dropped his gaze to her mouth, his thumb brushing featherlight across her lower lip. Cora's heart did a triple cartwheel into a back handspring and struck the landing. Was he going to kiss her? She felt like she was hovering at the top of a roller coaster right before the fall.

"Sometimes it hurts to look at you because I know I can't—" Liam squeezed his eyes shut, shaking his head with a muttered curse.

That didn't sound good. Her skin prickled with sudden awareness. He'd been about to say something important, and it was about the two of them being together. She'd bet her life on it. "You can't what?"

He shook his head again and stared at the elevator door.

Desperation flooded through her, and she fought to hold on to the thread of connection between them. "Does this have something to do with us working together, or living together, or whatever the heck makes you think we can't be more than friends?" When he didn't answer, it was answer enough. "You're wrong, Liam. We can if we want to. There's really nothing stopping us." She slid her hands up his hard chest and linked her fingers around his neck.

Liam sucked in a breath, his large hands opening against the small of her back, sending shivery trails of warmth over her skin.

As if on reflex, he pulled her closer. He made an almost desperate sound in the back of his throat, and for one blissful moment, Cora felt his grip tighten on her waist. She could almost feel the battle raging inside him, as if he were trying to resist her but failing. His heated gaze landed on her mouth again. A surge of giddy elation swept over her. Finally! Whatever his reasons were, none of them could negate this bone-deep connection between them, and he knew it. Cora stretched on her tiptoes, tilting her mouth toward his.

The elevator jolted to a stop.

Liam jerked back. Still gripping her waist, he set her away, holding her at arm's length. There was a war going on inside him; that much was clear. Even in her inebriated state, Cora couldn't miss the tension around his mouth. The sharp rise and fall of his chest. The banked heat in his eyes. Then, as if by magic, his expression smoothed into something bland and unreadable. "Time to go."

Cora felt stiff and unsteady on her feet as he led her into the parking garage. He kept his arm around her waist, but they might as well have been on opposite sides of the planet. Whatever intimacy they'd shared in the elevator was gone, and in its place was nothing but an empty pang of loss. He was rejecting her. Again.

Liam hurried toward the car with swift strides, forcing her to almost jog to keep up with him.

"Slow down," she said, trying to pull back.

He didn't seem to hear her as he guided her toward the car. When they were a few feet away, he pulled the keys from his pocket with his free hand and pressed the button to unlock the doors. Then he jerked open the passenger door and tried to guide her in.

"I've got it," she said irritably, shrugging out of his hold and lowering into the passenger seat. The happy buzz she had going earlier evaporated into frustration and angry resentment. Head pounding, she glared at him when he dropped into the driver's seat. "What's wrong with you?"

Liam didn't answer; instead, he adjusted the rearview mirror and began to put the key in the ignition.

On impulse, Cora snatched the keys away. "I asked you a question."

He held out his hand. "Give me the keys, Cora."

"No." She clenched them tightly in her fist. "Not until you tell me what your problem is."

"My problems are too numerous to count. Not the least of which is my inebriated roommate, who's keeping us from going home right now."

Roommate. His impersonal tone was like a crossbow arrow to the chest. If she'd been standing, she'd have staggered backward. Instead, she waved a hand in the direction of the elevator, demanding answers. "What happened back there?"

Liam gave her a questioning glance, all courteous and polite and unaffected. It made her want to slap the expression right off his face. "I don't know what you mean."

"You..." *said I was beautiful.* "We..." *almost kissed.* So many things hovered on the tip of her tongue, but his carefully blank expression stole them right out of her mouth. A tendril of shame flared in the pit of her stomach, but she blanketed her mind fast, smothering the flame before it could catch and stomping it down deep. He wanted to pretend nothing happened? Fine. She still had some dignity left. "Never mind."

"Let's go home, Cora," Liam said wearily. "It's been a long day. We'll both feel better if we can get some rest and put it all behind us. The important thing is, we got Magnus's phone, right?"

Put it all behind us. Cora's heart began folding in on itself, end over end like a crumpled piece of origami paper. She hoped by the time it was done it would resemble something entirely different. A lump of volcanic rock, perhaps. Or a military tank. Something impenetrable and unbreakable.

"Sure thing." She handed him the keys, knowing he saw straight through the brittle, plastic smile she was selling, but they were playing a game of pretend, so he bought it, anyway.

They drove in silence, Cora staring blindly out the window as the scene changed from residential buildings to a bustling downtown area filled with live music, restaurants, and Friday night revelers, and finally to the quiet, tree-lined street of her own neighborhood. She was suddenly so tired she just wanted to fall into bed and sleep for about a hundred years.

"Finn really came through tonight," Liam said suddenly.

"Mmm-hmm."

"We should invite him over for dinner this week."

She shrugged noncommittally, massaging the bridge of her nose with her thumb and forefinger. Her temples were beginning to throb, which was a clear precursor to tomorrow's main event: the hangover from hell.

"Would you like Finn to come over?"

"Sure."

"It seemed like you two were getting along quite well in the living room. I saw you laughing together. He makes you smile."

Something in his tone sounded off. Cora glanced over at him with suspicion.

"I just mean," he continued, shifting uncomfortably in his seat, "that you both seem to get along very well." There was a tightness around his mouth and a stubborn set to his jaw.

Cora narrowed her eyes. "We do."

"That's great. I'm glad." He nodded a little too quickly, as if he were trying to convince himself of something. "He's a good man. Don't you think?"

Oh, no. Was Liam trying to foist her off on Finn? *Please, no.* Anything but this. Her cheeks burned with mortification. It was bad enough suffering through his rejection, but it was downright insulting to realize he was trying to steer her affections toward someone else. Did he think she was some pathetic loser? That her emotions were such fickle things she could so easily be pushed into the arms of another man?

"And he knows how to throw a punch," Liam added thoughtfully. "It's not a skill you'd want to claim in polite company, granted, but any man worth his salt should know how to—"

"Stop." If she had to live through one more second of Liam's poorly concealed matchmaking, she was going to throw herself from the car. "I don't feel well. Can you just…not talk, please?"

Liam studied her for a long, uncomfortable moment in which she prayed he couldn't see the humiliation burning just under her skin. Finally he said, "Aye, I can do that."

Cora sank lower into the seat with a sigh. A few minutes later, they arrived home without another word spoken between them, a small mercy for which she was eternally grateful.

By the time the weekend ended, Cora vowed she would stop trying so hard to make the thing between her and Liam into something more. It was too painful to put herself out there when he clearly didn't want to be in a relationship. He'd even told her as much the first time she'd brought it up. So what if Suzette swore up and down that he was into her? Suzette had been wrong about guys before, and she had a trail of exes to prove it. Besides, Cora knew Liam was attracted to her on a physical level, but that wasn't enough to build a future on. Every jilted lover throughout history knew that. She couldn't keep going down this road if he wasn't even willing to meet her halfway.

Heck, he was speeding down a different track altogether if he was trying to throw her at Finn.

The embarrassment of that whole elevator incident still rankled whenever she thought about it. One minute she was locked in Liam's embrace while he said the sweetest things, every whispered word stealing away pieces of her heart like a thief in the night, and the next... They were having a stilted conversation in the car about how great Finn was. What hurt the most was how Liam seemed to believe she was so easily malleable, as if the feelings she had toward him could be diverted with just a few casual suggestions. If he believed that, then he had no idea how she truly felt. And maybe he didn't deserve to know.

From now on, she had to focus her energy on dreams within reach. The cottage at the edge of town, for example. She'd been wanting to buy it for years. It was going up for sale at the end of the summer, and she was finally in a financial position to make a competitive offer on it. The thought of living in her beautiful dream home with the picket fence and babbling brook should've been enough to lift her spirits. It always had in the past, but now there was a dull ache in the pit of her stomach she refused to identify.

Focus on what you can control, she reminded herself for the zillionth time as she headed into work Monday morning. Logically, it was good, sound advice. Now all she had to do was get her emotions to fall in line.

7

"HAPPY MONDAY MORNING, OFFICER O'CONNOR," Mavis sang out from the reception desk. Today the station receptionist was wearing a canary yellow sweater with matching dangly earrings, and her hair was puffed up extra high with some sort of invisible pomade.

Liam grinned and stepped into the sweet, citrusy cloud of perfume hovering around her desk. "Mavis, you're like a bright ray of sunshine this fine morning."

She gave a trademark giggle-snort and pointed to a box of doughnuts. "Bear claw? Better take one while you can. Otto just brought them in and they never last longer than thirty minutes."

Liam reached into the box and pulled out a flaky pastry, remembering a time when the closest he ever got to food like this was in his dreams. "Thank you, Mavis. This is just what I needed." Cora had left early that morning, making some excuse about meeting a friend for coffee, so he'd slept in by accident and didn't take the time for breakfast. He didn't often oversleep, but the tension between him and Cora was taking its toll, and he'd tossed and turned all night.

Before he could sink his teeth into the delicious pastry, Boyd called down the hall, "O'Connor, my office."

Liam let out a long-suffering groan under his breath, much to Mavis's amusement. Then he gave her a conspiratorial wink and turned to follow Boyd down the hall.

Cora was already seated in Boyd's office when Liam entered. She glanced up and gave him a perfunctory nod. This song and dance they'd been doing all weekend rankled on his last nerve. Ever since his slipup in the elevator, she'd been polite but distant. He hated that she felt the need to guard herself from him, but could he blame her? If he had that moment in the elevator to do over again, he'd never have allowed himself to embrace her and say the things he said. But she'd been so soft and sweet, and he'd lost his mind to the moment.

All weekend afterward, he'd mentally kicked himself for acting on impulse and being so reckless. It would've been so easy for him to just stay on the patio and let the scene inside Finn's living room play out as it should. Liam had gone out to watch the stars with the pretense of getting fresh air, but really it was to give them some time alone. He'd dozed off for a bit, and when next he woke, it was to the sight of Finn displaying his naked back to Cora. She was leaning over him, peering at the tattoo across Finn's shoulders.

Filled with jealousy, Liam had jackknifed off the lounge chair, then reminded himself this was exactly what he'd wanted. They were supposed to get close. They were supposed to *fall in love*. That was the whole reason he'd been tossed back to earth. Still, when Finn took his shirt off and Cora leaned in closer, Liam found himself yanking open the patio door without thinking. If he'd just stayed outside for a while longer, maybe things would've gone differently. But instead, he'd let his jealousy get the best of him. He'd been too pigheaded and stubborn to rein it in, and now here they were. That was always his problem when it came to her. Even with his soul on the line, he still couldn't get past his own selfish emotions. When was he ever going to learn?

Liam half hoped the angels would've paid him a visit on Finn's patio that night, but they were being evasive as usual. He doubted they'd do much more than chastise him for his actions, anyway, but even that had a certain comfort to it. Their presence reminded him that he wasn't alone.

"Do you understand?" Boyd asked, piercing Liam with his bloodshot, narrowed gaze.

Liam sat up straighter, trying to hide the fact that he hadn't been listening. For the first time that day, he took a moment to really study Boyd, and shock rippled through him at the man's appearance. Growing up together, Liam had witnessed his old friend hungry, angry, desperate, and beaten down. He'd seen Boyd harassed by landlords, townspeople, and even his unhappy wife. But Liam had never seen him like this.

Bloated from years of too much food and not enough exercise, he looked unhealthy. His skin was pasty from lack of sun, and his florid face reflected a clear lack of sleep and an overabundance of alcohol. There were deep, shadowed grooves beneath his red-rimmed eyes causing an almost ghoulish cast to his appearance. *Jesus, Mary, and Joseph*, Boyd looked worse than the time he'd hidden in the woods for three weeks avoiding a debt collector.

When Liam didn't answer fast enough, Boyd's neck began to grow red around his collar. Cora came to his rescue. "We understand, Captain Thompson. In fact, we're planning to interview Slice again today."

"The kid?" Boyd sat back in his chair, rubbing his chin as he considered it. "Yes. See if you can't scare any more information out of him. Arresting Wally Jensen from that dive motel was an exercise in futility. The man was useless. By the time he sobered up, all he could do was wail about his ex-girlfriend."

"He said someone contacted him anonymously, paying him to spray-paint over those cameras outside the Booze Dogs' compound the night the money was stolen," Cora said. "I was hoping there'd be more to the story."

Boyd shook his head. "We interviewed his ex, and she only repeated what we already knew. Someone in that motorcycle club is lying."

Or Magnus is lying, Liam didn't say.

Cora flicked a warning glance at him, as if she knew what he was thinking.

Boyd gave an abrupt nod. "Put the pressure on the kid. In my experience, it's the unassuming ones who hide the biggest secrets. The Booze Dogs are notorious for a variety of things, but being smart isn't one of them. Somebody there is bound to crack; we just have to administer the right incentive."

"Incentive," Liam repeated. There was a gleam of menace in Boyd's eyes he'd seen before a time or two. Usually, it involved roughing someone up, stealing something important, or blackmail.

"Yes," Boyd said flatly. "Do whatever it takes to get them to talk."

Cora shifted in her chair. "I'm afraid I don't understand."

"I believe he's saying we should consider using brute force," Liam said, not breaking eye contact with Boyd. "Blackmail. Whatever it takes. Isn't that right, *Captain*?"

Cora's gaze whipped to Boyd with a worried frown. "Surely, that's not what—"

"I never said that." Boyd glared at Liam. "It wouldn't be right for me to advise you to do anything unethical. I'm just pointing out that sometimes it helps to get…creative. Think outside the box. The Booze Dogs have always taken justice into their own hands, and they're not above fighting dirty. If you're prepared to beat them at their own game, then you need to be prepared to play by their rules." He glanced at Cora. "Within reason, of course."

Cora had stiffened beside him, and even without looking at her, Liam could tell she was bothered, but she remained silent. The irony in Boyd's suggestion was that they were already disregarding the rules. They'd broken into Magnus's home and used illegal surveillance equipment to gain access to his private information. Liam suspected Boyd would secretly be glad to know they'd employed such underhanded measures, except that their focus was on the wrong target.

They left Boyd's office to find his wife, Alice, standing impatiently outside the door, tapping her foot. Her glossy red lips were pursed into a moue of distaste.

"Alice, good to see you," Liam said, nodding. Her hair was smoothed into a loose updo, and she was dressed impeccably, as usual, in a tight blue shift dress, blue heels, and matching jewelry. Crystals dangled from her ears, and she wore an elaborate sapphire necklace with diamond filigree. Flashy and sparkly and crowd-pleasing. That was Alice Thompson.

When she caught sight of Liam, her angry expression bloomed into a flirty smile. "Liam O'Connor, we meet again." She said it like it was their destiny, but Liam knew better. Alice flirted with everyone, and the minute he walked away, she'd turn that coy smile on the next unsuspecting man who wasn't her husband. It didn't escape his notice that Alice completely disregarded Cora, barely glancing in her direction as Cora marched off to her desk. "I'm still waiting for you to fulfill your promise," Alice simpered.

At Liam's look of confusion, she let out a tinkling laugh,

smacking him playfully. Her hand slid down his arm like she was cataloging every muscle. "We were all supposed to go have drinks, remember? You were going to regale me with tales of you and Boyd growing up in Ireland."

"Oh, aye," Liam said, forcing a smile. "We'll have to all do that soon." And by soon, he meant never in this lifetime, or the next.

"I'm going to hold you to it." Alice glanced at him from beneath heavily painted lashes, fiddling with the sparkly sapphire necklace that hung between her impressive cleavage. It was a practiced movement, the purpose no doubt to draw his attention to her charms.

"Alice," Boyd barked from his desk. Her blooming smile withered on the vine, lips pressed flat and brittle as fallen leaves. Boyd didn't look happy to see her, either. "What are you doing here?"

She fluttered her fingers at Liam, entered the office, and shut the door behind her. Relieved, Liam hurried to find Cora, but she wasn't at her desk. He found her in the kitchen pouring coffee.

Before he could say anything, she spun around and gave the same breezy, careless smile she'd been throwing at him all weekend. The fake one that made him grind his teeth because he knew he'd put it there.

"How's Alice?" Cora asked, blowing on her steaming cup of coffee.

"Disturbing," Liam said moodily. "Every time I meet her, something about her rubs me the wrong way."

Cora lifted a delicate brow. "I think there are a lot of men who'd disagree."

"Boyd deserves more from his wife," he grumbled, remembering the way Alice had squeezed his arm like a farmer's wife assessing a piece of prime livestock. He rubbed his biceps as if he could erase the memory. "They're married."

"Not everyone honors the vows of holy matrimony," Cora said, glancing sideways at him. It was a casual comment, but she was making a point. Unfortunately, it was sharp and spiky and hit him right in the gut.

"Ouch." Liam jerked in mock pain. "I suppose I deserve that." He did have an affair with Margaret, John Brady's wife, though their actual affair happened almost two centuries ago. But thanks to the angels' infuriating setup, everyone in this life—including Margaret herself—believed the affair was a recent event. As a result, Liam almost became a suspect in John Brady's murder because he'd lied about his relationship with Margaret while he was working on the case. But Cora had helped clear his name. Her kindness and forgiveness had been humbling. Even now, shame prickled over Liam's shoulders when he thought of all she'd done for him. He was nothing but trouble for her. Always had been. Considering everything that had transpired between them, both past and present, it would take a lifetime to even begin making it up to her. Too bad he didn't have one to spare.

"Hey, forget about it. Bygones, right?" Cora headed for the door, giving him a warm smile, because that was who she was. She didn't hold grudges, and at her core, she was compassion itself. It humbled him all over again.

They made their way back to the pen. The place was alive with its usual activity. Rob Hopper was in a heated discussion on his phone. Otto was at his desk, using a sleeve to scrape pastry crumbs onto the floor. Happy was, well, anything *but*. He was scowling at Boyd's closed office door. Clearly, the captain must be spreading his surliness all over the station today.

"What do you make of Captain Thompson's advice just now?" Cora asked when they got to her desk.

Liam considered the veiled suggestions Boyd had been making back in his office. Cora may not have understood him, but Liam got the message loud and clear. "I think Boyd's almost at his breaking point. He's got a lot of people pressuring him to wrap these cases up, and he's willing to look the other way if we decide to— What was it he said? Ah, yes. 'Think outside the box.'"

Cora sank into her chair with a frown. "It's not like him at all. He's always been strictly by the book, so I'm still not convinced he meant for us to play dirty in order to get someone from the Booze Dogs to confess."

"Maybe you don't know Boyd as well as you think," Liam said.

She threw him a look. "Please. I've known him for years. Captain Thompson didn't just fall into this role; he has a reputation, and he's earned it. It's our job to uphold justice and enforce the law. He's been a stickler for the rules as long as I can remember."

"So have you, Cora." Liam leaned against her desk with a jaunty grin. "And *yet*."

She glanced sharply at him. "What's that supposed to mean?"

"Only that you withheld evidence for me back when I almost lost my job," he said with a shrug. "And now you're a willing participant in a clandestine operation to spy on Magnus Blackwell, even though it goes against the captain's direct orders. No one is above bending the rules once in a while. That's all I'm saying."

She opened her mouth to argue, then seemed to realize he had a point and snapped it shut. She looked so adorably disgruntled he wanted to lean down and kiss her until the little crease on her brow disappeared.

"I don't have time for this." She stood, grabbed her purse off the desk, then shouldered past him.

Liam fell into step beside her. "I'm only pointing out that even you've crossed the line on occasion. And if you can go rogue, *anyone* can. Is it so far-fetched to think Boyd wouldn't toe that same line? He's only human, after all."

"Keep your voice down," Cora hissed as a patrol officer passed them in the hallway.

"Admit that I have a point about Boyd," he said playfully, keeping pace with her.

Cora glanced back to make sure they weren't overheard. "You're going to get us into trouble. Just drop it, all right?"

"Why? Because you don't like empirical facts?" he teased.

She rolled her eyes. "Because you're annoying, and I don't like you."

"Ach, now you're telling lies just to impress me, lass," he said with an exaggerated Irish accent.

Cora pressed her lips together and marched on. "I wasn't lying."

"See? Another lie. It's almost second nature now," Liam said in mock wonder. "First, you break a few rules, and the next thing I know, deception just flies off the tip of your tongue like a common outlaw. I'm afraid you may be spiraling into a life of crime, Officer McLeod. Though I can't imagine you as a petty thief. Your talents would be wasted. You'd probably need to be something more…" He glanced at her expression. "Murderous. Aye, that's it. A sharpshooting assassin, perhaps."

"I do have a gun," she said coolly. "You may want to remember that." Cora waved to Mavis before pushing through the front door.

"Or maybe you'd be a cutthroat mercenary," Liam continued, pretending he didn't hear her. "Like a swashbuckling pirate—no, better. A swashbuckling *lady* pirate."

"Why is that better?" Cora blurted, still making a beeline for her car at the end of the parking lot. He could tell by the stubborn tilt of her chin she was trying to ignore him, but there was a smirk forming at the corner of her mouth.

"Because women are as fickle and unpredictable as the sea," Liam explained. "So, naturally they'd be more fearsome and have better adventures."

She opened her mouth to respond, but her phone chimed, and she pulled it from her pocket. "It's Finn. He's at Lindsey's gym right now and sent a picture." She turned her phone to show Liam an image of a photo collage board. On it were several snapshots of Lindsey Albright with friends. "He says one of the girls from her workout team was putting it on the wall outside the pool. Maybe she has more information. It's not much of a lead, but it's better than nothing."

Liam nodded. "Let's go, then."

"Not so fast." Cora rounded on him when they reached her car. "You have to go interview Slice Biddlesworth again, remember?"

He scoffed. "I'm not wasting my time on that."

"Captain's orders," she said with a shrug.

"Oh, *now* you want to follow the rules?"

She smiled sweetly, batting her lashes. "Guess I'm just fickle and unpredictable like that."

"Cora, we've already interrogated Slice," Liam said in exasperation. "The poor kid has been through enough, and he's still mourning the death of his woman. There's nothing more he's going to tell us. He doesn't trust the police. Anyway, I thought we agreed to focus on Magnus."

"We did, but someone has to keep up appearances so Boyd doesn't blow a gasket. From the looks of him these days, he could explode at any moment. Just go check up on Slice so you can report back, okay? Take him to lunch." She got into the car and added, "You love lunch."

Liam grumbled under his breath as she drove away. The woman was not wrong.

8

KICK START FITNESS WAS NOT CROWDED WHEN
Cora arrived, but that was to be expected for lunchtime on a
Monday. There were some die-hard weight lifters who looked
like they worked out for a living, a few runners on the tread-
mills, and three women at the smoothie bar in yoga clothes. Cora
knew the upscale gym filled up after business hours, and later
in the evening it would be hopping with people. On her own,
she'd have chosen to go when the likelihood of interviewing
more people who knew Lindsey was higher, but Finn seemed to
think the girl in charge of the photo collage was a close friend
of hers, so it was worth a shot.

"Hey, all right, all right. Awesome." A man with cropped
blond hair approached, clapping and grinning. Cora recognized
him immediately. With the jaunty spring in his step, the purple gym polo, and the deep suntan, Brad was the ultimate gym
evangelist, and exercise was his religion. He lived to convert all
the wayward souls who hadn't yet seen the light, one lazy body
at a time. As the lead personal trainer, he'd already done his best
to lure Liam and Cora through the pearly gates of Kick Start

Fitness, all for the low, low price of two hundred and fifty-nine dollars plus tax, but he hadn't succeeded.

"Hello again, Brad."

"You're back," he said with an enthusiastic handshake. "Couldn't stay away, could you? It's that special we've got going on. We've been slammed with new members."

"Actually, I'm here to meet my friend Finley Walsh."

Brad paused to consider the name, then bobbed his head. "Tall, triathlon guy, right? Brown hair? He usually only comes on the weekends, but I did see him come in today."

Cora hesitated. She had no idea if Finn was into triathlons, but at this point, she wouldn't be surprised. "He said he'd be at the pool."

"Yup, sounds like him. Here, let me give you a free day pass. That way, you can check out the facility after you're done meeting up with your buddy. Who knows? Maybe you'll change your mind about joining." He pointed a finger at Cora and winked. "I'll make a believer out of you yet."

Cora signed her name on the guest form, thanking Brad before heading down to the pool. She spotted Finn standing outside the men's locker room with a towel slung over one shoulder. He was talking to a young woman in a racerback swimsuit and running shorts.

"Cora," he said in surprise, hastily finger-combing his damp hair. "I was just heading upstairs to put you down as my guest."

"No need." She gestured to the plastic card on a lanyard around her neck. "Brad gave me a free day pass."

"Uh-oh. That comes with strings attached," the woman said with amusement. "He's going to make you sit through his spiel about the benefits of joining. My advice? Find someone to create a diversion so you can sneak out when he's not looking."

Cora grinned. "I've already gone through a partial spiel, so hopefully it won't come to that."

"I'm Jenna," the woman said. They shook hands as Finn made introductions.

"Jenna was on Lindsey's workout team," Finn said. "She's the one who made the photo memorial over there."

Cora glanced at the opposite wall to find a large bulletin board filled with snapshots of Lindsey Albright.

Finn excused himself to check his messages while Jenna led Cora to the poster board. Cora was surprised to find so many pictures of Lindsey outside of the gym. "These are from all over the place, not just Kick Start Fitness."

"Yeah, I contacted her parents on Facebook," Jenna said, standing beside Cora to look at the colorful collage of photographs. "I told them I wanted to make a memorial poster for her, and they kindly forwarded my request to Lindsey's contacts. It's really great how everyone came together. So many people sent me snapshots."

Sadness crept over Cora as she studied all the pictures from the vivacious young woman's life. There was a picture of Lindsey as a baby with her parents at the beach, and one of her with a gap-toothed smile graduating kindergarten. There was a picture of her carving a pumpkin for Halloween, a shot of her with a fluffy dog in the snow, and one of her on water skis as a young teen. There were several photos of her at summer camp, with friends ice-skating, and with her cheerleading squad in high school. There were snapshots of her in her college surrounded by friends at a football game, blowing out birthday candles, and standing in a field of tall grass with her head tipped back, laughing. It struck Cora, once again, how utterly unimaginable it was that someone so full of life, so filled with boundless energy and joy and love, could be alive one moment and gone the next. It brought into stark relief the magnitude of the crime committed against her, and it made Cora all the more determined to find justice for both her and John Brady.

"She was such a fun, vivacious person," Jenna said sadly. "I only knew her from our time working out at the gym, but she was always quick to laugh and so supportive. I really miss her good energy here. Our whole team does. It's hard to believe someone would want to hurt her..." She trailed off and swiped at her eyes, unable to continue.

"I'm sorry," Cora said. "We're going to do everything we can to find out what happened. Can you remember anything strange she might have said? Anything at all, no matter how small."

Jenna shook her head. "We mainly talked about our Booty Busters team so we could win the workout challenge."

"Did she ever mention friends?" Cora asked. "Her boyfriend?"

"I didn't even know she had a boyfriend until he emailed me that picture," Jenna said, tilting her chin to the photo board.

Cora searched the collage as Jenna pointed to a half-hidden picture in the corner. It was an image of Lindsey grinning under a streetlamp at night, her hair a tousled mess. Cora peered at it closely, recognizing it was a selfie. A shiver of awareness skittered down her spine, and she unpinned the photo from the board to scrutinize it.

"Her boyfriend said it was the last photo she ever sent him," Jenna said wistfully.

Cora's heart began thumping wildly. The picture was taken in front of John Brady's house. She recognized his front door in the upper left corner. "Are there any more like this?"

"I don't know," Jenna said, staring at the picture. "It's the only one he sent. You could ask him. His name is Slice."

"Yes," Cora said quickly. Her mind was spinning with possibilities. She remembered the day Lindsey had gone to the police station claiming to have a photograph from the night of John Brady's murder. Apparently, she'd taken a selfie in front of his house, and there were blurry images of people in his window. She'd thought the photo could be helpful, but it turned out to be a dud. But if Slice had more photos taken on this night, maybe there was another picture. A better angle. Maybe there'd be something in the background that would actually be helpful. Again, it was a long shot, but it was worth a try.

Cora held the picture up and asked, "Can I keep this?"

"Sure, go ahead," Jenna said. "I hope it helps."

"Cora," Finn called.

She glanced to the end of the hall where Finn was gathering his gym bag. There was a tense set to his shoulders as he waved her over. Cora thanked Jenna and hurried toward him.

"Something just came in." He reached into his bag and handed her Magnus's cloned phone. There was a text from a number she didn't recognize.

The diversion wasn't enough. Need to regroup and discuss strategy.

Magnus's only response was: When and where.

Will send details later.

Cora stared at the screen, excitement roiling in her stomach. "When did this come in?"

"About fifteen minutes ago. I just noticed it now."

"This could be a big breakthrough for us," Cora whispered, handing back the phone. "The diversion could mean the money Magnus must've planted in Lindsey's locker. Whoever sent this text message is our missing link."

"It's vague," Finn pointed out.

"Yes," Cora agreed. "Intentionally vague. That's what makes me believe it's from Magnus's accomplice. I have a gut feeling about this."

He nodded. "Me, too. I'll keep an eye out and let you know the second something comes up."

Back in her car, Cora quickly dialed Liam's number to tell him about the selfie.

He answered on the second ring. "Cora?" Loud music blared in the background, and she could hear people hooting and hollering over the noise. It sounded like he was at a raging frat party, complete with high-energy techno beats, shouts of laughter, and the occasional collective "ooh" and "aah" from a crowd of revelers.

"What are you doing?" she asked.

"Following orders, like you said," Liam shouted. "I'm having lunch with the kid." Someone hollered at him in the background, and Cora heard Liam say, "No, I don't mean you, Slice. I was talking about someone else. Yes, Cora's…kid cousin. Who I'm having lunch with… Tomorrow."

Cora shook her head in amusement. "Not your best save. Also, you sound like an old man when you call him 'the kid.'"

Liam said something she didn't catch. Cora pressed the heel of her hand to her other ear. "I can't hear you."

"Hold on," he shouted. Shuffling noises ensued, then a door slammed, and finally the noise was muted to a more manageable level. "Are you still there?"

"Where are you?" she asked.

"Hiding in a maintenance closet at the Teens in Action center," Liam said with a groan. "I got Slice to come when I told him there would be all-you-can-eat free food, which is the only upside to having lunch with a bunch of lunatic teenagers during a video game tournament."

"That explains all the noise." The teen center had been getting large, anonymous donations lately, and they'd been able to revamp the whole lounge area. With rows of new monitors, comfy chairs, and game consoles, the place had become more popular than ever.

"I knew Billy Mac would be here, so I figured I'd kill two birds with one stone and check up on both of them at the same time."

"What a Good Samaritan you are."

"Don't tell anyone."

"How is Billy the Mac? I haven't seen him in a while." It made her happy to know Liam had kept in touch with Billy, the fifteen-year-old foster kid who'd helped confirm Liam's alibi and clear his name. Billy was tough for his age, but Cora had a soft spot for him and often checked up on him to make sure he was okay. He spent most of his time prowling the streets like most kids with too much time and not enough supervision, but he knew a lot about the seedier side of Providence Falls, and sometimes had insight that helped her solve cases. Recently, Cora had been able to put an abusive criminal behind bars because of a tip Billy had given her, which ended up working in his favor. Without the man to harass him, Billy's home life had improved, and according to Liam, he was spending a lot more time at the local teen center.

Liam didn't talk about it much, but Cora knew he'd been showing up at the center to visit with Billy, often volunteering a couple of hours to grill burgers on weekends or assisting with group activities. The other volunteers loved Liam, and told Cora he had an easy, natural rapport with the kids—especially the ones who seemed aloof and unsocial. She wasn't surprised.

Liam's easygoing humor and natural charm seemed to work on everyone. Young, old, male, female—people were just drawn to him. Heck, even her cat, Angel, liked him, and Angel didn't like anyone.

"Billy's fine. He's moonstruck over that girl Katie," Liam said. "I saw him in the library pretending to read some hitch-hiking space book. He's been trying to catch Katie's attention, and I think he might be making progress." Someone thumped on the door, and Cora could hear Liam swear under his breath.

"Liam, I need you to ask Slice about some photos he may have of Lindsey," Cora said. She quickly filled Liam in on the selfie she'd discovered at the gym. Then she told him about Magnus's suspicious text conversation. "Finn said he'd let us know as soon as Magnus sets up a time and address to meet."

"Good man, Finn. He's been very resourceful and helpful with all this. Who could've guessed he'd turn out to be so... *likable*." Liam sounded genuinely baffled, which made her want to laugh. "He's changed so much in the short time I've known him."

Now she did laugh. "No, he hasn't; you're the one who's changed, Liam. When I first introduced you to Finn, you wouldn't even give him the time of day. You disliked him for no reason, which makes you the odd man out, because everyone likes Finn."

"Do you?"

"Of course I do." What a ridiculous question.

"How much?"

"I— What?"

"How *much* do you like Finn?" There was an odd tension crackling in his voice.

Wait, was he jealous? Hope unfurled inside her for the space of a single heartbeat, but she shut it down fast. No, she wasn't going to go down this road again. It was filled with potholes and detours and signs leading nowhere. Liam didn't want her. At least, not in any serious way. Just last Friday he'd tried to set her up with Finn! Liam had sung the man's praises like he was a car dealer and she was his gullible customer. No. Liam wasn't jealous; he was just trying to sell her down the river to another man. It made her skin prickle with the same humiliation she'd felt that night after the elevator incident. But this time, she wasn't going to spiral down into a slump. Whatever game he was trying to play right now, she wouldn't be a part of it. It was time she stopped trying to read into things and just focus on the future—on all the things she could change. Liam wasn't one of them.

Cora straightened her back and said in clipped, no-nonsense tones, "I like Finn a lot, Liam. Bunches and bunches. Now, if it's all the same to you, I'd like to get on with today's investigation. I'm heading back to the station to tell Captain Thompson about Lindsey's photographs. Just talk to Slice and find out if he has more of them."

"Cora, I'm—"

Someone pounded on the door and yelled Liam's name. She heard the door bang open and someone call out, "Come on, Liam. He's up." Triumphant shouts suddenly rose in volume, and the group of kids began chanting a name in the background.

Liam raised his voice to be heard over the din. "I have to go. I'll meet you back at the station in a couple of hours."

She frowned, annoyed for all sorts of reasons, not the least of which involved a cocky Irishman who gave her emotional whiplash and made her head spin. "Two more hours is a heck of a long lunch break."

"Aye, but it turns out Slice is an online gamer," Liam said with a laugh. "He's joined the teen tournament."

"But he's in his twenties."

"The kids don't care. They voted him into the circuit because he has some following on a channel, whatever that means. He goes by the name Blade Punner. Don't ask, because half the time, I've no clue what these young people are on about." He sighed wearily and added, "Kids these days."

"Later, gramps." Cora got off the phone, smiling in spite of herself. Yet another reason to be annoyed at him. Even when she wanted to stay miffed, he somehow managed to say or do something to amuse her. The really infuriating thing was that he wasn't even trying. It was like a superpower, and he just couldn't help himself.

She headed back to the station to tell Captain Thompson about the photo. For the first time in what felt like weeks, she was looking forward to bringing him some promising information about the case. To her disappointment, it had to wait, because when she arrived back at the station, Mavis announced he was gone.

"He took a personal day," Cora repeated, letting the words sink in as she stared at Mavis in confusion. The receptionist was busy wiping the front desk down with disinfectant wipes. "Are you sure that's what he said when he left?"

"Mmm-hmm. He said he had a doctor's appointment, which wasn't a big shocker, if you ask me. He's been looking pretty green around the gills these days." Mavis finished wiping the desktop and swapped a bowl of lollipops with a giant bottle of hand sanitizer. "All I know is, I can't afford to get sick right now. My nephew's wedding is on Saturday, and I can't show up there looking like a truck ran over me and feeling like it backed up again. Especially since I just spent a bunch of money getting my roots dyed. I even bought a new dress at the Fashion Shack."

Cora nodded in understanding, but her mind was still on the

captain's absence. In all the years she'd worked with him, he'd never once taken a free day for himself, let alone a vacation. Maybe he'd been battling some illness for a while and never told anyone. "I wonder if it's something bad."

Mavis suddenly looked wide-eyed and worried. "I mean, it's polyester jersey, so I'll have to wear Spanx, but—"

"No, I meant the reason for Captain Thompson's doctor appointment."

"Oh." Mavis cocked her head, considering that for a moment. "Actually, I think his leaving had something to do with Alice. She showed up to visit him, and ten minutes later, she flew out of here like a bat out of hell. Then the captain went after her like he was on a mission. That's when he said he was taking the day off. He seemed angry more than anything else."

"I suppose that's better than the alternative," Cora said. If the captain was sick, there wasn't much she could do to help. If he was having marital problems, she couldn't help with that, either. But if Slice came through for them with a useful photo that helped identify John Brady's killer, then that would do wonders for not just the captain's morale, but everyone else's. As for the mysterious text message on Magnus's phone, Cora felt hopeful about that, too. Captain Thompson wouldn't be happy that they'd gone against his direct orders and continued to investigate Magnus, but he wouldn't be able to fault them with the outcome if it helped lead to the solving of the money theft, and possibly Lindsey Albright's murder. It was an encouraging thought, and one she clung to for the rest of the day.

9

"THERE'S SLICE," LIAM SAID AS CORA PULLED INTO a spot in the Zippy Lube parking lot Wednesday morning. "Damn. He's got that ogre of a man with him today. He'd better not give us any trouble."

Slice Biddlesworth was in one of the garage ports leaning under the hood of a car while Bear, the huge biker who guarded the motorcycle compound, sat in a foldout chair in the corner. From a distance, the muscle-bound mammoth seemed relaxed and laid-back, which was a far cry from the way he'd been the day Liam and Cora tried to visit the Doghouse. Bear had been a formidable gatekeeper, refusing to let them inside. His flat gaze had dismissed Liam as forgettable but lingered on Cora with interest. Liam bristled at the memory of Bear flirting with her and inviting her to party with the Booze Dogs. He didn't like the man for that reason alone and, judging by the way Bear was now scowling at them as they exited the car, Liam wasn't likely to change his mind.

"If Slice has the pictures we asked for, then it'll be worth it," Cora said as she hurried eagerly toward the carport. It filled Liam with relief to see the spark of hope in her eyes. For the past few days, she'd seemed withdrawn and a little sad whenever they were alone together, though she hid it well. While Liam knew it was all his fault, he couldn't allow himself to dwell on it. The pain of knowing he was the cause for her unhappiness was too much to bear, and there was nothing he could do to change it. Instead, he fought to stay cheerful and upbeat, doing whatever he could to help with their investigation. Cora loved Providence Falls and the people in it. She'd be thrilled to solve the recent crimes and see that justice was served. At least he could try to make her happy in this way.

"Good morning, Mr. Biddlesworth," Cora said to Slice as they approached the carport. She ignored Bear completely, which gave Liam a rush of satisfaction.

Slice straightened from where he'd been leaning over the car engine, wiping his hands on a rag streaked with grease. His round, boyish face had a matching smudge across one cheek, and he gave Liam a nod before eyeing Cora warily. "What's up?"

"Officer O'Connor and I came to follow up on the request for more photos of Lindsey." Cora reached into her pocket and pulled out the picture she'd taken from the memorial board at the gym. The selfie showed a grinning Lindsey with the corner of John Brady's window in the background.

Slice glanced at it, and turned back to the car engine, mumbling, "I don't have anything else."

"Are you sure?" Cora sidled up to the car to show him the picture again. "It's very important. This was taken outside of John Brady's house the night of his murder. How did you get this one?"

Slice shrugged, then started adjusting a valve on the engine. "Lindsey texted me pictures all the time. That was one of them."

"You said you'd look for more when I asked you at lunch

Monday," Liam pointed out, joining them at the car. Up until now, Bear had remained in his corner, but he rose from his chair and began lumbering over.

"I haven't had a chance to look," Slice said, tugging on the collar of his gray coveralls. "Been busy."

"You said you didn't have any other photos," Cora told him, crossing her arms. "Now you're saying you haven't even looked. Which is it?"

"He's busy," Bear said tersely. "That's your answer. He'll get to it when he gets to it. Now, you and your partner best run along. We got work to do."

Cora's color began to rise, and Liam could tell she was about to go into feist mode. "All we're asking for is photos." She glared at Bear, then turned back to Slice and said evenly, "It shouldn't be that hard to—"

"Yeah, well, it is," Slice interrupted, stuffing a corner of the oil rag into his pocket. "I don't want to look at pictures of her right now, okay? It just reminds me she's gone and never coming back." He glanced away, a muscle ticking in his jaw. Then he cleared his throat and said, "I transferred them all onto my laptop right after I sent that one to her friend at the gym for their memorial board. Figured it would be easier if I didn't have to see her every time I opened my phone."

"And the laptop?" Cora asked. "Where is it now?"

"I'm not sure," Slice said with a tinge of annoyance. "I never use it, so I tossed it in a moving box and left it in a pile of stuff my mom was taking to storage. Like I said, I don't want to be going through photos of her right now, so—"

"Mr. Biddlesworth," Cora interrupted. "We don't have the luxury of ignoring potential leads because we're sad about what happened. It's our job to track down a killer. I understand what you must be feeling, and I'm so sorry for your loss, but—"

"Don't act like you know how I feel," Slice said angrily. "You didn't know Lindsey. You have no idea what I'm going through."

"I do," Liam said. "I didn't know Lindsey, that's true, but I've lost someone before. I know exactly how you're feeling, and that's why it's so important for us to get the photos. Not too long ago, Lindsey believed she had a photograph that could help our investigation. It turned out she was wrong, but if there are any others we could analyze, it might help. Maybe there was something she may have missed. More than anyone else, I know you want justice for what happened to your woman. Am I wrong?"

Slice dipped his chin, placing his hands on his hips. After a few moments, he slowly nodded. "Fine. I'll look tonight when I get off work. If there's any more of those—" he nodded to the photo Cora was holding "—I'll let you know."

"Let's go now. We'll help you look," Cora said, glancing hopefully at the mountain looming over them. "Bear can hold down the fort for an hour while you're gone, right?"

Bear looked at Cora like she'd just suggested he join a knitting club. "This ain't teatime, lady. This is a legit place of business, and Slice ain't gonna drop everything just because you flash a shiny police badge. So, unless you plan to arrest him, or you got a warrant to search his place, you best respect the boy's time and leave."

"This isn't your concern," Liam said, stepping into Bear's personal space. "We didn't come here for you, so I'll thank you to leave us to our business and go back to your corner."

Thunder rumbled in Bear's chest. "Make me."

Liam braced himself to do just that, but Cora gripped his arm to stop him, never taking her eyes off Bear. Her piercing stare was impressive, and Liam felt a surge of pride. "We're leaving now, but know this. If you try to hinder this investigation, for whatever reason, I'll come after you, and you won't like the consequences."

Bear smirked, his gaze trailing lazily down her body. "Don't be so sure, sweet cheeks."

Enough. Liam balled his hands into fists. It was time someone taught the man some respect. He lurched forward, but Cora blocked his path. "Don't," she said. "It's not worth it." He glared at Bear over her head. The infuriating man just winked.

"Come on." She tugged Liam's arm, and it took all his control not to punch the man's lights out. With effort, he reined in his emotions and turned back to Slice. "Call us as soon as you find anything."

Slice nodded, swallowing nervously. From the way he glanced back and forth between him and Bear, it was clear he didn't want trouble. Neither did Cora, which was why Liam let her lead him back to the car without another word.

Bear followed behind them like a guard dog, stopping at the edge of the carport to watch them leave with his sinewy arms crossed over his massive chest.

"I don't like the way that man speaks to you." Liam watched him from the side mirror as they drove away. "Someone needs to teach him manners the good old-fashioned way."

"And what might that be?" Cora asked with a laugh. It warmed his heart to see her smiling again. "Wash his mouth out with soap?"

Too easy. "Something like that." He was thinking more along the lines of a few good knocks to the man's thick skull, but he didn't bother to elaborate. It had been a while since Cora smiled at him, and he didn't want to say something that could change her mood.

"Poor Slice," she said with a sigh. "He's really broken up about losing Lindsey. At least he's still young and has his whole life ahead of him. Plenty of time to fall in love again. What's that saying? Time heals all wounds."

"Not always," Liam said. "Sometimes every moment without the person feels like an eternity, and time just amplifies your loneliness."

Cora glanced at him curiously. She seemed to sense there was a story, and she wanted him to elaborate, but he knew better than to go down that path.

"That's sad," she said softly.

Heartbreaking. Soul-crushing. "Aye, it is. But that's life." His life. Her life. They'd always ended in tragedy. Against all odds, he prayed that this time would be different.

10

BOYD DIDN'T RETURN FOR THE REST OF THE WEEK. There were a number of speculations buzzing around the station as to why, some of which Liam found downright amusing. The receptionist, Mavis, thought he'd been having some marital problems, and she was convinced he'd taken his wife on an impromptu vacation to smooth things over. Liam was unable to imagine any weekend with Alice going smoothly. If Boyd had actually taken her on a trip, then he was likely to return in worse shape than he left.

"Maybe he has some chronic illness, and he's not long for this world," Happy said matter-of-factly as he stared at his computer screen. Everyone glanced at him in surprise, not because of his morose comment—that was pretty standard for him—but because Happy rarely participated in office gossip. He always seemed too bored or grumpy to care. In fact, the only time Liam had ever noticed Happy looking somewhat eager was when he took off in the afternoons with his mysterious gym bag, and even then, he usually had a sour expression on his face.

"Captain doesn't have a fatal illness," Otto said around a

mouthful of bagel. "He's stressed out because of the unsolved murder cases, sure, but I see him in his office every day at lunch, and that man has the appetite of an ox. People with one foot in the grave don't have hearty appetites. It's a common fact."

"Pity," Happy said under his breath.

Otto let out a good-natured chuckle. "Yup, partner. Looks like you're going to be stuck with me for a long time. Lucky you."

Happy was staring at his computer screen, but Liam didn't miss the smirk hovering at the edge of his mouth. For a moment, Liam was dumbstruck. He'd never seen Happy display anything but boredom or distaste, and Otto was always kind to him, anyway. It suddenly dawned on Liam that the two men actually had a strange bond of friendship, even though their personalities were on opposite sides of the spectrum. Not for the first time, Liam realized how painfully shortsighted he'd been ever since the angels dropped him into this new life. He'd formed first impressions about people based on the way they seemed, and he'd used his own imagination to fill in the gaps. He'd never bothered to look any further because he was too wrapped up in his own goals to waste his time on anybody else. If he hadn't been so self-centered, things could've been so different.

By the time Liam walked into Dante's bar on Friday night after work, he was feeling disconnected and melancholy. He caught sight of Cora sitting in a back booth with Finn. They looked good together, easy and relaxed, in an animated conversation punctuated with occasional laughter. Cora's hair tumbled around her shoulders in a mass of wayward curls, and Finn was looking at her like the sun rose and set by her royal decree. A hollow ache thudded in Liam's heart, because he knew the feeling. How Cora managed to miss that Finn was head over heels in love with her, Liam didn't know. But it was a lucky thing, he told himself as he walked to the bar to order a drink. It meant the task the angels had left him with might not be insurmountable, after all.

"Hey," Suzette said from his elbow. "You look like you've got the weight of the world on your shoulders."

Liam glanced over at Cora's best friend. "Perhaps I do."

"Come on. Nothing's that bad," she said, waving at the bartender. She held up her fingers and mouthed, *Two*, indicating both her and Liam. "Let me buy you a beer and you can tell me all your woes."

"You don't want to hear it," Liam said, taking the bar stool next to her.

"Sure I do. I'm always up for hearing other people's problems. Especially if they're way worse than my own. It makes me feel better, so feel free to exaggerate."

Liam shook his head, staring at a bead of condensation as it dripped down the side of his glass. "You wouldn't understand."

"You think not, desperado?" Suzette dropped her chin in her hand. "Hit me with it."

"Fine." Liam ran a hand through his hair in agitation, then decided to just go for it. "The reason it looks like I've got the weight of the world on my shoulders is because I do. Thousands of future lives hang in the balance, and I've been reincarnated on earth, sent by angels to right a wrong I committed almost two hundred years ago in order to save the life of someone I love and my soul from eternal damnation. How's that?"

Suzette cocked her head to one side, studying him thoughtfully. What surprised him most was that she didn't seem shocked. Liam glanced around the bar, wondering if the faux flame torches on the walls were going to explode, or if a lightning bolt was going to strike him down. It was the first time he'd ever uttered the truth about his task to anyone, and it was strangely freeing. For a split second, he felt elated that there was someone to share it with. It made the burden less painful.

"Your presentation needs work," Suzette said after a pause. "It was a little over the top. Also, I'm pretty sure I saw that movie on TV."

The sudden elation he'd felt evaporated into a cloud of disappointment. "I wasn't lying; it's the truth."

"See, now you're just overselling it," Suzette pointed out. "When you do that, it looks like you're trying too hard. That's how you lose credibility. I'm a little disappointed in you, to be honest. Never thought a man with such a pirate smile could be such an amateur at subterfuge."

Liam took a few healthy swigs of his beer. Why bother? Even when he set out to tell the whole truth, he failed.

Suzette reached over the bar to snag a cherry from the condiment dish when the bartender wasn't looking. "But on the upside, I do kind of feel better about my own problems now."

"Glad to be of service," he said magnanimously.

"Here's the thing, and I'm only going to say this because I actually like you." She smelled like artificial cherries and beer as she leaned closer and enunciated, "You are a total and complete idiot."

Liam smirked. "I thought you were going to tell me something I didn't know."

"Okay. If you're so smart, then why are you letting a perfect woman like Cora slip through your fingers? No, don't try to deny it. I've seen you around her, and I know you're into her, so what's your problem?"

He opened his mouth to say something, but she cut him off.

"Your *real* problem, not the savior of humanity woo-woo stuff."

"Cora's too good for me." It was the only truth he could give her that she'd believe. "A man like me doesn't deserve her."

"Of course not," Suzette said easily. "She's brilliant and beautiful. She's kind to people even if they don't appreciate it. She's witty and funny and brave. She donates her time to charities and helps the community. I mean, if anyone deserves a halo, it's her, but just because she's too good for you doesn't mean you can't try to be deserving of her. Liam, she really likes you."

"I'm sorry." He glanced away, steeling himself. With a sick sense of resignation, he said the only thing he could. "I just don't feel that way about her."

Suzette snorted and gave him a "get real" look.

He forced himself to drive his point home. "Look, Cora is all the things you said, but I can't give her what she wants. I'm tied up in something else and can't be in a relationship with her."

"So, it's another woman, then." She said it like it was the only thing that made sense. The only way he'd even consider not jumping at the chance to be with Cora.

"No," he said hesitantly. But Suzette was like a dog after a bone, and Liam had a feeling she wasn't going to stop unless he shut her down. The best thing he could do was fall into the role she already expected. The role of a man unworthy of Cora. "It's more than that."

Suzette's mouth fell open, the fleeting astonishment on her face quickly morphing into distaste. "You're seeing multiple women right now?"

"Look, I'm not going to get into it with you because, with all due respect, it's none of your business. Just understand that I'm a man who likes his freedom. There's a lot of fish in the sea, and I don't want to tie myself down. Not now, and maybe not ever. I like Cora fine, but I'm not the right man for her."

He hoped the truth in that last part would convince Suzette he was sincere about the rest.

"But—"

"Jesus wept, woman. Leave me be already. Cora and I are never going to be together." His tone was harsher than he'd intended, but if he said anything more, he'd be "overselling it." Suzette glared at him like an angry lioness. He admired her for fighting so valiantly for Cora's happiness, but if she continued to press him, he wouldn't be able to keep up this facade of nonchalance. How strange. In the past, he'd never had a problem covering up his feelings and telling lies. The longer he stayed in this half-baked life the angels had thrown him into, the less he recognized himself. Cora was right. He had changed. Deep down, he should be glad of it, as it probably indicated he was becoming a better person, but it didn't make it any less disturbing.

"Fine." Suzette flipped a lock of flaming red hair over her shoulder, an angry flush across her freckled cheeks.

Liam made a show of checking out the two women who'd just sidled up to the bar. Even just the pretense of looking at other women made his insides roil with distaste, but he was playing the role and had to see it through.

The bartender set another round of beers in front of them. Suzette thanked him, then slid off her bar stool to leave. "I was wrong when I said you were a complete idiot, Liam. You are wise about one thing."

Liam dragged his beer closer, refusing to make eye contact lest she see the turmoil eating him up inside. "And what might that be?" he asked with an amused drawl. He made sure to sound arrogant, lazy, and slightly bored. Never let it be said he couldn't act.

"Cora is too good for you." Suzette looked at him like he was unwanted muck on the bottom of her shoe. "And from now on, I'm going to do everything I can to make her see that." She caught the bartender's attention and tilted her head in Liam's direction, snapping, "He's paying."

If he weren't so twisted up inside, he could've laughed at the irony. He was paying, all right. Suzette had no idea how much it cost him to push the woman he loved into the arms of another man. He took a long swig of beer.

She stalked away, leaving Liam to stare into the pale amber liquid, watching a teardrop of condensation slide down the glass until it disappeared into the wooden countertop like it never existed at all.

11

PROVIDENCE FALLS STATE PARK WAS AT THE BASE of the Blue Ridge Mountains, just west of the city. The lush foliage and picturesque trails made it a popular summer destination for local hikers, as well as a hot spot for traveling tourists. There were several hiking trails that branched out and reconverged, meandering along the river, with footpaths leading across charming wooden bridges flanked by a vibrant medley of evergreen, maple, beech, and oak trees.

For the more adventurous hikers, like Cora, the park had a gorgeous trail leading up toward a cliff overlooking a stunning waterfall that had been featured in many North Carolina magazines and travel guides. Aside from a handful of abandoned mines sprinkled throughout the area, the forest looked the same as it had for hundreds of years. To Cora, there was something awe-inspiring about standing in the middle of nature that had existed long before her and would go on existing long after she was gone. It was like stepping outside of her own life and being suspended in a secret world where time had no meaning and mankind was barely even a blip on the radar. Just as she'd hoped, getting out into nature today helped her to feel more grounded. With everything going on at the station, not to mention her personal feelings about Liam, this was exactly what she'd needed.

"I can't believe I let you talk me into hiking at this hour," Suzette grumbled as Cora led the way up the waterfall trail around eight o'clock on Saturday morning. "In my book, weekends are a sacred time for rest and reflection."

"This is restful," Cora said, gesturing to the beautiful forest around them. As if on cue, a cardinal swooped overhead, its brilliant red feathers glowing against the backdrop of greenery as a refreshing gust of wind rustled the leaves in the trees. They were about two-thirds of the way up the trail, and the air had grown cooler due to its close proximity to the waterfall.

"Not this kind of rest," Suzette said. "I'm talking about the cucumbers-on-your-eyes variety. The kind where you lounge around with a mud mask on your face while you reflect on the poor choices you made the night before."

Cora glanced at her friend, who was huffing and puffing along beside her with reddened cheeks. She couldn't be sure if the heightened color was just from exertion, or if Suzette was blushing. "What kind of poor choices are we talking about?"

"I saw Rob last night," Suzette said, holding up a hand to add, "By accident. I was on a blind date at Rookies, and it was awful. Seriously, Cora. This man danced like one of those inflatable windsock people at the auto dealership, and he was supermean to the servers. Anyway, I left early and ran into Rob on the way out. He said he wanted to talk, and I wasn't quite myself after dealing with Windsock Guy, so one thing led to another..." Suzette pulled a bottle of water from the pocket of her hoodie, took a long drink, and shrugged.

When she started to resume walking, Cora tugged on the

back of her friend's hoodie to stop her. "Oh, no, you don't. I have questions. First of all—"

"Yes," Suzette said, marching ahead. "The answer is yes."

"I didn't even ask my question," Cora called after her.

"I already know what's going through your head. So, yes."

"Really? You want to give me all your designer shoes because you and Rob have decided to elope to Minnesota to become farmers and live out your *Little House on the Prairie* dreams? Wow, that's so sudden. Tell me, when I visit you guys, will I need to bring my own bonnet, or can I just borrow one of—"

"Fine." Suzette whirled around, planting her hands on her hips. "Yes, Rob slept over last night. But nothing happened."

"I'm going to need a little more information, Ms. Wilson." Cora used her best "interrogation" voice, trying not to smile. Suzette was so clearly flustered; it was endearing and a little surprising. She usually acted very cavalier about the men she dated. "I thought you said Rob Hopper bothered you. What made you change your mind?"

Suzette plunked herself onto a fallen log. Her bright red hair danced in the breeze, and with the faint, whooshing sound of the waterfall in the distance and melodious birdsong overhead, she reminded Cora of a Disney princess from one of those woodland scenes. Except Suzette didn't look like she was about to break into song. Hives, maybe. She looked that agitated.

"What the heck happened, Suze?"

"We ended up at that all-night Italian restaurant. You know, the one where all the stoner kids go when they get the munchies? Rob ordered his favorite—pizza with Canadian bacon, bell peppers, pineapple, and extra sauce."

Cora propped her foot on the log to do calf stretches. "Hey, that's *your* favorite." She and Suzette had been best friends for so long they knew all those small, inconsequential details about each other that were unimportant in the grand scheme of things, but sacred within the circle of true friendship.

"I know," Suzette said in a hushed voice, like she was afraid of what it could mean. "At first, I thought it was just a fluke. But then we got to talking and I realized we have way more in common than I ever thought possible. Before I knew it, two hours had passed and we were still sitting in that corner booth, yapping away. I could've sat there all night, but I decided to be responsible and tell him I had to go home."

"And?"

"He ended up going home with me," Suzette said helplessly. "I told myself it was just for drinks, but we never even made it to the kitchen. I just opened my door, and *bam*! We started making out right there in the entryway, like two horny teenagers seizing the opportunity because we knew we'd be grounded for life in the morning. We somehow made it to the sofa, and here's where it gets really weird." She leaned forward with owl eyes. "Everything was going hot and heavy, and then Rob stopped. He just pulled back and got this really intense look on his face. He said he didn't want to mess things up with me, and I agreed we shouldn't rush into anything. So, we ended up just talking and…" Suzette wrinkled her nose in confusion. "Snuggling."

Cora blew out a breath. "Whoa."

"I know," Suzette said in exasperation. "Crazy, right?"

"Rob Hopper turned down sex in favor of just snuggling," Cora said thoughtfully. "That doesn't sound like him at all." When Rob saw a good thing, he was notorious for jumping right in, and Suzette was as good as it got.

"Eventually we just fell asleep on the sofa, and this morning, he gave me a kiss goodbye and said he'd call me later today."

"So, you guys are officially seeing each other?"

"I…" Suzette's cheeks turned red. "No, because that would

be so— I mean, come on. Rob Hopper? He's just..." She threw her hands up, shaking her head. Then her shoulders slumped, and she let out a defeated sigh. "I don't know. Maybe?"

Cora tried not to laugh at her friend's dejected expression. "You say that like it's a fate worse than death."

"It could be. Maybe I feel like I stumbled into one of those reality shows where the poor, unsuspecting fool gets pranked for everyone else's amusement." Suzette stood and began to pace. "I'm not sure what's going on with us. I'm afraid to even think about it. The whole thing is just bizarre."

"No, it's not. Suze, he's liked you for years. I've never known him to be hung up on someone for this long."

"That's because he's never had to be. Women tend to fall right into bed with him. They have a wild romp or two, and then he moves on to greener pastures. That's the problem. I didn't want to be just one of those girls."

"Trust me, you're not. I think he knows it, too; that's probably why he wants to slow things down." Cora remembered how upset Rob was when he'd talked to her at the station after Suzette refused to return his calls. He'd looked worse than she'd ever seen him, and now Cora felt certain his feelings for her best friend were genuine. "Not that it matters, but I just want you to know—and I can't believe I'm saying this about Rob Hopper—I approve."

Suzette had been biting her nails, but she dropped her hand, looking so relieved. "You don't think I'm crazy for even considering this whole thing?"

"Not at all. I just want you to be happy, and if he's the guy who does that, who am I to judge? Lord knows I've made my own share of mistakes, so it's not like I have a leg to stand on here."

Suzette's hopeful expression fell away, morphing into one of careful concern. "Cora. We need to talk about Liam for a minute." Uh-oh. Suzette looked way too serious, and Cora suddenly didn't want to hear whatever her friend was about to say.

"Let's not talk about him," Cora said in a rush. She knew Suzette believed Liam was in love with her, and it was only a matter of time before he caved, but Cora was sick and tired of putting herself out there when he didn't reciprocate her feelings. It was embarrassing, and a person could only take so much rejection before it just got pitiful. All she really wanted to do was forget about him this morning, which she'd been doing a pretty good job of so far. Not counting now, she'd already forgotten about him at least three times today. "It's not going anywhere, Suze, and I'm tired of trying to force something that's so one-sided. No, don't try to talk me out of it." She held up her hand when Suzette opened her mouth. "I've already made up my mind and—"

"You're right," Suzette interrupted.

Cora searched her friend's face in surprise. "I am?" For some reason, having Suzette agree with her was difficult to process, and it felt an awful lot like disappointment, though Cora refused to examine that. Suzette had been Liam's biggest champion until now, so if she'd fallen off the Team Liam wagon, then there really was no hope. What could've happened to make Suzette change her mind?

"I spoke with him at Dante's the other night," Suzette confessed. "And don't get mad, Cora, but I asked him about his feelings toward you."

Cora groaned. "Suzette—"

"I had to! It was the quickest way to get answers, and I was tired of watching you throw so much of your good energy into him. I needed to know if he was even worth it."

Cora didn't want to ask. The sinking sensation in the pit of her stomach already told her the answer. She suddenly wanted to turn and bolt down the mountain, jump in her car, and drive away. Just keep on driving like in those scenes in movies where the car drives off into the distance and the credits roll. The end. She needed to put this whole thing with Liam behind her. Why was it so hard to do? Why did every bone in her body seem magnetized to him every time he entered a room?

"I'm so sorry, Cora," Suzette said gently. "He said he likes you, but not enough to try for anything permanent. Apparently, there are too many fish in the sea, and he doesn't want to be tied down. Maybe not ever." She curled her lip with a moue of disgust. "Who knew he'd be such a walking cliché?"

"Right." Cora pretended to brush it off, telling herself the supernova-sized ache behind her sternum was relief, and nothing more. It wouldn't be the first time she'd embraced a lie when it came to Liam.

"He's so not worth it," Suzette said with feeling. "I can't believe I ever thought he'd be good enough for you. I think you should just write him off and move on to better things."

"I already have." Cora tried to sound casual and light, as if her feelings for Liam were just a passing fancy. Maybe if she pretended hard enough, she'd eventually believe it.

"Good," Suzette said with a bright smile. Too bright. Cora could tell Suzette was trying to help her pretend, which only made it worse. Both of them knew she was heartsick about this. "Speaking of better things," Suzette said in a valiant effort to rally. "Is Finn still planning to move to New York City at the end of the summer? Because I definitely think he's a great—"

"Suze," Cora said with a telltale hitch in her voice. She hoped her friend wouldn't notice. If Suzette started singing Finn's praises like Liam did, Cora knew she wasn't going to be able to hold it together. "Can we please talk about something else?

I came out here this morning to feel peaceful and think happy thoughts. I just need to clear my head and focus on things that are good for me right now. And if Liam really feels that way, it's fine. I'm totally okay with it and just want to move on."

Suzette studied her for a long moment, and Cora was afraid her friend could see straight into the very heart of her. To her infinite relief, Suzette gave her a decisive nod and started to back away. "Come on. Let's blow off some steam. I'll race you to the top. Last one there has to pay for breakfast."

Cora stood and dusted off her shorts, then loped up the trail after her. She could see Suzette's red ponytail swishing as she rounded a bend and disappeared. Instead of hurrying to catch up, Cora chose to walk in steady, measured steps, trying to ignore the piercing stab of sadness inside her every time she faced the facts.

Liam didn't want her. *Stab.*

Her instincts about him were dead wrong. *Stab.*

All those strange moments of déjà vu, the fragmented dreams where they seemed so connected, all of it meant nothing at all. *Stabbity stab stab.*

Cora's shoe caught on a stray tree root. She stumbled, grabbed a tree branch, and gave herself a mental shake. This wasn't working. She couldn't let the train wreck of her feelings for Liam ruin the peace she'd sought when she came on the hike this morning. Taking a deep breath, she squared her shoulders and forged on. For now, she was going to enjoy the beautiful foliage and breathe the fresh air, and just revel in the natural wonders of—

A rumbling growl came from her left as a dark shadow stepped out of the trees.

Cora let out a startled gasp.

Bear, the hulking man from the Booze Dogs' motorcycle club, looked just as surprised as she was. Surrounded by foliage in his namesake's natural habitat, he seemed even more intimidating than the last couple of times she'd seen him. The snaking tattoos around his muscular neck and arms only added to his menacing appearance. If not for the ripped blue jeans, bandanna, and faded Iron Maiden T-shirt, he could've been a barbarian warlord in one of those fantasy adventure movies from the eighties.

"What are you doing out here?" Cora asked, tamping down her surprise. She took a step back and did her best to sound cheerful and unassuming.

Bear's Neanderthal-like brows lowered into a scowl, and for a split second, Cora's self-defense training kicked into high gear. Knees slightly bending, she kept her arms loose and ready to move, making quick note of his areas of weakness: eyeballs, throat, kidneys, instep. He had no beef with her, as far as she knew, but it was hard not to feel nervous running into such a giant beast of a man in the woods like this.

After a slow perusal of her body, in which Bear took in her spandex running shorts, yoga tank, and hiking boots, his foreboding expression melted into a sly grin, which was so unexpected it was almost more alarming than the scowl. "Reckon I'm doing the same thing you are, sweet cheeks."

Cora ignored the nickname, keeping her weight balanced on the balls of her feet. "Hiking and enjoying the scenery?"

His grin turned almost feral as his gaze flew over her curves and crash-landed on her cleavage. "That's right."

Cora's back stiffened, and she crossed her arms to block his view. "I guess I didn't take you for someone who likes to exercise."

Now he looked incredulous, and maybe even a little offended.

"Outdoors," she added quickly. "In nature, I mean." Obviously, the man hit the weight rack. He looked like he ate kettlebells for breakfast.

"You don't know me, lady." He lifted his arm to rub a hand across the back of his neck, sending muscles rippling in places Cora didn't even know you could have muscles. She suddenly thought of Finn as an angry young teenager trying to fight Bear during that bar brawl. Cora marveled that Finn had the nerve to go up against the man. His sheer bravery and recklessness were undoubtedly what caught Eli Shelton's attention all those years ago.

"You're right. I don't." For all she knew, Bear could be a nature lover or a conservationist or an avid bird-watcher on the weekends. She glanced at his dirt-stained knuckles and the deep scrape on his forearm. Or maybe he just liked to uproot trees with his bare hands and haul them up the mountain for kicks.

"Anytime you want to get to know me better," he said with a wink, "you know where to find me."

Cora did her best not to roll her eyes, remembering his invitation to join the women who partied at the Doghouse on the weekends. "I'll pass."

Bear's deep chuckle sounded like a cascade of falling rocks. He glanced up the trail. "Where you headed?"

"To the top of the falls. My friend's right around the bend up there, so I'd better get going before she beats me. See you later." Cora turned and charged up the path.

"Girlie," he called after her.

Seriously? Cora kept walking. If he thought she was going to answer to that, then he was dumber than he looked, which was really saying something. He sounded just like the Booze Dogs' club president. Maybe Eli Shelton taught Misogyny 101 to all the new recruits. There was only so much she could take on a fine morning like this, and she was at her limit.

"Sweet cheeks," he hollered louder.

Past her limit. Cora spun and glared at him. "You've got to

stop with the derogatory nicknames. It's rude and makes you sound like you escaped evolution and are still dragging your knuckles on the ground." As far as self-defense techniques went, provoking an animal in the wild wasn't at the top of her list, but some things couldn't be helped. Besides, Bear wasn't looming over her anymore, and she was a fast runner. "I mean, sweet cheeks? Really? Do you honestly think that's an appropriate name to call a woman?"

Bear looked a little surprised and a whole lot amused. "Only when it applies, doll face. And for you…" He strained to look at her backside. "It applies."

Cora threw her hands up and turned to go. "I'm done here."

"Stick to the path," Bear said sharply.

She glanced over her shoulder. All the humor in his eyes dissolved until they were cold and flat and deadly. The man who looked at her now was as scary as his namesake. She dug her heels in, bracing to run if she had to. Even though he was built like a war tank, Bear didn't seem like a true threat to her, but she couldn't afford to take chances.

"There are dangerous animals in these mountains, and they don't like trespassers," he continued in a low growl. "Would hate for a pretty thing like you to stumble into one and get hurt." With that, he turned and lumbered down the trail, sending tiny birds fleeing from the bushes.

Cora watched him go with the uneasy feeling he wasn't talking about black bears and bobcats.

12

LIAM PACED THE BACKYARD OF CORA'S HOUSE, doing his best to sound respectful as he addressed the fluffy white clouds overhead. "Angels, I need to speak with you, if it's not too much to ask." He stopped near the fence, staring into the azure sky, waiting, but the angels didn't answer.

Blowing out a frustrated breath, he began to walk along the edge of the fence, his mind spinning in growing agitation. It never worked when he tried to summon the angels, but he only had two weeks left to complete the task they gave him, and he was desperate. He needed them now, more than ever.

Things between Cora and Finn weren't moving fast enough. Love between two people took time, everyone knew that, but Liam didn't have the luxury of sitting around waiting for things to progress naturally. The angels had given him extra knowledge and skills to help him navigate this world, but right now he needed something far more powerful than just one of their helpful "boosts." He needed an actual miracle. Unfortunately, they didn't seem inclined to come to his aid. Maybe if he called them by their names? In old Irish folklore, a name held power. It was worth a try.

"Agon?" Liam leaned a shoulder against the fence, praying they'd take pity on him. "Samael? I need help." He fought to remain patient, but after fifteen minutes of hearing nothing but the whoosh of occasional cars driving by and the melodious chatter of birds in the trees, he thumped the fence with his fist. Had they deserted him, then?

Marching back inside, Liam flopped on the living room sofa, stuck with the bitter reality that he was on his own without their guidance. Ranting about his predicament wouldn't get him anywhere. He needed a plan. His gaze roamed over the bookshelves filled with Cora's favorite books. The blank, flat-screen TV that sat on a console against the wall. The fireplace mantel with the small clock that chimed on the hour. He took comfort in the cozy room, letting the casual, familiar atmosphere ease his mind. When he'd first visited Cora's house, he'd found it strange and opulent, with its bouncy, overstuffed furniture, plush wall-to-wall carpeting, and mysterious modern appliances. The refrigerator alone seemed like a gold mine, stocked with enough food to feed an entire family. He'd enjoyed some of the modern conveniences right away, and balked at others. At first, he'd been reticent to use the dishwasher and clothes machine and lawn mower, finding the loud machines and complex mechanisms daunting, but eventually he grew comfortable with them. He'd learned a lot since then. Now, the place didn't feel unusual at all. It just felt like...*home*. But no matter how comfortable he felt living there with Cora, the reality was that the house—the life—none of it was his, and it never would be.

With a groan, Liam rubbed the heels of his hands over his eyes, wondering how he was going to get out of the mess he'd made. The angels had ignored him before, so this was nothing new, but their neglect seemed to cut deeper now. He could feel the urgent press of time embedded under his skin like a sharp splinter. No matter how much he wished he could ignore it, he couldn't escape the painful fact that time was running out. He had only two weeks left in this blasted life, and he had to make it count.

Cora's cat, Angel, meowed, slinking into the room to curl his body around Liam's ankle.

"Well, at least one angel has deigned to grace me with a visit." He scooped up the cat and brought them face-to-face. "I don't suppose you could hunt down a miracle, drag it back home, and drop it at my feet to show your appreciation?"

The cat twitched an ear and glanced away.

"No. I thought not, you mangy beast," he said affectionately. "What good are you to me, then?"

Angel bumped Liam's face with the top of his furry head and began to purr.

"Aye, I suppose there is that." Liam smoothed the cat's sleek fur. He never would've admitted such a thing in his old life, never even imagined it, but there was something both humbling and extraordinarily comforting about being on the receiving end of such dedicated feline devotion.

He heard the garage door open and gently set Angel on the sofa. Then he began to spin up a plan. If the angels weren't going to help him anymore, fine. He would just have to redouble his efforts on his own.

When Cora walked into the house, she looked flushed from her hike, but her mouth was pressed tight, and her expression was shuttered. She usually came back energized and happy after a workout, but today something seemed off.

"There you are," Liam said from his spot on the sofa. "Did you have a good run?"

She made a noncommittal sound and disappeared down the hall to her bedroom. A few minutes later, he heard the shower running and glanced at the cat. "She seems to be in a mood. We'll need to stay sharp."

Angel yawned, tucked into a circle, and settled in for a nap.

"Fine help you are," Liam muttered.

Cora came down the hall ten minutes later smelling like her favorite sweet, herbal shower soap. She was wearing baggy sweatpants and a tank top, and her freshly washed hair hung in damp ringlets down her back. Without glancing in his direction, she stalked past the living room and into the kitchen.

The clock on the mantel chimed, reminding Liam just how dire his situation was. Time was not on his side. Determined to bring her and Finn together no matter what, he followed her into the kitchen with renewed purpose.

Cora was standing at the counter making what she called "spa water," which consisted of a few slices of citrus fruit and a handful of raspberries tossed into a pitcher of water with ice. Liam had tried it once and been underwhelmed. Cora had said it was healthy and refreshing, but Liam didn't care. Raw kale was also supposed to be healthy, but that didn't mean he felt inclined to choose it over, say, a refreshing plate of chocolate chip cookies.

"We have juice and lemonade in the fridge," he told her, just in case she didn't know.

She shrugged a shoulder but didn't turn around. Her back was ramrod straight and her voice sounded strained. "I'm fine."

He fiddled with a stack of mail on the counter, glancing sideways at her. Something had her hackles up, and he had a gnawing feeling in his gut it had to do with him. "Are you...all right?"

"I'm fine," she repeated, methodically slicing oranges.

So, that was a definite "no." If there was one thing that he knew about women, no matter the century, "I'm fine" delivered in that tone could mean a great many things, none of which were the literal interpretation. But it was best not to poke a hornet's nest. Instead, he forged ahead with his plan. "Listen, I have an idea for dinner tonight. How about we barbecue and invite Finn over?"

Cora stopped slicing for a split second, then resumed as if she hadn't heard him. But now her posture was even stiffer than before, and her shoulders were almost to her ears. He'd somehow lost ground, but there was nothing for it. The best he could do was keep pushing forward because he was racing the clock. If time waited for no man, then he was currently the pitiful straggler in last place.

"We could throw steaks on the grill and make those frosty drinks you like." He walked to the freezer to check for the frozen bags of margarita slush. "There are three bags in here. One for each of us."

Cora tossed the fruit into the pitcher. "No, thanks."

"You don't want to barbecue tonight?"

"Nope." She made a blasé popping sound with the *p* at the end of the word.

"There's a new fast and angry race car movie showing at the theater," he said hopefully. "We could all go see that and get dinner afterward?"

"Count me out." She poured herself a glass of water and began to drink.

"Bowling, then," he offered, moving to the next item on the list of activities he'd mentally prepared. If not that, there was ice-skating, miniature golf, and some type of pottery painting activity, which, quite frankly, sounded abysmal. Who would willingly sit in a room painting dishes for hours on end? He'd rather walk blindfolded and barefoot across a floor full of tacks, but desperate times and all that. It didn't really matter what they did, as long as it involved Cora spending as much time as possible with Finn. "Finn seems to be quite a decent athlete. I'm sure he'd enjoy—"

"Will you stop?" Cora plunked her glass on the counter, her mouth pressed tight with annoyance. He'd expected that, but the sadness in her eyes made his heart ache, as if his suggestions were hurting her feelings. "Just stop, Liam. I know what you're trying to do, and it's not necessary."

He took a step back, curling his hands into fists so he wouldn't be tempted to reach for her. If he could just hold her for a while, it would make them both feel better, but he knew he couldn't do that. Painful or not, he had to remember the bigger picture. "I'm not trying to make you mad, Cora. I was just thinking we should spend more time with Finn, that's all."

She crossed her arms. "Both of us, or just me?"

"Both," he lied. "Finn has helped us a lot these past few weeks. He's a good man, and I just thought it would be nice if you—I mean, if all of us—"

"Enough." She shouldered past him to leave.

"What's the matter with you?" Liam asked in frustration. They'd never get anywhere if she wasn't willing to talk.

Cora spun to face him. "Do you think I was born yesterday? I know you're trying to set me up with Finn. I saw that coming a mile away, the moment you started singing his praises in the car last Friday night. And you know what's funny? I agree with you. Finn is a great guy. I know that probably better than you do, but I'm not going to jump his bones just because you've decided to throw me at him."

Anger suddenly flared, hot and bright. "I'm not throwing you at him." But it was another lie, wasn't it? He was trying to do exactly that, and though it couldn't be helped, he hated himself for it. The very idea of giving her up settled over his shoulders like a cloak of poisonous thorns he couldn't rip off. Even when he was forcing himself to do the right thing, the stinging knowledge that he was going to lose her permeated every waking moment. Sometimes, it was enough to drive him mad.

"Save it, Liam," Cora said, holding up a hand. "I don't need your help finding a man. I've done perfectly fine on my own before you, and I'll do just fine after you're gone."

After you're gone.

His anger suddenly dissolved into bleak despair, settling into the pit of his stomach like yesterday's ashes. Liam knew he wasn't long for this world. The concept was nothing new, but the reality of it hurt so much more when it came from Cora's lips. She thought she'd be all right after he was gone, but nothing could be further from the truth.

"You're wrong," he said, gulping past the geyser of bitter emotions welling inside him. Images of Cora's past lives flashed through his mind—the same images the angels had shown him in the Chamber of Judgment. Cora working in a factory during WWII...dying during an explosion. Cora as a young nurse, caring for soldiers during an outbreak of scarlet fever...dying in a hospital bed. Cora as a nanny, rushing to save a young child from the path of a runaway horse...dying in the street. "You're not going to be okay on your own," he said miserably. "You've made mistake after mistake, and it's always ended in tragedy."

"How dare you?" Hot splashes of color bloomed in her cheeks. "You haven't even known me long enough to comment on my dating history."

"Magnus Blackwell, for example?" Oh, it was a low blow. Liam knew it the moment he said the blasted words, but they cartwheeled out of his mouth before he could catch them.

Cora gaped at him in disbelief, pain flashing across her face before she could cover it up. Bloody ever-loving hell, he was an idiot of the highest order. This, right here, was why he didn't deserve her. *He* put that stricken look on her face. He would give his soul to take it back, but unfortunately, his soul was already wagered.

"Cora, I'm so sorry," Liam said in a rush. "It was an asinine thing to say, and I didn't mean it. Sometimes stupid things just come flying out before I think because I'm a damned fool. What happened with Magnus wasn't your fault; it was all him. You must know that I don't believe—"

"Magnus was a mistake," she said in a strained voice. "It almost cost me my life. That's true. But he was a one-off. I'll be much more careful when I choose to date someone new. Regardless, it's none of your business."

"You can't—" Liam broke off in frustration, choosing his words carefully. He didn't want to risk making her madder than she already was. The smart thing to do would be to back off and try his plan again in a week or so, but he didn't have the luxury of doing that. Taking a deep breath, he said, "You don't have to date someone new."

"Again," she said evenly. "None of your business."

"You're right. It's only that I want you to be happy, and… There's already someone in your life who cares very deeply for you. He's right under your nose and has been there all along." Cora looked guarded, yet so vulnerable. Liam wanted to embrace her and promise her everything was going to be okay, but he couldn't bring himself to lie to her any more than he already had. "I know you don't want to hear it, but if you could just give Finn a chance, you might realize how suited you are for each other. You deserve someone like him." If only he could tell her the truth about why it was so important. Maybe then, it would help her understand.

"You seem to be forgetting that Finn is packing up his life, as we speak, to move across the country," she pointed out. "For good."

"That's not carved in stone," he said quickly. "Things can still change." He had to believe that, or all would truly be lost.

"Nothing's going to change, Liam, because I won't let it. Finn is a good friend, and I'd never stand in the way of his career. I know what drives him to do what he does. His job is everything to him."

"That's where you're wrong," he said fiercely. Finn was as enamored with Cora in this life as he'd been back in 1844 Ireland.

"And how would you know?" she asked, scoffing. "You couldn't even stand Finn when you first met him, so don't act like these last few months have made you the expert on his feelings, or mine, for that matter. Why do you even care so much? Look, you've already made it clear you're not interested in this." She waved a finger between them, her voice trembling. The next words out of her mouth were like claws raking across his heart. "I'm not some pathetic person who needs you to play matchmaker or push me toward Finn like he's a consolation prize. I get it, Liam. You don't like me. And you know what? That's—"

"I don't like you?" he interrupted, reeling from the sheer absurdity of it. "*Like?* Jesus wept, Cora!" A jagged bark of laughter erupted from some broken place inside him. Was that truly what she believed? Every single action, every breath he'd taken since falling into this new life, was because he loved her. The whole reason he was in this predicament was because he couldn't *stop* loving her. And though it didn't serve his purpose, and because he was an utter fool, he had to set her straight right here, and now. He couldn't let her go on believing he didn't care.

"You have no idea what I've gone through these past few months, living with you under the same roof," Liam said. "Knowing your face is the first I'll see every morning when I wake. Your voice the last I'll hear every night slipping into my dreams. Feeling you so close every day, yet unable to…" He trailed off and dipped his chin before he bared everything—his hopes, his dreams, his imperfect, damaged soul. There was a fine line he still had to walk here, but it was hard when straining under the weight of so many secret emotions. With a ragged breath, he lifted his head, letting her see all the anguish and yearning and despair, telling her with his eyes all the things he couldn't allow himself to put into words.

"You are," he said reverently, "the very best person I've ever known, or could ever know. The way you care for others. The way you put their needs ahead of your own. Your adventurous spirit and bravery and willingness to see the good in people. You are dazzling in your grace and compassion. Everything about you is pure and fresh and hopeful as the dawn, Cora. And you don't belong with an ordinary man who's done terrible, selfish things—a man like me who will ultimately be your downfall. There's no world in which I could ever deserve to lo—" He stopped himself just in time before he said something that could ruin everything. "I care too much to see you end up unhappy. You deserve someone who's good down to the very marrow of his bones. Someone who will always do right by you and never hurt you or cause you pain."

Cora was standing before him with a stunned look on her face. A wave of understanding swelled in her gaze, turning her ocean-blue eyes soft and misty. He had the feeling she saw right through to his imperfect, damaged soul, anyway. He'd said too much, but fools often did. There was no taking it back now.

"So, that's what this is about." She said it like a revelation as she stepped closer. Dangerously closer. Her sweet, intoxicating scent enveloped him, making it difficult to focus. "You think you'll hurt me."

"I know I will. I already have." He was breathing hard. Angry with himself, and angry with her for being so damned tempting and making this so difficult. This conversation wasn't going at all the way he'd planned. They were supposed to be talking about Finn and arranging to spend the evening with him. "I'm not a good man, Cora. I never have been, and I won't see you hurt. I've made that mistake in the past, and I can't allow it to happen again."

Ever so slowly, she reached out and took his hand, tracing the lines on his palm. Liam felt the gentle touch like a spark of heat igniting him from the inside. Everything around him narrowed down to that slow, sweet drag of her fingertip over his calloused skin. "What if I said I was willing to take the chance?"

A fierce longing gripped him so hard it stole his breath. He'd waited so long to see her look at him like this he could barely force himself to choke out, "We can't risk it."

Cora dipped her chin and let his hand go.

He curled it into a fist, as if he could hold on to her touch forever.

"Suzette told me that you don't want to be tied down," she said, leaning against the counter. "You said there were too many fish in the sea?"

Liam glanced away with a silent curse. He'd been able to lie to Suzette, but there was no way he could stand in front of Cora and say something so absurd. Not after he'd practically bared his heart only moments earlier.

"It's true, I suppose," Cora mused, shrugging. "I mean, I'm nothing special."

His gaze shot to hers in angry disbelief. "Don't be ridiculous."

"Just one woman out of billions out there," she said with a melodious sigh.

"But the only one who matters," he said fiercely. Cora's slow smile made him feel like he'd been dipped in warm honey. Mother of God, he was in trouble. What was happening? Somehow, in the space of just a few minutes, Cora had gone from giving him the cold shoulder to giving him a sultry smile that felt like a gift he wanted very much to open.

"Do something for me," she said softly.

Anything. Everything. He'd harness the moon and bring it to her on a silver platter if he could.

"Kiss me," she whispered. "Just once."

Liam groaned, pressing the heels of his hands to his eyes. He was so far off the beaten path he'd stumbled into quicksand and was hanging on by a twig. If he didn't put an end to this, he was going to do something terribly, deliciously bad. "I don't want to ruin your life, Cora."

"You won't." This time, she stepped close enough that he could feel her soft breath against his face. She gently pulled his hands from his eyes, then peered at him from beneath thick, dark lashes tipped with gold. "It's just one kiss. If you hate it, we'll never do it again." Before Liam could answer, she stood on her tiptoes and pressed a soft, featherlight brush of her mouth against his.

Every rational thought was eclipsed by the sweet, raspberry-citrus whisper of his name on her lips. "Liam."

And that was all it took.

The twig snapped, and down he sank, spiraling into sweet, perilous oblivion and unable to care. Logic and reason scattered like dandelion fluff on the wind. He heard the need in her voice, and he answered.

Wrapping one hand around her waist, Liam slid the other up to cradle Cora's head as he pulled her tightly against him, claiming her mouth with his. Her soft moan of pleasure sank under his skin, stoking the fire inside him until it licked at his self-control. Her body was sweet and warm and lush, melting into all his hard edges until instinct crowded in and took over. Without breaking the kiss, he lifted her up and sat her on the counter, fitting his hips between her thighs. *Mine.* Everything about being with this woman, *his* woman, felt so inexplicably right, to believe otherwise seemed more like a sin than the one he was committing.

They had to stop. Deepening the kiss, he slid his hands over the luscious swell of her hips to circle around her narrow waist.

Nothing good will come of this. She trailed her fingers under his shirt, tracing along the bare, muscled ridges of his abdomen.

Liam groaned. *This is madness!* But she tasted so much like heaven that risking his soul to hell didn't seem like such a bad trade if he could just live here in her arms for a few moments longer.

Suddenly, his phone began to ring, the shrill sound echoing off the kitchen walls.

Cora pulled away. He fought against the driving need to yank her right back where she belonged. Instead, he tried to rise above his baser instincts, but he wasn't feeling particularly buoyant, so his voice fell flat when he said, "I should get that."

"Or you could let it go to voice mail?" she suggested.

Brilliant woman. That was a much better idea. Like magnets, they came together again, only this kiss was far more carnal, escalating quickly until their movements became urgent and more demanding.

A minute later, his phone rang again.

Liam growled like an angry lion, and Cora giggled against his mouth. He reached into the back pocket of his jeans and yanked out his phone. Slice Biddlesworth's name flashed across the screen. Liam held it up to show Cora.

She sat up straighter. "You'd better take it. Maybe he found the pictures."

In a tone far grumpier than he intended, Liam answered with a harsh "What?"

"H-hey, man," Slice said hesitantly. "I was just going to leave you a message."

"I'll hang up, then, and leave you to it." Mind already on the delectable woman who was smiling in amusement, Liam started to hang up, but she grabbed the phone.

"Hi, Slice. It's Officer McLeod." She put the phone on speaker. "Did you find the pictures?"

"No, because I still haven't found my laptop," Slice said. "I thought I threw it in with the boxes my mom was taking to storage, but there's a slight problem."

"What is it?" Cora scooted off the kitchen counter and began to pace the small kitchen. Already, he could see her lighting up as she slipped into investigative mode.

The caveman part of Liam's brain wanted to yank away the phone, crush it under his heel, and carry her down the hall to bed. Instead, he took deep, even breaths and tried to ignore the raging lust still pumping through his body like wildfire.

Walking to the sink, he gulped down an entire glass of cold water, then braced his arms on the counter and stared blindly out the window into the backyard. Slice couldn't have picked a worse time to call. Maybe in the grand scheme of things, this was divine intervention, but it felt more like a sadistic prank. Somewhere down there, the devil was laughing, long and hard.

"My stepdad was also doing a dump run that day," Slice was saying. "And he had a bunch of boxes in the garage, too."

Cora sank onto a kitchen chair. "Please don't say what I think you're going to say."

"There's a slight chance my laptop got thrown away by accident." Slice sounded nervous. "I know I said I'd call you guys that day you came to Zippy Lube, but I haven't been able to find it yet."

Cora tilted her face to the ceiling and sighed. "So, we're back to square one."

"Not yet," Slice said quickly. "I'm going to my mom's storage unit to go through the last few boxes, so it could still be there, but I just wanted you guys to know what's up. Just so you don't think I'm over here trying to hinder your investigation, or whatever."

"It's fine. Call us the moment you find anything." Cora said goodbye and hung up the phone. "That was our best lead."

"We'll find another." Liam took the chair on the opposite side to her. The flimsy wooden table was nothing. He could so easily reach across it. Drag her into his lap. Pick up where they left off. He stared at her with smoldering intensity, his mind flipping through all the wicked things he wanted to do with her. If only things were different. If only he was a different man. With a heavy sigh, he stuffed those thoughts down deep and prepared to do the right thing.

"Cora," he began.

"Liam." A soft smile played at the corners of her mouth as she nibbled her bottom lip. There was an adorable pink blush creeping up the sides of her neck. It was all he could do not to pounce on her like a feral animal.

"About all that," he said, waving his hand in the direction of the kitchen counter.

"You don't have to say anything," she said simply. "I got the answer I needed." Then she gave him a mysterious smile and walked away.

===================

13

CORA YAWNED INTO HER COFFEE ON MONDAY morning, waiting for that initial kick of caffeine to jump-start her day. For the past two nights, she'd had vivid dreams that jolted her awake and remained with her for long hours afterward. This time, the dreams had nothing to do with Magnus Blackwell and her near-drowning experience, which was a godsend. The newest dreams she'd been having were far more pleasurable because they featured her with Liam. Ever since meeting him, she'd had hazy visions of them together, the wisp of a fragmented dream or the odd déjà vu, but they'd never been as vivid as they were now.

On Saturday night after they'd kissed, Cora had a dream so real she woke up with the distinct scents of fresh air and distant wood smoke and newly tilled earth enveloping her senses. She could practically feel the grit of soil on her hands, and the rough linen of Liam's shirt brushing her arm as they sat, side by side, against a low stone wall sharing an apple. It had been dusk, or dawn—it was hard to tell. She'd been wearing an old-fashioned gown and a blue wool cloak, and she could still see the tiny flowers embroidered on her impractical soft slippers. It struck her how different their attire had been—hers made from fine silk and lace, and his from worn, coarse cloth faded by the sun. Though she couldn't remember their conversation, she remembered how they'd laughed together, and how he'd leaned close until their foreheads touched, whispering her name like a prayer. She'd been just as attracted to him in that dream as she was now.

Cora stole a glance at him now, sitting across the room at his desk in the Providence Falls Police Station. Even in clean, modern clothes, he still had a roguish, wild quality that no amount of grooming could change, and she loved that about him.

As if he could hear her thoughts, Liam glanced up and gave her a secret smile that was just for her. The bustle and noise of the station suddenly faded away until all she saw was the rougher, old-fashioned version of Liam from her dreams superimposed against the more modern version of the man looking at her now. Two different timelines, but the same person. Even the same devilish smile. She blinked, and the vision vanished as the busy police station came whooshing back into focus. Cora rubbed her forehead. This type of thing had happened before, but just like the recent dreams she'd been having, it was much more vivid.

"McLeod, O'Connor." Captain Thompson strode through the pen looking surly and unapproachable, as usual. "My office." It was his first day back from his impromptu time off, but he seemed no more rested than before.

They followed him inside, and Cora noticed his desk was exactly as he'd left it—littered with stacks of papers, an empty fast-food bag, stained coffee mugs, a bottle of Tums, and—to Cora's surprise—a pack of cigarettes. She remembered him commenting a couple of years ago how his wife was nagging him to quit, so he'd gone through nicotine patches and eventually kicked the habit. If he was starting up again, then he really must be having a tough time.

"We were all surprised when you took the week off, Captain," she said, taking the seat next to Liam on the other side of the desk. "Is everything okay?"

Boyd looked annoyed. "Are you asking to feed the latest gossip at the watercooler, or just because you're curious?"

His comment stung, but she did her best not to show it. "Just concerned. I've never known you to take time off, that's all."

He popped a couple of antacids and washed them down with a gulp of soda. "Alice's mom is unwell, so we went to visit for a few days. I had to get back, but Alice will be staying there to help care for her."

"I'm sorry to hear that," Cora said. "How long will she be—"

"Not sure," Boyd interrupted. "Could be weeks, maybe months. Now, if you two don't mind, I have a meeting with the mayor in an hour, and I'd really like to bring him some good news." He sat back and steepled his fingers, staring expectantly at her and Liam. "Fill me in on your progress with the Booze Dogs."

"We have a lead, but it's iffy," Cora said, glad she had at least something hopeful to report. "Do you remember when Lindsey Albright came in with that picture she took outside John Brady's house on the night of his murder?"

Captain Thompson nodded. "I saw it, and it was useless. I spoke to her myself."

"Yes, but she took several pictures that night. Apparently, there were others."

That got his attention. He sat up straighter. "She said there was only that one."

"Not according to her boyfriend."

"Why would she lie about that?" He swiveled his chair to face the wall for a moment, deep in thought. The scowl on his face grew more pronounced, and Cora noticed his neck was turning an alarming shade of red. Added to the rest of his overall demeanor these past few weeks, he was beginning to look like the poster child for Heart Attacks R Us. This wasn't good. He needed to take better care of himself, but that was up to him. The best she could do to help was to solve the cases and help ease some of the pressure.

"Lindsey probably meant it was the only useful photo," Cora said quickly, hoping to appease his growing agitation. "It's possible she sent him a few others and forgot. At any rate, we'll know soon enough because the good news is, Slice has the rest of those pictures on his laptop."

"The bad news," Liam added dryly, "is he's misplaced the laptop. He put it in a box and thinks it might've accidentally been tossed at the dump. Says he'll get back to us soon if he finds it."

The captain pressed his mouth into a grim line, then thumped the desk with his fist. "Damn that kid."

When his phone began to ring, he didn't answer, just stared at it, lost in thought. Cora couldn't blame him; she'd been overwhelmed with everything for weeks, but the feeling had almost become familiar to the point where she could accept it, like a frog in hot water. She'd been simmering under the pressure of first John Brady's murder, then Lindsey Albright's, and then the Booze Dogs' theft, and things just kept getting hotter and hotter with no relief. The captain was under even more pressure than the rest of them because he had to answer to the mayor's office, and he'd been gone for a week. Coming back to everything after spending an emotional few days with a sick relative was enough to shake even the most steadfast person.

"Captain?" Cora asked hesitantly.

He didn't answer right away. When his phone finally stopped

ringing, he blinked a few times and looked around as if he were coming up for air.

Liam had been silent for most of their conversation, but now he leaned forward and rapped his knuckles on the desk. "Boyd, are you all right, man?"

Captain Thompson blinked again, then turned to Liam and said coldly, "I've told you not to call me that, O'Connor."

"Oh, aye," Liam said with a nonchalance that bordered on disrespectful. "So sorry, *Captain*. It's only you're beginning to look a bit like a teakettle someone forgot on the stove, and I didn't want you to boil over."

Cora cringed. Liam's cocky attitude was a bad move. The captain was already angry, and this wouldn't win them any points. She kept her face politely blank but kicked Liam's foot with the heel of her boot. She was going to do more than that if the captain went nuclear—and he looked like he just might. Where was Liam's sense of self-preservation?

The phone began ringing again, and this time the captain reached for it. Without looking at either of them, he said gruffly, "That'll be all."

Once they were in the hall, Cora elbowed Liam in the ribs. "You need to check that attitude, Officer, or you'll find your-self pushing pencils at your desk while the rest of us do all the fun stuff."

"My humblest apologies," he said with a devious smile. "The last thing I want to do is miss out on all the fun stuff with you." Just like that, Cora was inundated with visceral images of their heated kisses back in her kitchen last Saturday. Paired with her vivid dreams of him over the weekend, her entire body flushed with desire and a hot blush scorched across her cheeks. They hadn't discussed what happened, afterward. For the rest of the weekend, they'd gone about their business as usual. In fact, Cora even let Liam invite Finn over for dinner on Sunday night. It had been an altogether pleasant time, especially for her, because she now knew without a doubt that Liam cared for her. He liked her a *lot*, and that gave her renewed hope. Even now, she felt lighter and more content because—as Liam had said—nothing was carved in stone. There was still time for things between them to grow into something more.

Liam burst through the police station doors and into the bright sunshine outside. He kept walking and didn't stop until he was halfway around the block. Images of Cora's flushed cheeks, the way her lips parted, the way her azure eyes grew soft and dreamy, threatened to break his careful composure. He knew he was playing with fire when he made that comment, but he couldn't help himself, and it was clear she'd been thinking about their kiss over the weekend. So was he. He hadn't stopped thinking about it ever since it had happened, and it was becoming a huge problem. Right now, all he wanted to do was storm back into the police station, toss her over his shoulder, and drag her back home, where he could ravish her properly.

Ignoring what had transpired between them was an exercise in futility. It had taken all his control to go about the weekend pretending like nothing had happened. Desperate to fix the slipup, he'd suggested dinner with Finn and was shocked when she agreed. Finn, true to his nature, had been charming and easygoing and the perfect dinner guest, and he'd even made Cora laugh a few times. Liam's jealousy had been alive and well, no matter how hard he tried to fight it. Logically he knew it was good for Cora and Finn to get along. But deep down, he still wanted all her smiles and all her laughter for himself, especially now that he'd had an intimate reminder of just how good it could be. He wanted *so badly* to hold her. To imagine a future with her. Every time she walked past him now, all he could think about was the sweet taste of her, and the way her body had felt, molded against his, and how very much he wanted to do it again.

Liam let out a growl of frustration, startling a jogger on the sidewalk. The man gave him a large berth and crossed the street. Turning back to the station, Liam steeled himself to do what needed to be done. He could still succeed with the task the angels had given him. All he had to do was steer clear of anything physical with Cora. It didn't help that she seemed to feel just as strongly for him as he did for her, but he could still fix this. It would improve his chances if he had more time on his side, but it wasn't absolutely necessary. Though people often grew into love, easing into a romantic relationship over the course of many years, it wasn't the only way. Sometimes people crossed paths on the street for the very first time, and all it took was a single glance. One heartbeat of time when a soul recognized its match. Hadn't the very thing happened to him? He'd climbed through Cora's bedroom window all those lifetimes ago, and within their first conversation, he was already falling for her.

By the time Liam reached the police station parking lot, he'd managed to wrestle the memory of their shared kisses into the background of his mind. *Barely*. It helped to focus on what he needed to do next, so with renewed determination, he began plotting another evening for Cora and Finn. Time was not on his side, but they could still fall for each other as long as he took himself out of the equation. All was not lost. Love was nothing if not surprising and unpredictable, and this could still work. It had to. He was betting his life on it.

14

"THERE HE GOES AGAIN WITH THAT GYM BAG," Otto said as Happy stalked out of the station on Tuesday afternoon.

Liam watched the tall, lanky police officer disappear down the hall. Happy was a private man who didn't like to mingle with the rest of the officers, but it didn't faze Liam. Some people were just born quiet and contemplative, and making the effort to engage in small talk was draining for them.

"Maybe he's having a late lunch with the captain," Mavis chirped as she added a ream of paper to the copy machine in the corner of the pen. "Although something tells me his wife, Alice, wouldn't put up with Happy being the third wheel on her weekly lunch date with her husband."

"Why would anyone willingly want to have lunch with Happy?" Rob asked from his desk as he repeatedly tossed a rubber ball into the air. It had been a slow day, and with the captain out, the atmosphere was more laid-back than usual.

"I would," Otto said cheerfully. "Happy's not that bad, once you can look past his gruff exterior."

Rob snorted. "Speak for yourself. Happy's gotten more and more surly over the past few months. Although, when you get right down to it, having lunch with his charming mug staring at you couldn't be any worse than having to eat lunch with Alice." He gave an exaggerated shiver of distaste.

"Rob," Cora admonished. "That's not very nice."

"But." He held up a finger. "You can't say it's not true."

Liam had to give the man that. Alice looked nice enough, but underneath, she was bitter as sour ale and tough as hardtack. He'd rather guzzle coffee than spend time in her presence, though the muddy sludge of a drink was only slightly less offensive. Granted, he didn't know much about Alice in this lifetime, but her personality seemed the same as it was back in Ireland, and she'd nagged Boyd incessantly.

Cora waved Rob off and walked up to Liam's desk. Today she was wearing jeans and a fitted top the color of Irish bluebells. It matched her eyes and highlighted her curves to perfection. He tried to forget the memory of those soft curves pressed against him, but it was futile. She was standing too close. He had to force his attention back to his computer lest he do something unforgivable like drag her onto his lap and finish what they'd started in that kitchen.

"I'm in the mood for lunch at the Rusty Spoon," Cora said, leaning against the edge of his desk. The faintest trace of lavender and sun-warmed vanilla floated over him, making him ache. "Want to come with me?"

Yes. A hundred times, yes. But that wasn't the correct answer. Liam bit the insides of his cheeks and forced himself to say, "I'm very busy right now."

She leaned over to see what he was working on. "Browsing YouTube?"

He minimized the screen. "I was researching something."

Nothing in particular, but ever since he discovered these fascinating videos, they served as a great diversion. It seemed like anything under the sun was there to learn and explore. It was unfathomable how much information people shared just for the hell of it. In his old life, when people didn't know something, they just shrugged and said, "I guess we'll never know," and moved on. Here, the moment you posed a question, you could satisfy your curiosity with just the push of a button on a computer. It was a form of decadence he'd never even dreamed of, something that went beyond material things like food and shelter. More importantly, it was a powerful form of distraction, which he desperately needed.

"Come on, Liam. That stuff will be there when you get back. Let's go get cheeseburgers. With the crispy onion straws?" She gave him a knowing smile, and he felt his resolve crumble because, well, he was only human.

"Fine." He rolled his chair back and forced himself to add, "I'll just call Finn and see if he wants to join us." From the look on her face, that was definitely the wrong answer, but he pretended not to notice her disappointment.

"I was hoping—" Cora's phone began to ring, cutting off whatever she was going to say, which was probably a good thing. She pulled it from her pocket and checked the screen. "Speak of the devil." Throwing Liam a look, she answered on the third ring. "Hey, Finn. Were your ears burning? We were just— Where? Got it. We'll be right behind you." She got off the phone and checked to see if anyone in the pit was listening. Then she said in an excited rush, "It's happening. Magnus got a text from that number and they're meeting in ten minutes at the east parking lot of Providence Falls State Park."

Liam jumped to his feet. "That's almost thirty minutes away. We'll take your car, but I'm driving." To his relief, Cora didn't argue. Usually, she insisted on taking the wheel because she said his driving gave her whiplash, but some occasions called for speed, and this was one of them.

"Finn said he was making arrangements with movers, so he didn't see the text until just now," Cora said a few minutes later as they peeled out of the parking lot. "But he's a lot closer to the park than we are. If we're lucky, he'll at least get there in time to see who Magnus is working with." She smacked her hand on the dashboard. "We'll never make it in this traffic. If only we could fly."

Liam gave her a devilish smirk. "Your wish is my command." He punched the gas and swerved through traffic with expert precision, taking the shoulder of the on-ramp to zoom past cars until they were speeding west down the highway. They'd be even faster if they could use the siren, but that would draw too much attention. Magnus couldn't suspect he was being followed.

Cora gripped the grab handle near the ceiling when Liam sped past three cars, broke through an opening in the middle lane, and shot ahead. "You really do drive like a maniac."

"Admit that it's thrilling," Liam demanded with a laugh.

Her lips twitched. "Never."

"Come now, it's just the two of us here. You can be honest."

"I refuse to encourage you, speed demon." But her voice was tinged with amusement. "You're far too cocky as it is."

Liam switched lanes to bypass a truck and punched the gas as they made their way toward the mountains. Soon the wide, flat lanes of the open freeway became a narrower, tree-lined highway meandering through foothills dappled with sunlight. With every passing mile, it felt as if they were leaving the modern world behind and entering a place untouched by the passage of time. Liam had always loved the forest, and he understood why Cora enjoyed hiking in the area. Nothing could compare to the peaceful, steadfast presence of trees. It was comforting to know they'd stood timeless, sentinels over the earth, unbothered by the fleeting cares of mankind. By the time the sign for Providence Falls State Park appeared in the distance, he'd managed to shave off several minutes.

"There it is." Cora checked her watch. "Magnus's meetup should've happened by now. Finn's sure to be here, but he isn't answering my text messages."

The east parking lot was empty, save for a minivan and one sports car. "That's Magnus's car," Liam said, pointing to the silver sports car in the far corner. He slowed to a crawl before parking on the shoulder of the road, making sure they were hidden by an outcrop of tall shrubs.

"I didn't see Finn's car on the way here," Cora said, checking her phone again. "He's still not answering."

"Maybe he parked on the other side of the lot and made his way on foot so he wouldn't draw attention to himself." Liam turned off the engine. "We should do the same. If we stick to the tree line, we can get closer without being noticed."

"Wait," Cora said, peering through the shrubs. "Something feels off. If Magnus was supposed to meet someone, where's the other car?"

"There's that minivan," Liam said, pointing to the blue, boxy vehicle parked near the road.

She hummed in consideration. "No, I don't think so. It's on the other side of the lot. If you were meeting someone, why park so far away?"

"For appearances, perhaps. Maybe they don't want to be seen with each other."

"Let's give it a few more minutes." Cora unbuckled her seat belt and checked her phone again. "Finn will text back soon.

In the meantime, we can keep an eye on Magnus and see what he does."

Liam could just make out the back of Magnus's head in the driver's seat. "There's no one else in the car with him. Maybe he's on the phone."

They waited for a few minutes in tense silence. Two ladies eventually appeared down the main road, their ponytails swinging as they laughed and talked. They were pushing jogging strollers with wide-eyed toddlers munching away on baby biscuits. The women strolled up to the blue minivan and began settling their kids in the vehicle and folding up the strollers.

"Rules that out," Liam said. "Magnus's accomplice must be running late."

"Unless we missed their meeting altogether. But then, why is he still sitting there?"

The minivan pulled out of the lot and drove away, but Magnus stayed where he was. For the next thirty minutes, they continued watching his car in silence. Liam began to get antsy. "This is useless. He hasn't even moved, and we're wasting time. I say we stick to the tree line and make our way over there."

"Agreed," Cora said, frowning. "This whole thing doesn't feel right, and I don't like that Finn hasn't responded." She clicked a button on the side of her phone and reached for the door handle. "Turn your ringer off, so we don't make noise."

They skirted the car and used the trees to cover their approach as they made their way toward the far end of the lot. It was midday, and the humidity level was off the charts. Liam's shirt clung to his body within seconds, and if it weren't for the trees to provide shade, they would've been boiling. They followed a line of dense, flowering shrubs running along the edge of the parking lot. When they got within fifteen feet of Magnus's car,

Liam jerked to a stop with a grim realization. He tapped Cora's shoulder to get her attention.

"I know what's wrong," Liam said, eyeing Magnus's profile through the leaves. "Listen to the sound of the engine."

Cora cocked her head, then stared at Liam in shock. "It's not on."

"Which means he's not running the air conditioner. Now look at the windows. No one in their right mind sits in their car in the blazing heat for this long without rolling the windows—"

Cora was already running toward the car. She yanked the driver's-side door open with a choked gasp, stumbling back as Magnus Blackwell's body slumped halfway out of the car. His glassy eyes stared unseeing at the sky.

Her face blanched. "Not again."

Liam crouched beside the open door, noting the dark bloodstain on Magnus's shirt. "He's been stabbed." He searched inside the car for clues, but everything appeared neat and orderly. Not even the water bottle in the holder had been overturned. "Looks like he was taken by surprise. There's no sign of a struggle."

"Whoever did this was someone he knew," Cora said in a methodical voice. Liam could tell she'd managed to wrestle her initial shock under control and gone into detective mode. "We have to call this in."

Liam pulled his phone from his pocket and made the necessary call. After hanging up, he joined Cora, sitting next to her on the curb to wait for the ambulance and police. "When Boyd asks later, I'll tell him we got an anonymous tip and came out here to investigate."

Cora nodded and dropped her head in her hands. "Why would anyone kill Magnus?"

"I imagine the man has many enemies."

"Everything just keeps getting worse," she said wearily. "This makes three murders in as many months, and now our biggest lead shows up dead. What the hell is happening to my city?"

Liam shook his head. "We need to talk to Finn."

Cora reached for her phone and dialed Finn's number. There was no use texting since stealth was no longer necessary. After a minute, she tried again, then shut her phone. "He's not answering. What if he saw, what happened, and he's somehow in trouble?"

A cold finger of dread brushed down Liam's spine. He jumped up and began to pace. "I'm sure he's fine. We'll try again in a few minutes." Finn had to be fine. Liam couldn't allow himself to imagine otherwise.

"But he always answers when I call," Cora said. "This isn't like him."

They sat in the blazing sun until the paramedics, several officers, the coroner, and Captain Thompson arrived. Soon the area around Magnus's car was taped off and the entire parking lot was blocked from pedestrians. A small crowd of people had gathered behind the police lines to gawk at the scene.

"Did you see anything? Anyone?" Boyd asked when he stormed out of his car. His face was mottled with splotches of red in what Liam could only assume was anger. Though he'd only been standing outside for a couple of minutes, he was already covered in a sheen of sweat.

"Nothing, Captain," Cora said. "We got an anonymous tip and came out to investigate. We found Magnus Blackwell in his car like this."

"Anonymous tip." Boyd narrowed his eyes with suspicion. "What exactly do you mean by that?"

"A note on my windshield," Liam said quickly. "It said to check the parking lot at Providence Falls State Park, so here we are." The lie rolled off his tongue, smooth as silk. It was a skill he'd honed from his past life of thieving, and while he wasn't proud of it, in this case it served him well.

"Show me the note," Boyd demanded.

"I tossed it away before we came out here." Liam did his best to look sheepish. "It was a mistake; I realize that now. But I thought it was just kids playing a prank. We almost didn't come here at all. I had no idea we'd find something of this magnitude."

"That's sloppy-ass police work, O'Connor," Boyd said with disgust. "Sometimes I wonder how you got into this profession at all." With a glare, he walked off to talk to the coroner.

It was several hours before Liam and Cora were finally dismissed to go home. Everyone had been shocked by Magnus's murder, and tension at the station was higher than ever.

Back at home, Liam slumped wearily onto the living room sofa, staring at the blank television. This time, he didn't bother trying to summon Agon and Samael. If they were trying to teach him a lesson by making him deal with the chaos on his own, then so be it. He could do this without them...but he couldn't do it without Finn.

"Any luck?" Cora asked as Liam set his cell phone on the coffee table that evening.

"None." They'd been calling Finn for hours, to no avail. They'd even driven by his penthouse on the way home, but he didn't answer the door and his car wasn't in the parking garage.

"What if something's happened to him?" Cora asked worriedly. "Finn would never leave us hanging for this long without at least checking in."

Liam feared she was right. There was only one other thing he could think to do, but Cora wouldn't like it. "If we still haven't heard back from him by noon tomorrow, we'll go to his place and have a look around. Maybe there will be clues inside as to where he's gone."

"You're talking about breaking and entering again," she pointed out.

"If he's in trouble, we can't waste any time on protocol. Besides, if one of us were missing and Finn suspected foul play, he wouldn't let anything stop him from helping us. He'd do whatever it took. You know that."

"Fine," she said with a groan. "But let's hope it won't come to that."

The next morning at the station, the hours dragged by with still no word from Finn. Liam tried to lose himself in browsing the internet, but his mind kept circling back to all the terrible things that might've befallen Finn. That only led to internet searches for various reasons a person might disappear, which only made Liam feel worse. Shark attacks, kidnappings, alien abductions, serial killers, falling into wet concrete—all of it was disturbing, and Liam soon learned the downside to having information always at one's fingertips.

Just before noon, Cora surprised Liam by marching up to his desk and placing her car keys on top. "Let's go. Whatever's going on with Finn, it's not good. I can feel it in my bones. There's no way he'd let almost twenty-four hours go by without contacting us, especially when he knows how we've been trying to get answers about Magnus. I can't sit still any longer. I need to *do* something."

"Now you know how I feel." Liam swiped the keys off his desk. "Come on."

They arrived at Finn's building close to noon, and Liam's stomach churned with foreboding when there was still no sign of his car in the parking garage. He tried to tell himself Finn was probably running errands and lost his phone, or maybe he got caught up with some last-minute details at the law firm, but instinctively he knew Cora was right. They had to find Finn, and fast. Liam had only ten days left, and while Cora and Finn had grown closer as friends, they still had to be in love by the time the month ended. With the window of opportunity rapidly closing, Liam felt like he was riding the razor-sharp edge between determination and despair, and tipping toward the latter.

They took the elevator up to Finn's penthouse and knocked for several minutes. No sounds came from within.

"Keep watch while I open it." Liam knelt beside the locked door and pulled a set of lock picks from his pocket.

Facing the elevators down the hall, Cora glanced back at him. "When did you get that?"

"This morning," he said, inserting the tension wrench and rake. "I found it in the lockup."

"I'm surprised you didn't already own a set," Cora said dryly. "Something tells me this isn't the first time you've done this."

"Actually, it is," Liam said. "I've never broken into a place with this type of lock, but it should be fairly simple. It's a standard pin and tumbler. This particular design came around in the latter half of the nineteenth century. It's common enough, but it's not very secure. Most locks aren't. They make people feel better, but it's just an illusion of safety. Almost anyone can get past them with minimal skill and the right motivation."

"Let me guess," Cora said. "You know all this because you honed your lock-picking skills during your wayward youth."

"No, something much simpler." Liam heard the lock click and he beamed up at her. "YouTube."

Finn's door swung open, and they entered, shutting the door behind them with a soft click. It was cool and quiet inside, the muted shades of blue and gray on the walls lending to the peaceful atmosphere. Several empty packing boxes were stacked along the living room wall.

"Finn?" Cora called. She headed down the hall toward the bedrooms, calling his name again.

Liam searched the kitchen. There was a box on the counter half-filled with dishes, but everything else seemed undisturbed. The living room and patio were just as neat, and aside from a pile of folded laundry and a half-emptied bookshelf, there was nothing out of the ordinary.

"Nothing," Cora said, coming from the back room. They switched places and continued looking, and ten minutes later came up empty-handed.

Cora blinked back tears as they left the penthouse and took the elevator to the parking garage. "I just don't understand where he could be."

This time, Liam didn't stop himself from drawing her into his arms. "Don't worry, Cora. We'll find him." His words rang with conviction, but dread gnawed like a trapped animal inside him, desperate to break free. He was running out of time. They all were. Even if Finn was okay, the likelihood of Liam succeeding in his task was minuscule, at best.

"We have to tell Captain Thompson we suspect Finn's in trouble," Cora said as they drove back to the police station.

"What do we tell him when he asks why?" Liam pulled to a stop at a red light and glanced at her. She looked so tired and sad he reached for her hand and gave it a gentle squeeze. "Boyd's going to demand an explanation."

"We can't tell him we went against his direct orders and were secretly conducting an undercover investigation with Finn's help. That's not going to get us anywhere but suspended," Cora said, staring out the window. "We'll say it's a hunch because he's gone radio silent. If nothing else, it will document our concern."

"It's only been a day," Liam said, hoping to lift her spirits. "Finn may surprise us by showing up with a good explanation."

Cora nodded glumly, but it was clear she didn't think it was likely. Liam didn't, either, but he'd been hoping for miracles ever since the angels tossed him into this new life. What was one more added to the list?

Back at the station, Boyd stared them down in his office. "Magnus Blackwell was on the Booze Dogs' hit list, and yesterday someone from that gang finally took matters into their own hands. We need to find out who, and we need to find out now."

"We have no proof it was the Booze Dogs, Captain," Cora said. "It could've been—"

"Their stolen money was found at his lake house," he said flatly. "Surely you, of all people, haven't forgotten that."

Liam saw Cora flinch at the reminder of that terrible night. He suddenly wanted to punch Boyd in the face. It was a gut reaction he sorely wished he could follow up on, but it wouldn't do to make more trouble. Instead, he pierced Boyd with a steely glare. "You said Magnus was innocent. You ordered us to stop investigating him."

"I said there was *no proof* he'd done the crime. He claimed he was set up, and we didn't have enough evidence to keep him behind bars. But now he shows up dead, and that's three people murdered in my city in less than three months." Boyd was almost yelling now. A vein pulsed in his temple, and he visibly struggled to rein in his emotions. After a few shallow breaths, he leaned back in his chair. "Look, I'm tired. We're all tired. The sooner we can connect these cases, and bring in the gang members responsible, the sooner we can all sleep at night. Magnus Blackwell was wrapped up in something, and all signs point to that gang. Lindsey Albright and John Brady were tangled up in it somehow, too."

He glanced at Cora and his features suddenly softened, but Liam could tell he was forcing it. "McLeod, you're one of my best detectives. I'm counting on you to get to the bottom of this. Can you do that?" He didn't even acknowledge Liam, which was an obvious slight, but he wasn't surprised. Boyd may have been his friend a lifetime ago, but he didn't seem to like him much in this one. And as far as Liam was concerned, the feeling was mutual.

"I'll do my best, Captain," Cora said with a worried frown. "But there's something more you should know. We believe Finley Walsh may be in trouble."

Boyd's face blanked. "Who?"

"Finn, the man who helped me rescue Cora," Liam said through clenched teeth. Most days he was able to tamp down his growing dislike of Boyd, but it was getting harder and harder.

"Ah." Boyd nodded absently, and began sifting through papers on his desk. "And what makes you think that?"

"He seems to be missing. He hasn't returned any of my calls or texts within the last twenty-four hours," Cora told him.

Boyd glanced up from one of the reports he was holding. "McLeod, when a man doesn't return multiple phone calls and texts within twenty-four hours, that's usually called avoidance."

"The *man*," Liam said, glaring at Boyd, "is our friend Finn, an attorney who happens to work at the same law firm as Magnus Blackwell. Finn also represented Slice Biddlesworth when we brought him in for questioning. There's enough of a connection with the case to give us cause for concern."

"It's not like him to go radio silent like this, Captain," Cora added. "We stopped by his home earlier and he's not there. Call it a hunch, but something just doesn't feel right."

Boyd rubbed the stubble on his jaw, focusing on the wall behind them. He had the same calculating look that Liam remembered from his past life—the look he got when they were working on a plan. "It seems too coincidental, if you ask me."

"What do you mean, Captain?" Cora asked.

"This man Walsh goes missing the same time Magnus shows up dead," Boyd said with a sudden burst of renewed energy. "Maybe they were rivals."

"I don't like where you're going with this," Liam said in a warning tone.

"Maybe he met Magnus at that park, planned to talk to him, and things got out of hand." Boyd shrugged. "Maybe Finn killed Magnus, panicked, and went into hiding."

"No," Cora said, shocked. "I've known Finn for years, and he was a friend of my father's. Captain, there's no way he'd commit murder, no matter how he felt about Magnus Blackwell."

Boyd looked a little too pleased with himself. "So, you're confirming he has a problem with Magnus."

"He doesn't care for him, that's true, but Finn is no more a murderer than we are," Liam said with annoyance. "Finley Walsh is the only person I've ever met who mirrors Cora's passion for justice and determination to help others. There's no way in hell that man is guilty of murder. We're concerned for his safety, Boyd, and that's why we brought up his absence. That's the only reason." Liam didn't miss the way Boyd's mouth thinned at the use of his first name, but this time Boyd didn't bother to correct him.

"Your concern has been noted." Boyd turned back to the reports on his desk. "And now that we're all concerned about Finley Walsh, I'd like you to find him and bring him in for questioning. That will be all."

After leaving Boyd's office, Liam followed Cora to her desk and sat on the edge with folded arms. "That went well."

"Are you serious?" She looked at him like he was off his head. "The captain just put Finn on the list of murder suspects."

"And nothing will stick because we know he's innocent,"

Liam said. "The important thing here is, we got what we wanted. Direct orders to search for Finn."

She slumped into her chair with a sigh. "You're right. At least now we can devote more time to it."

"Exactly. We'll find him, Cora. I'm sure there's a reasonable explanation for why he's not around."

Cora didn't look convinced, and deep down, neither was he. For the rest of the day, he kept telling himself that there was still hope, that the other police officers would be on the lookout for Finn, too. But no matter how much Liam tried to stay positive, nothing could ease his growing sense of doom.

15

CORA STOOD IN THE SUPERMARKET PRODUCE aisle, absently tossing apples into a plastic bag. It was Thursday night, and neither she nor Liam had found time to go grocery shopping all week. They'd been so focused on work and searching for Finn it seemed as if the days were beginning to blur together, and they'd barely had a chance to come up for air. After yet another evening of fast-food burgers and fries on the way home, Cora had decided to stock the fridge with something a little less artery-clogging.

She wandered over to the vegetables, tossing several prebagged salad kits, extra cucumbers, and a bag of baby carrots into the cart, then backtracked to the fruit aisle again to grab some oranges. Normally, she was a lot more efficient when she shopped, not zigzagging around in random directions like one of those robot floor vacuums, but her mind was too busy spinning on the same hamster wheel she'd been hung up on all week. *Where is Finn?* No one had been able to locate him. They'd checked his penthouse repeatedly, even calling the building manager to find out if Finn had been in contact. They'd gone to the gym to ask around, but Finn hadn't made any recent appearances there, either. Cora even tracked down the number for his sister, Genevieve, in New York City, asking if she'd heard from Finn lately. She hadn't. It was as if he'd just vanished into thin air, and with every day that passed, Cora's fear and worry for him grew. She was beginning to lose sleep.

On top of all that, she'd been having increasingly vivid dreams of her and Liam again, always in those old-fashioned clothes and in the same rural setting. Sometimes they walked hand in hand along a forest path. Sometimes they sat in a field near an old stone wall. And sometimes they stood in a dark garden beneath a million stars, sharing kisses so filled with heat and passion the whole world could've fallen down around them, and they wouldn't have noticed. Those were the dreams that made Cora wake gasping, her body thrumming with desire, limbs tingling with the loss of the man she'd been holding. It was often hard to go back to sleep afterward, especially knowing the star of her dreams—the modern-day version, anyway—was sleeping in the very next room.

Cora pushed her grocery cart toward the wine section of the supermarket, thinking about her impromptu make-out session in the kitchen last Saturday with Liam. They still hadn't talked about it, but she didn't mind. They'd been so busy, and most importantly, she wasn't worried because she was no longer in the dark about Liam's feelings for her. Sometimes she blushed just thinking about how heartfelt and sincere he'd been when he said all those wonderful things to her. She knew it was only a matter of time before everything clicked into place for them. They shared an undeniable attraction, and every day that passed seemed to bring them closer together. Just thinking about it made her smile as she rounded the grocery aisle and—

"Oh!" Cora's cart smacked into a woman who was standing

in front of the sparkling wine. "I'm so sorry! I didn't see you there. Are you all right?"

The woman snorted. "Usually, unless someone clips me with a shopping cart." She appeared to be checking her white tennis shoes for smudges, then glared up at Cora in annoyance.

"Alice," Cora said in surprise. "I didn't recognize you."

Captain Thompson's wife pressed her lips into a thin line, patting her hair self-consciously. She was usually dressed like a celebrity, with matching bags and shoes and sleek, fashionable clothes. In all the years Cora had worked at the police station, she'd never seen her without heavy makeup, lash extensions, and a spray tan. But tonight, Alice was wearing a pair of joggers, an oversized T-shirt tied in a knot at her waist, and not a stitch of makeup. Her eyes were glossed over, and she looked like she'd been drinking.

With a start, Cora remembered what the captain had told her. "I'm so sorry to hear about your mom being sick."

Alice cocked her head, frowning.

"Captain told us you were going to be taking care of her for a while," Cora added softly.

Alice closed her eyes and began shaking her head.

"It's so great that your mom has you there to help," Cora continued, giving Alice a chance to pull herself together. "I hope she feels better soon."

Alice had dropped her chin into her chest, bending slightly at the waist. To Cora's dismay, her shoulders began to shake. Poor woman. Her mother must really be sick, or had she already passed away?

A wave of sympathy swept over Cora, and she wanted to comfort her. Alice wasn't a touchy-feely person—at least, not with women—but Cora reached out to pat her on the back, anyway.

"Ha!" Alice jerked her head up with a gasp, her mouth

stretched into a wide grin that didn't quite reach her eyes. She was…laughing? "He told you my mom was sick?" She wiped a hand over her mouth, then turned abruptly and grabbed a bottle of wine from the shelf. "Of course he did. Figures Boyd would say that, the lying dog."

Cora's mouth fell open in surprise. "I'm not sure I follow."

Alice spun around, pointing at her with the neck of the bottle. "Let me tell you something, Courtney."

"Cora." Jeez, they'd met over a dozen times. The woman should know her name by now.

"Right." Alice jammed a hand on her hip. "You want to know what's really going on? Here's a hard, cold fact for you, Detective. Men are pigs. All men. No matter how good they seem in the beginning, or how much they shower you with compliments and promises and—" Alice stopped abruptly, her pretty face suddenly scrunching into a sneer as she studied Cora from head to toe. "Is it *you*?"

Cora glanced around, wondering how much Alice had been drinking. Did she drive herself there? If so, Cora was going to have to call her a ride because she couldn't let Alice drive herself home like this. "I'm Cora, Alice," she said patiently. "From the Providence Falls Police Station?"

"I know who you are," Alice said angrily. "Are you the one having an affair with my husband?"

Cora jerked back in shock. "Good God, no. *Captain Thompson?* Are you serious?"

Alice continued sneering, then rolled her eyes in dismissal. "Whatever. You know what? I don't even care if you're sleeping with him."

"I am absolutely *not* having an affair with the captain," Cora insisted. "Let me make that very clear." She could go on and say that she found the captain to be extremely unattractive, both physically and in his utterly joyless attitude about life in general, but she didn't want to insult Alice. She'd married him, after all. The captain was good at his job, but Cora could never be in a relationship with someone so stoic and jaded. He was like one of those cantankerous uncles who got invited to Thanksgiving dinner even though nobody really wanted to talk to them. A romantic relationship with Captain Thompson? Cora barely suppressed a shudder. Just, *no*.

"I've spent ten years with that jerk," Alice said, grabbing two more bottles off the shelf. "And in all the time we've been married, he never once took me on a fancy vacation. Did you know that? No trips to Fiji like he promised when we were dating. No summer house in the Hamptons like I used to dream about. It's always 'Not this year, Alice' and 'That's too expensive, Alice' and 'You should know better than to ask, Alice.'" She was getting louder, and Cora barely resisted the urge to shush her. "But he's a liar. He made promises to me about what our life would be like, and it went from pie in the sky to mud in my eye." She let out a harsh laugh. "And here I am, ten years older with nothing but a closet full of clothes I have to buy on credit cards behind his back because he says it's—" she made air quotes with her hands "—frivolous spending. But then what do you suppose I find when I'm going through his stuff?" She was growing angry again, spittle flying from her mouth like a hissing cobra. "A ritzy necklace in one of those velvet boxes. You know, like from those bigwig jewelry stores? But it's not for me. *Not for me*," she emphasized bitterly. Then her voice cracked, and the rest of her words came tumbling out in jagged pieces. "That's what he said. 'It's not for you, Alice.'"

Cora's heart ached for the dejected woman. She clearly believed her husband was having an affair, though Cora couldn't imagine the captain having time to cheat on his wife. He always seemed so stressed out, but maybe this was one of the contributing factors. Maybe he really was seeing someone behind her back. Alice was now openly weeping, and Cora searched for something to say. Anything to ease her suffering. "Alice, I'm—"

"There you are, hon," an older woman said, ambling up to Alice.

Alice quickly swiped at her tears and straightened her spine.

The woman was shaped a bit like a teapot, with gray hair, navy stretch pants, and a flowery tunic top. She had a bedazzled denim purse slung over her shoulder and a slushy drink in her hand. "I've been waiting in the car, but it's too hot even with the windows rolled down, and you know that air conditioner's broken. You coming, or what?"

"I'll be right there, Mom."

"Mom?" Cora watched the older woman leave. She didn't look sick at all.

"Yup. That was my mom," Alice said in a bitter, singsong voice. "Alive and well. So now you know the truth, Courtney. I left my cheating husband and I'm back to cornflake casseroles and *Jeopardy!* marathons with my mom. Ain't life grand?"

Before Cora could answer, Alice walked away.

16

LIAM TRUDGED INTO HIS BEDROOM ON SATURDAY evening, kicking his shoes off and flopping onto the bed with a groan. He'd spent the past twenty-four hours scouring the town for Finn with no luck, and time was running out. He felt like he was trapped inside an hourglass, and every second that passed was a falling grain of sand threatening to bury him. In just a handful of days, the month was going to end. And what did he have to show for it?

Angel jumped onto the bed, snuggling in beside him.

"Nothing, that's what," he told the purring cat. Not even the angels were helping him anymore. What he needed was a sign. Some last vestige of hope to keep him going. Otherwise, if he was only going to fail, what was the point of trying anymore? He was so tired of fighting this uphill battle, and nothing he did ever seemed to work in his favor.

"Liam!" Cora rushed into his bedroom, holding up her cell phone. "I got a text from Finn."

He jerked upright. It was a sign. It had to be. "What does it say?"

Scooping up Angel, Cora sat beside him on the edge of the bed and read the text aloud. "'Apologies for not responding sooner. Had to take care of some personal business out of town. Be back in a week or so.'"

As Cora read the text, Liam's heart began to thud against his rib cage until her voice faded to a low buzzing in his ears. *Be back in a week or so.* His stomach churned and his head began to pound as he stared at the text message, trying to breathe through the dread now coursing through his veins.

"I mean, I'm glad he's not hurt or anything," Cora was saying as she smoothed the fur on Angel's back. "But it's unlike him not to give us more details."

"Tell him to get back here right now," Liam said harshly. "We need him."

"I just tried calling, but he didn't answer."

"Keep trying. Text him; maybe he'll respond to that."

Liam reached for his own phone and dialed Finn's number. As expected, it went to voice mail. He squeezed the rectangular glass-and-metal device, barely refraining from throwing it against the wall.

"He's not answering," Cora said, shaking her head. "It's kind of rude, don't you think? Which, when you get right down to it, doesn't sound like Finn at all. He could've at least sent us a text before he took off. Whatever he had to do must've been pretty important to just disappear on us like that. And he didn't mention anything about Magnus's meeting at the park, either, so he must not have made it out there. It sounds like whatever he had to deal with was an emergency." She sighed and nuzzled her face into Angel's fur. "I guess we can at least rest easy knowing Finn's okay."

"Aye, rest easy," Liam said bitterly. There'd be no rest for him ever again, now that Finn was officially out of the picture. He stared at his phone screen, the date and time glowing back at him like a digital harbinger of doom. Taunting him. *Be back in a week or so.* Liam squeezed his eyes shut, tossing the phone on the nightstand. Even if he wanted to go track Finn down, he wouldn't even know where to begin. He'd said he was out of town. In this world of cars and freeways and high-speed trains and commercial airplanes, "out of town" could mean the next city over or the other side of the planet.

"Don't lose hope," Cora said, nudging him with her shoulder. "We'll still solve the cases."

"You don't understand," Liam said, dropping his head into his hands. "We *needed* him."

"Yes, he was a great help, but we still have each other." Cora leaned her face close to his and gently pulled one of his hands away so she could see him. She gave him a sweet smile that reminded him so much of the first time he'd met her, in another century when she was the young and impressionable squire's daughter. He suddenly yearned for that simpler time, before everything went to hell, when they were so desperately in love and full of shared dreams and hope for their future. He wished so badly that he could confide in her and tell her the truth. "We've still got time to figure things out," Cora said softly. "Right?"

"That's just it." Liam stared bleakly into the bluest, truest eyes he'd ever known. He wanted to lay his head in her lap and weep. "I'm out of time."

Her forehead creased in confusion. "What do you mean?"

He opened his mouth to tell her, but he'd been so careful to keep all his secrets he couldn't bring himself to utter a word of it. "It's...nothing."

For long minutes, they didn't speak, but Liam's head was filled with the growing noise of regret and despair.

"I have an idea," she finally said, dragging the quilted comforter off his bed. "Come with me."

He followed her down the hall, out the back door, and around the side of the house to the metal ladder leading up to the roof. Within minutes, they'd climbed to the same flat section above the garage where they'd once watched fireworks. Cora laid out the comforter and sat, drawing her knees up and linking her arms around them.

Liam settled beside her, then tipped his face to the night sky. The full moon glowed against the backdrop of stars, a clear reminder that some things never changed. There was a small comfort in that. If not for the jasmine-and-magnolia-scented breeze, and the occasional whoosh of a car driving by, Liam could almost pretend he was back in Ireland all those lifetimes ago. He had Cora beside him, just like before, back when life was so much harder in some ways, yet so much simpler in others.

"I sometimes come up here just to clear my head, or when I feel overwhelmed," Cora said, staring up at the glowing moon. She waited a few moments, then stole a glance at him. "Liam, I hope you know you can trust me. Whatever you're going through—whatever burden you're carrying—I want to help."

"I know, *macushla*, but there's nothing anyone can do," he said wearily. He was falling from grace, every passing hour just a slow descent into eternal darkness, and even the angels had abandoned him. His soul ached with the burden of knowledge that he'd failed. Finn and Cora would never embrace their destiny now, and the rest... Images of the future the angels had shown him—the energy crisis, the senseless wars and ravaged landscapes and political upheaval—all flashed through his mind in a painful kaleidoscope that stole his breath. The future chaos might not happen in this lifetime, but the trajectory was set in motion now. Liam swallowed past the jagged lump in his throat. "Some things are beyond fixing, and they just must be endured."

"But you don't have to endure it alone. I'm here with you, and there's nowhere else I'd rather be." She turned to face him and reached for his hand. "All I want is to ease your burden."

He stared at their linked fingers, her small, pale hand such a stark contrast against his rough, calloused skin. The delicate lines of her bones looked fragile in comparison, like finely sculpted porcelain. But she was so much stronger than she appeared. Even back in his old life, he'd been amazed at her bravery and capacity for kindness. She'd been a motherless child raised by an overprotective father in a drafty, aging house with nothing but a sour old nursemaid for company. Cora's only joy had been the books from her father's library, where she could live vicariously through the characters' adventures and dream of a life outside of Kinsley, Ireland. There'd been no warmth and laughter to lighten her days, nothing but the monotonous confines of her small world, yet she'd never wilted as so many in her place would have. She'd been bright and hopeful and quick to laugh and, like now, a brilliant light in Liam's otherwise dreary life.

"Liam," she said, leaning closer. "Please tell me what's wrong." A lock of her hair caught in the breeze, brushing across his cheek like the gentlest caress.

In spite of everything, he smiled. It was getting harder and harder to push her away, and with his imminent failure on the horizon, he was beginning to wonder why he should. In this whole messed-up world the angels had dropped him into, Cora McLeod was the only thing that always felt right. If his future was going to be fire and brimstone, he'd be a fool not to embrace the last few days of heaven he had left. Before he could allow himself to change his mind, he dived in.

"Cora, I'm going to tell you a story," Liam began, taking her other hand. He shifted to sit in front of her, staring into her eyes. "And it's going to sound unbelievable. You will think I'm crazy, and I won't blame you. But when I'm done, there's one truth you must know above all else. I need you to believe it, no matter what."

She was looking at him with so much compassion that he almost leaned forward and kissed her, but he forced himself to continue. "I love you."

Her eyes grew round with surprise and a tremulous smile played at the corners of her mouth.

"I've loved you long before we ever met," he continued, "and I'll go on loving you even after the world stops spinning and the stars burn out. Everything I've ever done has been because I've always wanted you above all else. You were the dream I never dared hope for. You've always been in my heart, and you always will be. If you believe nothing else, please believe that."

Myriad expressions flitted across her face, almost too fast for him to catch, but when she launched herself into his arms, Liam knew she believed him, and his heart felt near to bursting with gratitude.

"I love you, too," Cora said, squeaking when he hugged her too tight, their mingled laughter a sound he wanted to burn into his memory so he could remember it for later when he was gone. The idea sobered Liam enough to grip her arms and lean back to see her face. She was smiling, and for a moment, he wavered. He didn't want to tell her the rest, because he didn't want to kill the sheer happiness reflected in her eyes. If only he could live here forever with her, just like this.

"Tell me your story, Liam," Cora said, squeezing his hands. "And know that, no matter what, I'm here for you."

He swallowed and withdrew his hands from hers, because it was too hard to think when they were connected like that, and maybe he was also trying to distance himself for the rejection that would undoubtedly come when she heard the truth. "Cora... Do you believe in reincarnation?"

Her delicate brows rose, and then she surprised him by saying, "Before I met you, I never gave it much thought. But now... Maybe?"

"What makes you say that?" he asked as an ember of hope flared inside him.

"Nuh-uh," she said playfully, shaking her head. "Tell me your story first. I've been waiting too long for this to get sidetracked."

"All right." He took a deep breath and let it out in a whoosh. "I'm not from here. I'm from a tiny village in Ireland called Kinsley. I don't even think it exists anymore."

She cocked her head. "Why wouldn't it?"

"Because..." He glanced nervously at her. "It was 1844 when last I was there. I looked it up. It isn't on any maps I've seen, so I think it was absorbed by neighboring counties."

Cora blinked. Humor faded to confusion, and Liam felt his stomach drop. This was it. The moment where she pinned him as a lunatic. "What do you mean, you were there last in 1844?" There was a strange look on her face he couldn't decipher.

With nothing left to do but forge ahead, Liam continued. "We knew each other in another life. I was a worthless thief, a peasant with no prospects, and you were a squire's daughter engaged to another man. But I climbed through your window one night with the intent to rob you, and against all odds, we became friends. Eventually we became more than friends."

Cora looked thunderstruck, but she surprised him by whispering, "Go on." Why wasn't she freaking out yet? Was she humoring him?

He lowered his head, unable to look at her when he admitted, "You were destined to marry your fiancé, but I altered the course of your fate. We were never supposed to fall in love, but we did, and it led to nothing but disaster."

She tilted her head. "What kind of disaster?"

Liam stared at her like she'd gone away with the fairies. "Are you not hearing what I'm saying, woman? I'm your reincarnated lover from another life."

She nodded. "I heard you."

He waited a few beats, but she remained unruffled. "Why aren't you calling the nearest insane asylum to have me committed?"

"Well, for one thing, we don't have those anymore," she said with a shrug. "And for another, the reincarnation thing makes an unusual kind of sense to me. I've been having strange dreams of us, too. In each dream, we're wearing old-fashioned clothes and sitting against a stone wall in a field, or walking under the stars at night, or traipsing through the forest. They've grown more vivid, and sometimes they feel so real. Your story has more detail, but—"

"Cora, I'm not telling you about a made-up story," he said carefully. "I'm telling you about an actual life I once lived with you in it. We tried to run away together, but it all went wrong. It was raining that night, and you fell from your horse and..." Liam's throat closed up, but he forced the words out, anyway. "You died in my arms."

"What happened to you afterward?" There was the hint of a tremor in her voice, as if she could somehow feel the dread of the aftermath, even though she hadn't lived through it.

Reflexively, Liam laid a hand on his throat, allowing himself to remember those darkest moments for the first time in over a hundred and seventy years.

17

Kinsley, Ireland,
1844

IT WAS THE RAIN THAT FINALLY CONVINCED LIAM
to rise shakily to his feet, gripping his beloved Cora in his arms
like a small child. Her delicate face was as pure and beautiful as
the day they'd met, but the bloom in her cheeks had disappeared
over the hours he'd rocked her, begging her to come back to
him. Raindrops splashed against her skin, marring her perfect
face, the icy rivulets drenching her hair and clothes, plastering
her golden curls to her skull and weighing down the heavy wool
cloak she was wearing. It had to be uncomfortable for her, especially on a night like this. It just wouldn't do. She deserved
better than to be kept in the freezing cold, and he suddenly be-
rated himself for not trying to warm her up sooner.

"I've got you, *macushla*," he murmured, stumbling over the
muddy forest floor as he gripped her body against his chest.
"I'll take you back home, where they'll—" Liam choked on the
burning sensation in his throat. "They'll take good care of you."
Somewhere in the back of his mind he recognized that her soul
had flown, but the logic of it couldn't put a dent in his need to
protect her and care for her. The horror of what had happened

was hovering at the edge of his thoughts, as if his mind was shielding him from a pain too overwhelming to handle.

He carried her for hours, or years, or centuries. The passage of time meant nothing because he was frozen inside, trapped in the single-minded task of putting one foot in front of the other, moving closer and closer to Cora's salvation. He told himself if he could just get her home to where she was safe, then she'd be okay. It was a fool's lie, but he was both a fool and a liar, so he let it fuel his resolve until, finally, he stood in front of the squire's house with Cora in his arms.

Liam kicked the door with his boot, the harsh sound of it resonating through his frozen limbs like a gong portending doom. "We're here now," he whispered. "I've brought you home. Everything will—"

The door flew open, and Cora's father, the elderly squire, stood on the threshold with a candle in his hand. "What is the meaning of this?" With a gasp, he dropped the candle and reached for his daughter. "Cora!"

A servant who was standing behind the squire rushed forward, and they tried to pry her from Liam's arms.

"What has happened?" the squire shouted. "Give her to me!"

Liam was trying, but his body didn't want to release her. Somehow, it knew that once they took her from him, the bubble he'd sealed them into would burst, and the terrible reality he'd been ignoring would come crashing down around him.

"Unhand her this instant," the squire's manservant said in a cold, hard voice. It was his lack of emotion that jolted Liam into compliance. The demand was a simple one. Nothing unusual. Nothing earth-shattering. Just a normal request like it was any other regular day.

One by one, Liam's frozen fingers uncurled, and then they took his beloved Cora away. In the dim light of the manservant's candle, he watched his world fade into the darkness as they carried her deeper into the house.

Liam remained on the doorstep, unblinking as rivulets of rain coursed down his face. Everything felt muffled and slow and terribly wrong. Like a helpless insect trapped in amber, he stood frozen in place. It felt safe, somehow, like he'd found a way to exist between one second and the next. If he didn't move, then he could pretend the world wasn't moving, either. Every gust of wind would cease. Every drop of rain would hang suspended in the air. And the agony knocking at the back of his mind would remain locked out forever. He'd never have to acknowledge or feel it. But Liam didn't get what he wanted; he'd already learned that. The world kept turning, and his treacherous heart kept pumping, every beat like the worst kind of betrayal. It felt wrong that he was standing there, terribly, achingly alive, when she...

"Squire McLeod!" An angry shout came from beyond the garden gate. The dull thud of horses' hooves and the sound of a carriage rolled up behind Liam. He didn't turn around to look because nothing mattered but that long stretch of hallway and the woman who'd disappeared into the gloom.

"*There he is.* Just the gutter rat we're looking for."

Liam barely recognized the voice of John Brady, Margaret's husband, right before he was seized by the neck and shoved against the hard stone wall of the house. He didn't resist, only vaguely aware of the craggy rock scraping against his forehead and the cruel grip of the old man's hands. One of the paving stones near his foot had a small crack, Liam noted dully. A tiny weed had somehow taken root, reaching toward the sun. John Brady was hissing accusations in Liam's ear, but he barely heard. It wasn't until the heel of the old man's boot crushed the tiny weed into a pulp that Liam seemed to notice what was happening.

"Let him go, Mr. Brady," another man said in a cool, clipped tone. "I'll handle this."

The grip on Liam's neck loosened, and he turned to face the two men.

John Brady's mouth was stretched over yellowed teeth, twisted in malevolent fury. Beside him stood the town magistrate, whose reputation preceded him. Tall and whip-thin, the man was like a frozen pond in the dead of winter, cold and unforgiving.

"This is him, Magistrate." Spittle flew from John Brady's wrinkled lips when he leaned into Liam and hissed, "You *killed* her."

Liam squeezed his eyes shut, trying to stave off the tidal wave of pain rising inside him, but it was no use. He had, hadn't he? He'd killed her. It was all his fault. He'd killed his beloved Cora. A keening, wild sound erupted all around them, like a tortured animal in a snare. With an odd sense of detachment, Liam realized it was coming from him.

Squire McLeod appeared out of the gloom with tears coursing down his doughy, agonized face. "What has happened to my daughter? My sweet girl. What did you do to her?"

I killed her. Liam began to shake, unable to speak past the sound bleeding from his throat. *She's gone forever, and it's all my fault.*

Fast as a lightning strike, the magistrate shoved Liam against the wall and snapped restraints on his wrists. Then he gave him a hard shake. "Quiet, you."

"Squire McLeod," John Brady said. "I have reason to believe this man killed my wife, Margaret. The servants found her at the bottom of the stairs, and her jewelry was stolen. This man violated my wife. On more than one occasion. He murdered her."

"No." Liam struggled with the iron on his wrists, trying to

focus. He felt disconnected from his body, like he was watching through a hazy dream. "That isn't true."

"Shut your lying mouth, you filthy swine," John hissed. "My servants are loyal to me. They saw you sniffing around my wife's skirts whenever I was out of town."

No, that wasn't right. Liam tried to push away from the wall to face him, but the magistrate gave him another warning shake. "Is it true?" he demanded. "Did you rob and kill Margaret Brady?"

"No," Liam said in a broken voice. "I w-would never do that."

The magistrate, who'd been searching his pockets, suddenly yanked out a glittering jeweled necklace. "Oi! What's this, then?" He held it within inches of Liam's nose.

Liam stared at the sparkling necklace in confusion. "I don't—"

"Margaret's necklace," her husband sputtered in outrage. Something cracked the back of Liam's head. Pain lanced through his skull in sharp, agonizing pinpricks of light. From the corner of his eye, he could see John Brady shaking his heavy walking cane with a demonic glare. "You filthy thieving son of a wh—"

"Here, now, Mr. Brady," the magistrate said harshly. "I'll thank you to leave the punishment of this man to the law. He'll get what he deserves." He turned Liam around to face them all.

"Mr. O'Connor." There was a dazed, haunted look on Squire McLeod's face, as if he hadn't quite absorbed the enormity of his daughter's death yet. "What happened to my Cora?"

Liam struggled to speak past the pain ripping through his heart, his lungs, his head. The horror of that night loomed over him like a guillotine. "I'm sorry," Liam said brokenly. "We were in love, you see."

"Hugh McLeod's daughter in love with a stinking peasant?" John Brady cackled like an evil specter. "The man's delusional, clearly."

"We were running away to America." Liam forced himself to continue, for the sake of Cora's devastated father. He deserved to know the truth. "Cora's horse slipped in the rain and she… She fell. I tried to save her, but… It's my fault, you see." He could barely breathe around the shards of glass that seemed to be lodged in his throat. "It's all my fault."

"There you have it." John Brady slammed the end of his walking cane on the paving stone like a judge with a gavel, addressing the squire and magistrate. "He admits his own guilt. This piece of filth is a murderer and a thief." He turned to Liam with a triumphant glare. "You'll hang for this, by God. I'll make sure of it."

Squire McLeod stood speechless, mouth opening and closing like a stunned, dying fish. If he'd resorted to shouted obscenities and furious accusations, it would've made sense to Liam. He deserved nothing less. But the look of abject sorrow and pity coming from Cora's father was soul-crushing. Liam wanted to sink into the ground until he was nothing but dust.

The magistrate began pulling Liam toward the carriage. "Come along, you. Don't give me any trouble or I'll knock you out cold myself."

Liam didn't struggle. His beloved Cora was gone and, along with her, every shred of hope and light left in his bleak heart. Nothing mattered anymore. In the days that followed, he was trapped in a nightmare of murky vignettes where nothing felt real. It wasn't real when they threw him in the freezing jail cell. Not real when, a few days later, he was sentenced to the gallows, and not real when he was shoved up the wooden steps and they wrapped a rope around his neck. Even through the sounds of the jeering crowd, the ominous *snick* of the trapdoor under his feet, and the sharp, blinding snap of pain, none of it was real. Because if he accepted it was real, then it meant he'd lost her forever, and he refused to let this be the way their love story ended. Somehow, no matter what happened next or where he ended up, he would find his beloved Cora again.

18

CORA LISTENED AS HE FINISHED THE STORY, flinching when he recounted in a detached voice how he'd been wrongfully hanged. Blinking back tears, she ached at the thought of Liam dying like that—with no loved ones around, no honor, and no hope of justice. It was wrong on so many levels, and heartbreaking that such a vibrant, beautiful soul as he could lose everything in such a terrible way.

She was sitting cross-legged on the blanket facing him, holding his large hand in hers and squeezing tightly, as if she could siphon some of the pain from him through physical contact. She wanted to cry, but she refused to let the tears fall. Liam had just recounted a terrible ordeal from a past life, and if he'd had to endure that by himself, then the least she could do was be strong for him now and remind him that he wasn't alone anymore.

He was rubbing his throat, grimacing through remembered pain. Cora had thought her own dreams were vivid, but his had to be even more so for him to have such a visceral reaction.

"That's why you hate wearing ties, isn't it?" she asked gently. "You gave me such a hard time when I tried to get you to dress up for that formal event back in June, but it all makes so much sense now."

He nodded, blinking from the memories as if he were coming out of a dark cave into the light. "I can't stand to have anything around my throat. I don't like to dwell on the reason why, but that's it."

"Liam, how long have you been having these dreams of our past life together?" Had he been experiencing them longer than she had? All her dreams seemed to start after they'd first met, but from the way he talked, it seemed his visions were more intense, and he'd been having them for years. She'd been so confused by her dreams, never quite understanding what she was seeing, but now she was grateful for their ambiguity.

"They're not dreams, Cora. That's what I've been trying to tell you. I've actually lived through it. It all happened in the past, and I was given a second chance to come back here to make things right. You and I were never supposed to fall in love—not back then, and not now. Your destiny was with Finn. My goal was to try to get you and him together in order to redeem myself and help the world."

Cora sat up straighter. "Okay, first of all, who told you my destiny was with Finn? And secondly, you can't tell me how to feel. *I* choose. Is that why you've been trying to push me in his direction so hard?"

"I know it all sounds crazy, but I was…" He trailed off, running a hand across the back of his neck and stealing a glance at her from beneath his thick lashes. "I was visited by angels. They told me all of this."

Cora's eyes widened in surprise. "What, like you had a vision and angels spoke to you?"

"Aye, in a sense." His brow furrowed in concentration, like he was struggling to find the right words to tell her things. Finally, he just shook his head. "I promise you, I've not gone mad, though sometimes it feels that way. Everything I'm telling you is true. Do you believe me?"

She nibbled on her bottom lip and picked at a frayed thread from the blanket as she considered what he'd told her. Of all the things Liam was secretly dealing with, she never would've guessed it was epic failure from a past life and visions, or visitations, from angels. But as unbelievable as it sounded—and it was truly far-fetched—the things he was telling her made sense when compared to the strange way he'd been acting toward her all summer. His overprotective behavior, as if she belonged with him. Those times when it was so clear he wanted more from her, but he never allowed it to go any further. And then there were those inexplicable moments of déjà vu where she'd see flashes of him from another time, or those vivid dreams where, now that she thought about it, their surroundings did seem like a rural place in Ireland. As crazy as it all seemed, she couldn't bring herself to discount him.

"I want to believe you," she finally said. "It's just a lot to take in. I've built my entire life on logic and facts and weeding out the truth, and this is something way beyond my comfort zone."

"Mine, too," Liam said. "Trust me, ever since I arrived here in Providence Falls, nothing about this task set before me has been comfortable. Do you have any idea how hard it's been for me, living day in and day out with the woman of my dreams, unable to show her how much I love her?"

A pleasurable heat rose in her cheeks, and her heart felt near to bursting. "Careful. A girl could get used to pretty words like those."

He leaned forward and drew her into his embrace, nuzzling his face in the crook of her neck. "If I could find a way to spend the rest of eternity reminding you how wonderful you are, I'd do it."

"Wait," she said, leaning back before she lost herself to the intoxicating feeling of being in his arms. "The angels told you to get me and Finn together because it would right your past wrongs and help the world. What does 'help the world' mean?"

Liam's face shuttered. "It's...complicated."

"It can't be any more complicated than what you've already told me."

"You and Finn," he began, then stopped. Again, he appeared to be having one of those internal struggles until, finally, he said, "Every action we make in life affects the future and people in it. I'm not talking about small, everyday things. I'm talking about something on a grander scale."

"Like the butterfly effect." At his blank look, she explained. "It's a theory that one small change can cause a ripple effect over time that eventually changes something in a monumental way in the future."

"Yes," he said with a firm nod. "That's exactly it. If I'd succeeded in getting you and Finn together before the summer was over, then it would've...helped the future in good ways."

"Why before summer's end?" Cora asked, tilting her head. "Why not in a year, or two?"

Now he looked nervous again. He pulled away, and she instantly missed the warmth of his embrace. "I was only given three months to complete my task."

"And then what, I live happily ever after with Finn, and you just go on your merry way?" She didn't like that idea at all. Never going to happen.

"And then... I'll be gone." His statement was devoid of hope, the tone so hollow it echoed through her bones. "Either way, Cora, I was never going to be allowed to stay here, no matter how much I wish otherwise. The angels gave me three months, and I'm nearing the end. Whether I succeeded or not, my days here were always numbered. My time is almost up."

"Like hell it is," she said forcefully. "Liam, I can believe your story because I share some of the same dreams, visions, memories—whatever you want to call them—as you do. I've felt this connection between us, and deep down, I *feel* in my heart that this is real. But if you think I'm just going to sit here and accept that you'll leave or disappear in the next few days? You can think again." Adrenaline was pumping through her veins, and she felt ready to go into fight mode. "I refuse to accept it."

"It's not a matter of whether or not we accept it," he said with a resignation that alarmed her. "It isn't up to us. I've failed, so the bad things that happen now, both to you and the future world, will be all my fault."

He turned away from her, head bowed. He looked so hopeless and dejected Cora wanted to shake him.

"No," she said fiercely, gripping his arms. "No, Liam. You can't beat yourself up over something you have no control over. I get that you were told by the angels to fulfill a task, but let me just tell you right now, *nothing* you did would've made me fall for Finn. It wasn't going to happen. Not this summer. Not next summer. Not ever. I don't want him like that; I want you." She shrugged helplessly. "I think I wanted you from the first day we met, though I tried so hard to fight the feeling. And I'm sorry, but I refuse to believe the world's future is at stake because of who I decide to *love*. No one should carry that kind of an emotional burden, certainly not you. Love is not a punishment; it's something to be celebrated because, in the end, it's all that really matters. Look, I don't know much about what happens after we die, but I do believe love is the only thing we get to take with us. The love we gave and the love we were given. And I know you believe you failed in getting me and Finn together, but you have to understand it was never up to you. The heart is unpredictable and can't be steered. We don't get to tell ourselves who to fall in love with. That's why they call it 'falling.'"

Liam was staring at her in stunned silence. Then he began to smile. Relief washed over her like cleansing rain. His expression was caught somewhere between pride and wonder. "Something tells me the angels would have their work cut out for them if they had to hear your opinion on the subject."

"Let me at them," Cora said with a stubborn tilt of her chin. "I'll set them straight."

"If anyone could, it would be you." He cupped her cheek with his large, calloused hand and gave her a look that radiated so much warmth and admiration she wanted to burrow into the moment and bask in it forever. When he pulled her close, his powerful arms hugged her so tightly she almost couldn't breathe, but she didn't care. If she died right here, she'd go happy. Liam eased up and planted a tentative kiss on her temple, then trailed his lips, featherlight, down the side of her cheek and jaw.

"I wish we could stop time." She shivered as his warm breath tickled the sensitive spot near her ear. "Just surround ourselves in a protective bubble where all our troubles and uncertainty couldn't reach us."

"Mmm," Liam agreed, drawing his mouth up to hover over hers, their lips almost touching. His smoldering gaze did hot, swirly things to her insides. "If only there was a way."

Cora felt like she was hovering at the edge of a precipice, about to tumble off into the unknown, and she welcomed it. She wanted nothing more than to throw caution to the wind and take this leap. "I have some ideas."

Liam chuckled, the dark sound of it sliding over her skin until she shivered again in delicious anticipation. It struck her, in that moment, what an excellent thief he must've been. All it took was one devious smile and she'd give up everything like Persephone to Hades.

"Do you now, lass?" His Irish brogue was suddenly back in full force, which, if she'd been on the fence at all, would've tipped her right over the edge. "Tell me," he demanded.

"I'd rather show you," she whispered against his lips.

And then they were kissing.

It wasn't the tentative, slow-burn kind of kiss they'd shared before. This was an all-out wildfire, a single spark of flint and tinder roaring to life until she was burning up with need for him. Without pulling away, Liam lowered her to the blanket until the full length of his body was pressed against hers. Cora reveled in the intoxicating feel of him, and she let out a soft whimper that made him growl low in his throat.

He broke the kiss and said huskily, "I want you."

Cora nodded and tried to pull him in for another kiss, but he resisted, his chest rising and falling with barely restrained emotion. "Tell me you do, too, *macushla*, because I swear by all that's holy I will stop right now if you're not ready. Or at any point, at any time, if you decide you can't, tell me and I promise—"

"Don't you dare stop now, Liam O'Connor," Cora said, nipping his bottom lip and dragging it between her teeth.

He let out a sound that was half laugh, half groan, then jerked her hard against him until she squealed. Their soft laughter mingled with the sound of the breeze rustling through the trees. A dark lock of hair fell over his eyes, the moonlight highlighting the sharp angle of his jaw and the fullness of his lips. Against the backdrop of stars, he looked like a dark prince from a fairy tale who'd come to steal her away. *Yes, please.* Cora arched up with a throaty sigh.

He bent to kiss her with more urgency this time, and she answered his call with wholehearted abandon, clutching his shirt as she tried to pull it over his head. "Take this off," she whispered urgently. "I want to feel you."

He shot up and whipped it off, flinging it so far it sailed over the edge of the roof. Cora might've been amused, but she was too busy drinking in every magnificent muscled inch of his body, from the smooth swell of his pectoral muscles, down the hard ridges of his abdomen, to the contoured V-shaped line of muscle that disappeared beneath the waistband of his jeans.

She gently ran her fingers over his taut stomach and decided she needed more. Much more. Hooking her fingers into his waistband, she added, "This, too. I want to feel all of you."

Liam stood, pinning her with his molten gaze as he slowly removed the rest of his clothing until he stood before her wearing nothing but moonlight and shadows. Cora felt her breath catch at the beautiful, impressively aroused man standing before her. Everything about him was so overwhelmingly perfect—from his fallen-angel face, to his powerfully built body, and most importantly, to the way he was looking at her like she was his entire world.

They reached for each other at the same time. Every vein in her body was thrumming with the delicious, wild heat that emanated off him, melting into her. Between lust-filled, drugging kisses and whispered words of endearment she could barely hear over the rapid beating of her own heart, Liam slid her clothes off until they were both pressed skin to skin.

"Cora," he said with a purely masculine groan that made heat pool low in her belly. "I've waited so long to hold you like this."

She curled her arms around his neck, silently pleading with him to hurry, not wanting to wait any longer.

He kissed her again, then slid into her in a slow, claiming thrust. Cora almost sobbed with the blissful intensity of it. The *rightness* of it. Liam stilled for a moment, placing soft kisses on her forehead, her eyelids, her lips, as if he wanted to prolong the moment of their joining, to imprint it in his mind forever.

"My beautiful Cora," he whispered, gazing down at her in awe. "You're so..." His soulful, midnight eyes glittered with emotion, and he buried his face in her neck. "Mine."

"Yes." She brushed her fingers through his unruly hair, clasping him tightly to her chest. "I'm yours."

Liam's entire body was shaking with the effort it took him to hold back. Cora could feel the wild need inside him, straining to be unleashed, calling to something equally powerful in her. She tilted her hips instinctively, wanting more. Needing more. She was ready to beg for it, if she had to. When he finally began to move, she dropped her head back with a soft gasp. The deep, velvet glide of him inside her was so much better than she'd ever imagined. It was more than just the aching fullness and the hypnotic rhythm; it was the intense closeness of sharing such a profound moment with *him*. The man who'd invaded her dreams and stolen her heart. Cora had never felt this way about anyone else in her life, and she knew with perfect diamond clarity that she never would. In the past, she'd always held a piece of herself back, but not now. With Liam, she could truly let go. She could lose herself in his embrace, knowing he'd take care of her.

And he *did*. Again and again.

They must have succeeded in stopping time because Cora had no recollection of how long they lay on that roof under the moon. They were too lost in each other to notice or care. It wasn't until Liam kissed her awake and they came together a final time that she realized dawn was fast approaching. There was a frantic undercurrent in their lovemaking now, as if they had to steal as much joy as they could before it disappeared with the light of day. When her desire finally peaked and she came apart in his arms, Liam held her like he'd never let her go, whispering her name like a prayer—like she was his salvation—until he joined her, and they fell together.

———————————————

19

LIAM LAY BESIDE THE WOMAN WHO WAS DEARER to him than his own soul, reveling in the feel of her nestled against him for hours. His gaze traced the delicate lines of her face just visible in the light streaming through her bedroom curtains. They'd climbed down from the roof in the early hours of the morning, linking hands as they entered the house to float down the hall toward her room. Together, they'd tumbled into her bed in a tangle of limbs and soft sighs, giddy and exhausted and drunk on each other. Within minutes, Cora had slipped into a deep sleep, but Liam couldn't. He'd spent lifetimes dreaming of having her in his arms like this, and he didn't want to waste a single second on sleep when he knew it couldn't last.

"How will I go on without you?" he whispered, brushing a curl from her face as she slumbered. He traced the line of her cheekbone with his thumb, skating lightly down her jaw to her full lower lip. Cora's mouth twitched, and she smiled in her sleep, snuggling closer and sliding her leg over one of his.

The sound of her contented sigh was sweeter than a lullaby, and as final as a funeral dirge. Time snapped back into place like a lightning strike, and he wanted to weep. For hours, he'd kept his worries at bay, refusing to think about what came next, so he could stay in the moment with her, but now it was too much. Despair rose up from some dark ocean inside him like a leviathan from the deep, threatening to drag him under. As perfect as it had been, Liam couldn't deny that their time together was almost over. He had to accept all of this for what it really was—just a long goodbye. With careful movements, he untangled himself from Cora's embrace and slid from the bed to pad blindly down the hallway.

It was too much for any man to endure. The sheer joy of loving her, and the crushing defeat of knowing he was going to lose her. Liam found himself stumbling into the backyard to the maple tree, propping himself against the trunk with one arm as he bent over, gasping for breath. This must be an inkling of what hell felt like—the knowledge that you'd once touched heaven, but never would again. He turned to lean against the trunk, sliding down until he sat in the dirt.

When the first white feather drifted down to land at his feet, followed by another and another until the downy wisps fell like snow, kissing his eyelashes and the tip of his nose, Liam began to laugh. It was a rusty, bitter laugh that scraped across his rib cage and burned from the irony.

"Your timing is impeccable," Liam said with a hitched breath, staring up at the two celestial beings perched in the tree above him. "Have you come to gloat, then?"

The angels glowed with otherworldly light as they hovered in the leafy branches. Samael, the blond angel, floated down to stand before Liam. His round face was softened with compassion, which Liam found more alarming than his usual stoic demeanor. Agon, the tall, dark-haired angel, joined them on the grass. His kind smile lacked the usual cheer, and there was a hint of sorrow on his countenance that Liam had never seen before.

For long moments, no one spoke. Liam had never felt more like a sinner as he sat under their heavy regard. He finally broke the silence. "I've been calling you."

"We were not allowed to interfere," Agon said sadly.

"We'd already shown you the future and given you everything we could," Samael added. "The rest had to be up to you. This was a journey you needed to finish on your own."

"Yet you're here now." Liam's gaze darted between them, alarm unfurling like a poisonous bloom inside him. "Why is that?"

Samael looked slightly uncomfortable. It was the most human emotion Liam had ever seen from the angel. "We've been sent to fetch you back."

"No!" Liam shot to his feet, adrenaline pumping and dread roiling in his gut. "It's not the end of the month yet. I still have time."

"You *had* time," Samael corrected. "Three months to succeed in the task you were given. In light of the fact that you failed so spectacularly at getting Cora and Finn together, last night's *activities* adding to a colossal part of that failure, it's become abundantly clear there's nothing more you can do with your time here."

"You can't take me yet," Liam cried, backpedaling from the angels. "Please. I'm begging you." He tried to run, but his body was stuck in a holding pattern. His legs were moving but he stayed in place, like a helpless hamster on a spinning wheel. "I know I've failed," he said frantically. "I'm sorry for that, but I couldn't stop loving her. I know it was wrong, but she loves me back." He finally stopped trying to run and pleaded with them. Was there no mercy in their cold, immortal hearts? *"She loves me back."*

"We know, Liam O'Connor," Samael said quietly. "That is not in question."

Liam felt like the world had tilted sideways and he was sliding down the surface toward oblivion. Mind slipping into despair, he scrambled for a way out. What could he say to convince them to allow him the few days he had left? "Look, I know I never deserved her, and I still don't. But I'm not ready to say goodbye yet. I can't just leave her like this. It would break her heart, and I'm not ready." His throat ached and tears pricked the corners of his eyes as he repeated, "I'm not ready."

"No one is ever truly ready," Agon said with compassion.

"But I want to do better," Liam said desperately. "I can still do better. Even now."

"It's irrelevant," Samael said. "Your presence here serves no purpose beyond the task you were given."

"But I can still do some good here," Liam insisted. "Even knowing my own soul is lost, I still have a few days left to help in some way. Think of the butterfly effect!"

Samael and Agon tilted their heads in unison. If they were human, Liam would say they looked mildly interested.

"The idea that one small action can be the catalyst that changes something in the future," Liam said quickly, running with it. "I've failed in what I was supposed to do, yes, but I can still do some good, even if it's on a much smaller scale. Cora and the rest of the police force have been trying to solve these murder cases. My own soul is already lost, I know that, but I can help try to bring the guilty to justice and help protect the innocent people from evil. And I recognize there's this selfish piece inside of me, a piece of me that just wants more time to spend with the woman I love. It's true. I'm not denying that because I can't, but I also want so badly to make a difference. I don't want to leave this world not having made at least *something* better. Please." Liam lifted his hands beseechingly at them. "I've done a lot of things wrong and caused a lot of heartache. Please give me these last few days so I can try to do at least one thing right. Even if I don't see the results of my actions before I go, I can leave knowing I tried."

Samael and Agon shared a long look, and it was clear they were having a silent conversation.

Liam stood there quivering on the knife edge between hope and utter despair, praying silently that the angels' answer would tip him in the right direction. Everything he'd just told them was true. He'd never felt more strongly or more committed to a cause than he did now. Maybe it was the fact that he had so little time to make a difference, or the fact that he'd been learning from Cora for the past few months. He'd watched how she worked so hard to protect and help others, how her very life was a manifestation of her love, and he remembered what she'd said so passionately to him. Love was the only thing you could take with you when you went. The love you gave and the love you were given.

"Very well, rogue," Samael said, tilting his head in somber acquiescence. "You may stay for the remainder of the month."

"Yes!" Liam's heart leaped with gratitude, and he ran toward them with his arms outstretched.

Samael's choirboy face looked mildly shocked, and Agon just chuckled as Liam's arms passed straight through them.

He stumbled, clutching at nothing, then turned back to them in surprise. "Sorry. I got carried away. Can you not take a hug, then?"

Samael blinked rapidly. "A human hug is…not something we require."

Liam considered that, then asked, "But what if the human requires it?"

Samael looked momentarily stumped, but he recovered quickly. "Gestures of comfort are not our department."

"I don't see how it could hurt," Agon said thoughtfully, gliding closer to Liam. He held out both his arms, then slowly curved them around Liam's shoulders and gave him two perfunctory pats on the back. *One. Two.* As hugs went, it needed work, but what Agon lacked in technique, he more than made up for in angelic power. Each pat was like a thousand volts of pure, unrestrained goodwill rocketing through Liam's system. He felt the glorious zap of it, from the top of his head, to the tips of his ears, nose, fingers, and toes.

"Good *God*," Liam choked out, stumbling back a step.

"Yes," Samael said primly, turning to Agon. "If you are quite finished, we—"

"That was the very best hug I've ever had," Liam said, grinning like a mad fool as he stared at Agon in awe. The initial zing of joy was beginning to fade, but the residual effects filled Liam with a glowing sense of warmth and good cheer.

Agon's sunny smile was an exact reflection of what Liam was feeling on the inside.

"I feel so light and carefree," Liam said in wonder. Powerful stuff, angel hugs. Heady and addicting. "I feel like I could *fly*."

"A temporary side effect, nothing more," Samael assured him. "It will dissipate in a moment."

That was a shame. If Liam could hold on to the feeling by sheer force of will, he would. In the brief time Agon had bestowed the hug, Liam had forgotten all his troubles, which was almost unfathomable. Liam glanced hopefully at Samael and held out his arms with a crooked smile. "I don't suppose you'd…?"

"Thank you, no. We must go now." Samael gave Agon a

pointed look, and they began to disappear in a flurry of sparkles. "May the time you've been granted help ease your conscience, Liam O'Connor, before you're gone forever." His voice echoed inside Liam's head, even after they'd disappeared. "We shall see you soon."

20

LIAM STOOD BESIDE CORA IN THE OFFICE KITCHEN late Wednesday afternoon while she made a cup of coffee. He deliberately brushed up against her as he reached for a mug from the cupboard, enjoying the slide of his arm against hers. "Pardon me, Officer McLeod."

"Liam," Cora whispered, glancing at the doorway. She nudged him away with her shoulder, but her secret smile mirrored his own. "Someone will see you."

"Let them." He leaned down until their faces were inches apart. "Let them see I'm with the most beautiful woman in the world and I'm completely under her spell." Cora's cheeks flushed pink. He loved teasing her like this, even though she'd reminded him at the beginning of the week that they had to keep their relationship under wraps for professional reasons. For the past three days, they'd been trying to act as if things were business as usual between them. It was almost impossible for Liam, especially because he knew they had so little time left together. As far as he was concerned, he didn't care what anyone thought; he was going to spend every last moment he could with the woman he loved. Cora didn't seem to believe he would truly be gone in a few days, and he didn't have the heart to convince her otherwise. It would only make her worry more, and since it wouldn't change the outcome, he wanted to bask in her happiness for as long as he could. Smiling, he bent and planted a lightning-quick kiss on her nose.

Cora spun away just as Otto ambled into the kitchen. She gave Liam an "I told you so" look.

"Hey there," Otto said cheerfully, oblivious to the fireworks going off in the room. He went to the fridge and pulled out a half-eaten cinnamon roll in a plastic bag. "Anyone seen Happy? He left a while ago and hasn't come back."

Cora shook her head. "Where'd he go?"

"No idea," Otto said, grabbing napkins from the dispenser on the table. "Late lunch, I guess."

Liam pulled his phone from his pocket to check the time. It was four o'clock, and there was an alert on his phone. "Slice just called," he told Cora. "I had my ringer off, so I didn't hear it. But he left a message."

"Finally," Cora said with relief. "Please tell me he found the laptop and has more pictures. I don't want to have to meet with Captain Thompson today with nothing new to report."

"Captain's not here, so you're off the hook," Otto said.

"We were supposed to give him an update at five o'clock," Liam said. "Are you sure he's gone?"

"I saw him leave a while ago," Otto said around a bite of cinnamon roll. "Mavis said he'd be out the rest of the day." He waved a hand at both of them and left the kitchen.

"Well, I guess that's a good thing," Cora said with a sigh. "What's the message say?"

Liam lowered himself into a chair and pressed the button for voice mail.

"You gotta help me, man!" Slice sounded frantic and out of breath. *"I found my laptop and the picture like you wanted. I even called your station and reported it, but now he's here. The guy from the picture, and he's trying to—"* A crash sounded, and then heavy thumping, and then the message ended.

He was in trouble. Liam shot up from the chair. "We have to go."

Moments later, they were in the car, speeding toward Zippy Lube. Liam handed Cora his phone as he wove through traffic at breakneck speeds. She replayed the message several times on speaker.

"Why would Brady's killer go after Slice?" Cora asked.

"He must have found out there was a picture linking him to the murder."

"But how could he know that? Slice only just found the picture today," Cora said as the Zippy Lube sign appeared at the end of the street. Liam gunned the engine and they shot toward the parking lot, coming to a screeching halt just outside the Zippy Lube carports.

"Oh, my God," Cora breathed. Slice lay crumpled on the garage floor, with a tall, gangly figure crouched over him. "Is that...?"

"Happy," Liam said grimly, jumping out of the car and running toward them.

Happy Blankenship jerked his head in their direction. He was crouched over Slice with both hands on the young man's shirt. Happy's hands and sleeves were stained with blood, along with the cell phone on the asphalt beside him. With snapping eyes and messed-up dark hair, Happy looked furious and even a little unhinged, which came as a shock to Liam. The sour-faced man was never a barrel of laughs to be around, but he'd always been calm and in control. Now he looked like he was ready to commit murder.

Liam bolted toward him, clamping a fist on the back of his shirt collar.

"Officer Blankenship," Cora said, pulling her gun and aiming it at Happy. "Back away from him right now."

"Don't be ridiculous," Happy snapped. He jerked against Liam's hold, glowering at them with impatience as he pressed down on Slice's stomach with both hands. "He's been *stabbed*. I just called it in, and I'm trying to save him." He jerked his chin to the workstation against the wall. "One of you grab a clean rag and help me."

Liam uncurled his fist from Happy's shirt. He had no idea what the hell was going on, but it was clear they had a more pressing problem. Slice Biddlesworth lay pale and shivering on the ground, his wispy, wheat-colored hair plastered to his round, boyish cheeks.

"Easy, now." Liam placed a hand gently on Slice's arm as Cora brought a small stack of clean rags from the workbench. "What happened here, man?"

"Captain Thompson happened," Happy spit through pinched lips as he used a folded rag to stanch the wound. "He did this."

"What?" Cora stared at him in shock. "What do you mean?" Liam watched the color leach from her face. He should've been shocked, too, but somehow he wasn't. Had he known on some subconscious level that Boyd was capable of this?

"The captain was the man in the picture." Slice's chest hitched as he fought for breath. "It was him. I didn't know when I found the pictures because they were blurry." He struggled to speak, growing visibly weaker. Liam bent closer in order to hear. "I called and told him I found my laptop with the pictures. I didn't realize it was him all along..." Slice's voice grew reed-thin, and he trailed off with a grimace.

"Save your breath," Happy commanded. "You've done well, and now you need to stay strong. The ambulance is on its way. I'll tell them the rest." When he glanced back to Liam and Cora, his expression was even more dire than usual. "Captain Thompson called him a few days ago, saying if he found the laptop or pictures, he was to contact him directly. Slice didn't realize the captain was the murderer in the window because the pictures were too blurry to tell."

"The lab can enhance those images," Cora said. "It's not always reliable and it would depend on the original files, but sometimes it works."

"That's why Thompson must've panicked when he got the call. He came out here to get rid of Slice and the evidence, just like he did with Lindsey Albright, but I showed up before he could finish the job. When he saw me, he jumped in his car and drove off. I couldn't leave Slice to bleed out, so here we are."

Liam ground his teeth together. Damn Boyd and his unending greed. He'd always known he took the law into his own hands back when they were friends, but he'd never resorted to outright murder. At least, not as far as Liam knew. But how well did he really know Boyd, then or now? Not well, clearly. Liam couldn't help feeling like this was somehow his fault. Boyd had always had a dark side, and he should have been paying closer attention.

Slice flailed a hand toward Liam, trying to grab his sleeve.

Liam laid his palm on his arm to calm him down. "Shh, you must rest."

"He knows." The young man trembled with exertion but managed to grip the edge of Liam's shirt. His words became slurred, and Liam had to lean down to hear him. "G-go to church."

Liam stared into his pain-filled eyes. He wasn't making any sense. Maybe he thought he was dying, and he wanted a priest. "All right, man," Liam said soothingly. "All right. But you're going to be fine. Just rest now. We'll take care of it."

Slice closed his eyes and stopped struggling, clearly worn out from the effort it took to speak.

"I can't believe Captain Thompson did this," Cora said, looking stricken. She'd been sitting on her heels, and now she'd slumped to sit directly on the ground beside Slice's shoulder. "How did you know it was him, Happy?"

"I've been watching Thompson for months," Happy said flatly. "One night back in May I overheard him in his office, talking to someone about a deal. It was unusually quiet because everyone had left for the bar, and the evening shift was hanging out in the kitchen. I think he thought he was alone in the pit because his door was cracked open. I heard him say 'take the money' and 'stay quiet.' It sounded suspect, so I started watching him. I followed him whenever I could, and I even trailed him on the weekends. I didn't tell anyone because I had nothing concrete yet. It was his wife who finally gave him away."

"Alice?" Liam asked in surprise. It didn't sound like something she'd willingly do. Alice was even greedier than Boyd. If Boyd was taking bribes or making extra money on the side, it wasn't likely that she'd complain about it, no matter how dirty the money was.

Happy nodded. "Alice never said a word, but I saw all the evidence I needed with my own eyes. When she came to visit, and they had that fight the other day at the station, she was wearing a sapphire necklace. I thought it was odd because it seemed over the top for just a daytime outfit, even for Alice. The night of John Brady's murder, his safe was left open, and he'd been robbed. I remembered reading through the report and seeing the insurance claims. That sapphire necklace was one of the stolen items."

"Oh, my God," Cora said. "I ran into Alice at the store the other night. She was angry and said she left him because she believed he was having an affair. She said she found a necklace while going through his things, but he told her it wasn't for her."

"She must've found it and worn it to spite him that day," Happy said. "Maybe to accuse him of buying it for another woman."

An ambulance siren wailed in the distance, and Happy glanced down at Slice. "They're here now. Just hang on." But Slice was beyond hearing. He lay pale as a ghost. If not for the shallow rise and fall of his chest, he might've been beyond helping.

The ambulance came screaming into the parking lot. Three paramedics jumped out and ran toward them. They immediately began administering to Slice, and Happy filled them in on what had transpired as two squad cars pulled up.

In the melee of activity, Liam pulled Cora aside. "We have to go after Boyd." There was so little time left for him, and he vowed he'd do everything he could to help Cora find justice for the innocents who'd died. Now that he knew it was Boyd, he was more driven than ever. A chilling anger had begun growing and spreading inside him ever since Happy told them Boyd was the killer. Liam should've seen it. How could he not have detected that Boyd was so evil? Because Liam had a history with Boyd, and they'd been on the other side of the law together back in his old life, he felt almost responsible for what had happened. He should have known.

"Happy's calling it in right now, but we have no idea where he went. And Captain Thompson's too smart to stay in his own car. He'll know we're looking for him. I just can't believe he'd do something like this," Cora said, looking ill. "Taking bribes and stealing is bad enough, but *murder*?"

"You don't know Boyd like I do," Liam said darkly. "There's not much a man won't do if he's desperate enough. Back in Ireland life was brutal. There was no opportunity for a better future. We were hungry and angry and hopeless. We were thieves, Cora."

"But you didn't kill people." She stared at him with absolute conviction, and it was humbling.

"No, of course not," Liam said. "I would never have done anything like that. But I can't say the same for Boyd. He was always hotheaded and stubborn. He didn't always think things through. I don't know exactly what happened the night of John Brady's murder, but I wouldn't put it past Boyd to kill someone if they stood in the way of him gaining a fortune. Look what he was willing to do to Slice just to cover it up."

The paramedics were strapping Slice onto a stretcher when Eli Shelton and Bear rode up on their motorcycles. The growling roar of the engines was nothing compared to their angry faces.

Eli swung a leg over his bike and shot toward the paramedics like a swarm of angry hornets. "What the hell happened to my boy?" Even though the president of the Booze Dogs was an older man and not physically in his prime, he looked mad enough to do serious damage. Bear, the supersized muscle head, was slower to get off his motorcycle, but he looked just as deadly.

Liam caught Eli's upper arm to keep him from interfering. "There's nothing you can do right now. Leave them be. You'll just be in the way."

Eli barked out a litany of swear words and tried to yank his arm away as Liam tightened his grip. "If you want him to live, you'll leave them to do their jobs. Every second they have to deal with you is a second you take from Slice."

"Let him go," Bear snarled, advancing on Liam. The man's legs were so swollen with muscle it was a wonder the ground didn't shake beneath his feet. Liam released Eli and braced for a potentially painful fight. Bear was huge, but Liam was fast. What he lacked for in bulk, he could make up for in speed. He knew from experience men like this packed a powerful punch, but that only counted if they could catch him. He just had to stay alert and remain fast on his feet.

"Enough," Cora said, her voice ringing with authority. "There isn't time for this. And Liam's right." She held her hand out to stop Bear from going any farther, and to Liam's surprise, it worked. It never ceased to amaze him how she managed to stay visibly unruffled in times of stress. "Slice was stabbed," she continued evenly. "But our officer arrived when it happened, so was able to call the paramedics in time."

"Tell me who did this." Eli was so angry spittle flew from his mouth as he closed in on Cora. "Slice called us not fifteen minutes ago, saying he was in trouble."

"I'll tell you," Liam said. "But first, back up and give her some space." He didn't like the way both bikers were looming over her.

Cora glanced at Liam as the two men took a step back. She lowered her voice and murmured, "Liam, we shouldn't tell them anything until there's been an official statement."

"They have a right to know," he told her. "Slice is one of theirs, and it's only a matter of time before everyone finds out." When she gave a reluctant nod, he turned to Eli and Bear. "It was Boyd Thompson."

Eli's eyebrows shot up, and then lowered into a murderous scowl. "That captain scum tried to kill our boy?" He barked out a string of curse words too fast for Liam to commit to memory. For a normally surly individual, Eli was angrier than ever. Heaving like he was about to breathe fire, with his crimson face twisted into a mask of fury, Liam caught a glimpse of what a formidable man the bike club president must've been back when he was in his physical prime. "This is why I hate doing business with you filthy, no-good, lying pigs," Eli spit. "Where is he?"

"We don't know where the captain is," Cora said, ignoring his insults. "Only that he drove away right before we arrived. Did Slice say anything else to you when he called? Anything that could help us locate him?"

Eli shared a look with Bear, then said flatly, "No."

"But, Prez, the captain could be headed there *right now*," Bear growled. "We can't let him get away."

"I said *no*," Eli hissed.

"The longer we stand here, the better Boyd's chances of disappearing," Liam said, noticing the flicker of indecision on Eli's face. "Tell us what you know."

Eli jutted his chin. "No, I'll take care of it. Most of my men are at an event right now. It'll take me some time to call them in, but we'll deal with it."

Cora crossed her arms. "If you're talking about one of your Wednesday night cage fights at the old barn, they're too far away. By the time you call your guys in to search for Captain Thompson, he'll be long gone."

Eli's eyes narrowed into dangerous slits. "What cage fights?"

Liam wondered the same thing. Cora had never mentioned anything about that before.

"We're losing time," she said in frustration. "I've known about your operation for a while now. I just haven't reported it yet."

"No idea what you're talking about, girl." Eli feigned boredom, but there was an underlying threat in his tone that made the hair on the back of Liam's neck rise. He took a step forward, instinctively moving closer to Cora.

"Cora, Liam," Happy called from across the parking lot as the ambulance drove out. He jogged up, his pinched face coolly assessing the two bikers. "We've got people moving out to search for Thompson now. But there's something you should know. We just found Finley Walsh's car down a ravine near the state park."

Cora sucked in a breath. "No! Not Finn." Her face blanched like she was going to be ill.

Liam felt the same. Not giving a damn who was looking, he curled an arm around her shoulders for support, trying not to show the whirling vortex of dread churning in his own stomach. Though he hadn't wanted to admit it, a tiny part of him had still hoped things could work out, for some miraculous moment where Cora and Finn might end up together. But even aside from all that, Finn was a good man and deserved so much better than this. The last thing Liam wanted was to find out Finn had met an untimely death in such a violent way. Even though Liam had failed him—failed everyone—he still wanted to imagine that Finn would go on living his life instead of dying in some ravine all alone. "Did they find him?"

"No," Happy said with a puzzled frown. "They searched the whole area and there's no sign of foul play. It's odd. Almost as if his car just rolled off the edge of the road on its own. I'm heading back to the station, and then I'll check on Slice."

Liam suddenly remembered what Slice said right before he passed out. "Get him a priest."

Happy pursed his lips in disapproval, as if Liam insinuating that Slice wouldn't make it was in poor taste. "The paramedics said there's a very good chance he'll pull through."

"Still, it's what he wants," Liam insisted. "He mentioned

church, remember? Far be it from any of us to deny a man the right to his religion when he's knocking at death's door."

Bear pulled Eli aside, and they began talking in rushed, angry whispers.

Happy tilted his head in their direction. "Can you two find out what they know and report back?"

"Already on it," Cora said, squaring her shoulders. She'd somehow locked her emotions away and now appeared calm and collected again. "Can you call us if you hear anything about Finn?"

Happy nodded and hurried toward his car.

"Finn could be dead, Prez," Bear was saying to Eli. "After all he's done for us over the years, it ain't right. We can't risk letting that scumbag captain get away with this. Magnus Blackwell's death. Finn's car. The locations can't be a coincidence. Both those accidents are too close to where we—"

"Fine!" Eli snarled. He spun toward Liam and Cora, scowling like they'd just flipped him off and set his bike on fire. "I'll be damned if I let your captain get away with everything he's done."

"What else do you know?" Cora asked. "Something tells me you've got a lot more dirt on the captain than we do."

"I could tell you stories that would make your pretty little head spin, girl, but I ain't got time for that. Still, I've got too much at stake here, and I'm not letting that man take anything more from me. But first…" He grimaced like he'd just drunk back-to-back shots of diesel fuel. "I need you both to do me a favor."

Cora jammed her hands on her hips. "A favor from a couple of no-good, lying pigs like us, huh?"

"Don't you sass me, girl. I remember your father, and he was squared away. He walked the line back in the day, and he raised you, so I'm going to have to take a chance that I can trust your word."

"Spit it out, man," Liam said in frustration. They were losing time. "What do you want?"

"I reckon I know where your captain's going, but I can't round up my men to get there fast enough. You can make it if you leave now. But I need your promise you won't call in the location for at least an hour. Give my guys that much of a head start."

"I don't understand," Cora said. "I need more information before I agree to this."

"You don't gotta understand, lady," Bear said irritably. "Just give him your word you won't tell your police buddies where we're headed for at least an hour, and we can get on our way."

"Fine. Yes," Liam answered for both of them. "You have our word. We'll give you a head start before the police arrive."

Cora blew out a breath of annoyance but didn't disagree. It went against her better judgment, Liam knew, but even she understood the magnitude of what they were up against. Boyd, the captain of their police force, was a lying, scheming murderer who'd been committing acts of corruption for years, and all behind the guise of a trusted pillar of the community. They couldn't let him get away.

Eli nodded once. "Bear will go with you. He can keep an eye on you, just in case your fingers get antsy and you feel like breaking your promise and making an early phone call. He knows the way out there. Just follow his lead."

"To where?" Cora threw her hands up, clearly impatient with all the subterfuge. "Captain Thompson knows he's been made. And now he's on the run. We've got officers out looking for him already. He can't access his bank accounts or use his phone because he knows we'll track him. Where would he go at a time like this?"

Eli's grin was the kind a shark makes just before it bites. Cold and deadly. "He's gone to church."

21

LIAM FOLLOWED BEAR'S DIRECTIONS AND DROVE
west toward the mountains. The overcast sky gave way to dark
clouds, and sheets of rain began hitting the windshield as they
sped away from the city, which didn't seem to bother Liam at all.
Unlike Cora, who was certain they were going to slide across the
road and roll the car at the next hairpin turn, Bear sat in the back
seat with a begrudging smirk on his face. He seemed to enjoy
the way Liam was tearing hell-for-leather down the highway.

"Respect, man." Bear thumped a fist to his chest when Liam
swerved between two semitrucks and shot ahead. "I never ride
in tin cans if I don't have to, but at least you make it interesting."

"Can you please tell us exactly where we're going now?"
Cora asked.

"You heard Eli," Bear said. "We're going to church."

"Then we're definitely on a fool's errand," Liam said. "I've
known Boyd a long time, and I can promise you, the Lord's
house is the last place he'd go, even if the devil himself were
chasing him."

Bear made a sound that almost passed for a chuckle, but Cora couldn't be sure. He stretched out in the back seat, taking up most of the space. "Church is a limestone cave. Part of a whole network of tunnels and caves. It's the old meeting place for the original Booze Dogs. They were bootleggers back during Prohibition. Had a secret still and stored barrels of whiskey up there. Among other things."

"The only caves I'm aware of are on the other side of the ridge," Cora said. "I didn't realize we had any here."

"Most people don't know," Bear said, "and we want to keep it that way, you get me? But this thing with the captain is personal, and we need to catch him fast, so here we are."

"Why would Boyd want to hide in the caves?" Liam asked. "If it were me, I'd take as much money as I could get my hands on, steal the fastest car I could find, and flee the country."

"That's probably his plan," Bear said. "He's not looking to hide. We store a lot of stuff at church. Ever since the Doghouse got robbed, Eli's been having us stash more money from our business operations up there, too."

Cora glanced back at him. "Stolen money?" She didn't expect him to answer truthfully.

"Aw, you think we'd steal, sweet cheeks?" He slapped his hand against his heart, mocking her. "Now, that just hurts my feelings. All the money we put up there is earned."

Right. Earned through an illegal gambling ring. She wanted to point that out, but Bear was helping them track a killer. Though it was tempting, she couldn't afford to punch this gift horse in the mouth. "So, the captain is after your money," Cora said. "But if it's so well hidden, how does he know where to find it?"

"Maybe he followed one of the Booze Dogs when they were making a run," Liam said. "That's what Slice meant when we were waiting for the ambulance. *'He knows. Go to church.'"*

Bear made a growly sound in the back of his throat. "That scumbag lawyer Blackwell was in on it, too. They're always working together."

Cora turned in her seat to face Bear. "What does he have to do with this?"

"Magnus Blackwell was messing around with Wally Jensen's woman."

Cora remembered the drugged-out biker from the Fantasy Palace motel weeks ago. He'd been trying to skip town with the two-thousand-dollar payout he got from the anonymous source, and he'd also been trying to impress his girlfriend in that honeymoon suite from hell. Both she and Wally were still in jail.

"She wasn't supposed to know about church, but Wally's always been a pussy when it came to her, and he must've let it slip," Bear said. "She's the one who convinced Wally to paint over the security cameras that night. Wally thought he was doing it for an anonymous source, but his girl knew all along. Blackwell must've sweet-talked her into helping. Maybe he promised her a fancy life. She ain't too bright, that one. Anyway, Magnus didn't just steal that money. He stole something much more valuable. Eli kept a map of the cave networks in his office. Old as dirt, drawn out by the original Booze Dogs back in the day. It was stolen the same night the money was taken."

"Eli never mentioned it," Cora said. She definitely would've remembered something like that.

"That's because he only just realized it was missing."

Cora began to realize why Eli was so spitting mad today. It wasn't just the fact that Magnus had stolen two hundred thousand dollars from his office, which was enough to make anyone livid, it was that the Booze Dogs stood to lose so much more now that outsiders knew about the location of church.

Cora gave Bear the side-eye. "So, Magnus took your map... and now he's dead."

"Before you high-jump to any fancy conclusions, I'll tell you right now, we didn't kill him," Bear said, glowering at her. "We only just found out about Magnus's connection to Wally's woman yesterday when our men were mucking out Wally's old room at the Doghouse. She left a bunch of her stuff in his closet, and one of Magnus's business cards was in there. We asked around and found out she'd been seeing Magnus on the side. One of her girlfriends knew the whole story, and eventually we got the information we needed. That's when Eli put two and two together, and he realized the map had been stolen, too."

"I still don't see how Boyd fits into this," Liam said, turning the windshield wipers on high. The rain was coming down in sheets now, lending a hazy quality to the highway and forested area beyond. "I'm not at all surprised about Magnus sleeping around and stealing treasure maps, but—"

"Those two are thick as thieves," Bear said. "Your police captain and Blackwell have been making deals and taking bribes for years. The captain uses the Booze Dogs as his scapegoat whenever it suits him. Anytime something goes down and he needs an out, he points a finger at us. That's why Eli hates him so much. The Booze Dogs don't deal in drugs or nothing like that. We keep our business to ourselves. But we've been an easy target for the captain, and there's not a whole lot we can do when he's got that dirtbag lawyer in his pocket."

"My God," Cora said, shaking her head. "How long has this been going on?"

"Longer than you been around, doll face," Bear said. "I'm guessing your captain and Blackwell have been working together to try to find church for a while now. Slice is one of our guys who runs the money up there after the..." He caught himself before he said something incriminating, like *cage fights*. "After we pull in profits from our business endeavors. They must've followed him on one of his runs. Turn there." He pointed to a sign up ahead on the right. The rain was coming down in heavy sheets now, but Cora recognized the Providence Falls State Park sign.

"You were at church that day," she said to Bear in surprise. "When I ran into you on the hiking trail."

He grunted, which she assumed was an affirmation, but he was too busy searching the near-empty parking lot as they drove to the entrance of the park. The heavily forested trails were hidden beneath a canopy of spruce, pine, and deciduous trees, the rich medley of verdant shades etched in sharp contrast from the rain. Liam pulled the car to a jarring stop right beside an old blue station wagon. It was the only other car in the lot. Captain Thompson's car was nowhere to be seen, but he could've dumped it and commandeered this one to stay under the radar. He was a bad man, Cora now knew, but he wasn't stupid.

"Stay close," Bear said when they stood at the bottom of the trail. "Where we're headed, there ain't no path, and it's tricky even when it's not raining like this." The torrential downpour from a few minutes earlier had eased into a light drizzle, but the mud was going to make it harder to navigate. Bear took off at a fast clip, and Cora broke into a jog to keep up. Liam was right behind her.

"I have a bad feeling about this," Cora said under her breath as she scanned the darkening forest around them. She didn't trust the captain anymore, and he could be anywhere. She wanted to call in reinforcements, but she'd promised Eli an hour, and she'd keep her word.

"Nonsense," Liam said cheerfully. "We're following an angry bear into the woods. What could possibly go wrong?"

"Tracks." Bear pointed to large shoe prints in the mud ahead of them. The impressions were fresh, with deeper indentations on the balls of the feet like he was running.

"We have to hurry," Cora said.

They picked up their pace, trudging through the rain until Bear turned left at a rotting log, leaving the main trail to charge through the underbrush like a bulldozer. Cora stayed as close as she could, but it was hard to go fast when the mud sucked at the bottom of her tennis shoes. She wished she'd worn her hiking boots, but she hadn't planned on wading through a forest when she went in to work that morning. Wet branches slapped at her face, and her clothes were completely drenched, but she was so driven by their goal that she barely felt it.

Bear stopped suddenly in front of her. She bumped into him before she could slow down, but he didn't seem to notice. "Sorry," Cora said, rubbing her forehead. He was like hitting a brick wall.

"We're headed that way." He was pointing across a deep ravine.

"Sure thing," Cora said, staring down into what looked like a hundred-foot drop. "Where's the bridge?" The gaping maw of the ravine was riddled with sharp rocks that jutted out like teeth near the bottom.

"There's a suspension bridge about fifteen minutes' hike from here, but this way's much faster." Bear walked over to a tree and yanked something from a crevice. It was a weathered-looking rope as thick around as his fist, with a large knot at the bottom. The top of the rope was secured to an overhanging branch above the ravine.

"I want to go first," Liam said, rubbing his hands together in excitement.

Cora rolled her eyes. "You would say that."

Liam grinned as Bear dropped the rope into his hands. "Come, Cora," he said, holding out one arm. "I'll carry us across."

"Hard pass," she said, taking a step back in case he tried to insist. "This isn't *Star Wars*, Liam, and I'm not a damsel in distress. Besides, it's raining, and that rope doesn't look like it could hold two people. Just go. I'll do it myself."

Liam looked like he wanted to argue, but she threw him a look that shut him down. With a nod, he pulled back, placed one foot on the bottom knot, and swung out. Cora cringed as he swooped over the ravine, then felt a wave of relief when he landed effortlessly on the other side. He tossed the rope back with a look of pure, boyish glee. Cora half expected him to ask to go again.

Bear swiped a paw out and caught it. "You're up next, sweet chee—"

"Don't," she said sharply, yanking the rope from him. "My name is Cora. Or Officer McLeod. Not *sweet cheeks*, or *girlie*, or *doll face*. If you call me any more of your derogatory nicknames, I'll—"

"Okay, okay," Bear said, holding his hands up in surrender. "You got it, babe." When her eyebrows shot up, he quickly corrected himself. *"Cora."* He stood back and swept his arm out toward the ravine with a mocking bow. "Please be my guest, Cora."

Cora wasn't fooled by his obsequious attitude for one second, but she had other things to worry about. Like swinging from a ratty-looking rope over a dangerous cliff. Refusing to think on it too long, she gripped the rope with both hands, placed her feet on the knot, and swung out. She didn't realize her eyes were closed until Liam's arms wrapped around her like steel bands.

"I've got you," he breathed in her ear. He waited until she was steady, then tossed the rope back to Bear.

Bear joined them and secured the knot on a small branch nearby. "We're making good time, but no more talking from here on out. We're getting close, and we don't want to be heard."

"How much longer?" Cora asked, checking her phone. "We promised Eli an hour. In exactly twelve minutes all bets are off, and I'm calling in reinforcements."

Bear glanced at her phone, then smirked. She didn't like the look on his face, and it suddenly dawned on her.

"You've got to be kidding me." She wanted to slap her forehead in frustration. Or better yet, slap Eli. He'd played them like a fiddle. How could she have forgotten something so basic?

"What's wrong?" Liam asked, glancing between her and Bear.

"There's no cell phone reception this high up the mountain," she said in disgust as Bear started to chuckle. "That's why Eli made us promise to give him an hour. He knew where we were headed, and he knew we'd likely be out of range. Now we can't call the station for backup."

"You aren't going to need it," Bear said, continuing through the woods. "Booze Dogs are heading here soon, and if you can agree to quit yapping, we'll get your captain even sooner. Now, come on."

"And you say *we* can't be trusted," she muttered to the solid wall of his back, angrily kicking up dirt as she trudged after him.

Bear didn't respond, and by unspoken agreement, they all stopped talking. The rain had picked up again, muffling the sounds of their footsteps through the underbrush. They took several turns, zigzagging in an odd pattern around jutting rocks, fallen logs, and other unnoticeable landmarks that Bear seemed to be familiar with. Finally, they came to a large rock formation surrounded by trees. Cora could hear the roar of the waterfall off in the distance.

Bear stopped in front of a gnarled, rotting trunk surrounded by bushes. Then he turned sideways and disappeared behind the trunk. She did the same, only to discover a crevice in a wall of rock that was hidden from view. It was cooler inside, and the air smelled like damp earth that had never seen the sun.

"Limestone caves," Liam murmured from behind her. "Fascinating."

It was dark as pitch, but Bear's face suddenly loomed in front of them. "Follow me," he said, turning on a tiny penlight that must've been hidden near the entrance. "Do not turn on your phones. Too much light, and he could see us, depending on where he is in the tunnels. Keep your left hand on the wall and stay close. There's a lot of places you can drop off if you're not careful."

That sounded ominous. Cora trailed her hand along the wall, keeping her eye on the small pinprick of light Bear was using. The limestone walls were rough under her fingertips, and the ground was uneven under her feet. The farther into the caves they walked, the darker it got, until all ambient light from the entrance was long gone, and they were engulfed in an inky blackness that felt eternal. The air felt dank and stale as a tomb, and Cora was grateful for Liam's steady presence behind her. She told herself that all she had to do was turn around and follow the cave wall back outside into the sunlight, but the thought wasn't very comforting. This place was like a maze, like nothing she'd ever experienced before. When she was a young girl, she'd gone on a trip to caves with her father, but that tourist attraction had been well lit, with tour guides leading the way. This cave system seemed infinite, and far more inhospitable.

Bear's light stopped moving, and she slowed with her arm outstretched until she felt his massive back. Liam's hand came to rest on her shoulder.

"We're going to make a right turn in a minute," Bear whispered. "You'll need to step only where I step, because there's about a ten-or twenty-foot drop on both sides."

Cora gripped the back of Bear's shirt, not caring whether he liked it or not. The idea of slipping into the gloom was worse than anything he might do. Bear started to move forward, and Cora reached back and grabbed for Liam until they were holding hands. When Bear veered to the right, Cora shuffle-stepped behind him, keeping her eye on the penlight like it was a lifeline. It was slow-going, and an icy breeze began to swirl around them, ruffling her hair and clothes. Even though Cora knew the displaced air was likely due to the fact that they were now walking across some kind of natural bridge with precarious drops on either side, it still felt eerie, like skeletal fingers reaching out to hold her back. She shivered, and suddenly lost her footing.

With a gasp, Cora yanked on Bear's shirt but lost her grip. She stumbled and fell hard on her left knee. When she tried to gain balance with her right foot, it caught nothing but air. The realization that she was so close to the edge made her cry out.

Liam's strong hand suddenly grabbed on to her arm like a steely vise. He yanked her up and she fell onto her left hip, gasping for breath. *Safe.*

Before Cora had a chance to process what was happening, she heard a scrape behind her, a muffled curse, and then…nothing.

"Liam!" she cried, reaching behind her. Nothing but uneven rock scraped across her palms. He was gone. "Liam! Where are you?"

Far below, she heard a grunt, and the sound of heavy breathing. "Here."

"Oh, my God, Liam, are you hurt?"

She could hear a scraping sound like he was dragging himself across the ground. "I'm all right."

Cora reached blindly for Bear. "We can't leave him down there. We have to get him."

"With what?" Bear scoffed. "Unless you've got a rope and grappling hooks in your pocket, lady, he's staying where he is. We can come back for him later."

"Are you out of your mind?"

"He's on the bench," Bear said. "Best he can do is take a nap and wait for us to get back."

If it were bright enough to see, she'd have slapped him for sounding so blasé.

"Bear's right," Liam called from below. "We're running out of time."

"I don't want to leave you," she said as a lump formed in her throat.

"We gotta go," Bear said. "Or we lose our chance to catch your captain. That's why we came, ain't it?"

"Go with him, Cora," Liam told her. "I'm not hurt, and I'll wait for you."

Cora felt tears prick the corners of her eyes. Logically, she knew he was right, but she hated the idea of leaving him all alone in this place that felt like a catacomb. Like a place for the dead. "I'll come back for you," she said fiercely, swiping at a tear that escaped her eye.

"Be careful," he said.

She felt Bear grip her wrist and slap her hand against his belt. Miserably, Cora curled her fingers into his belt as he began to move forward again. The darkness felt ominous, and a chasm of emptiness opened up inside her. With every footstep, Cora couldn't shake the feeling that she was leaving a piece of her heart behind.

22

LIAM LAY PROPPED AGAINST THE CAVE WALL, breathing heavily. The fall had knocked the wind out of him. His backside felt bruised, but he'd broken no bones and sustained no internal injuries. As frustrated as he was to be sitting useless in the dark, it could've been much worse. It could've been Cora who'd taken the fall, so he was grateful she was all right.

He rolled a small rock in his hand, then threw it into the pitch dark with a heavy sigh. If there was one thing Liam hated to do, it was wait. He'd never been good at sitting still and doing nothing. *"Bollocks."*

"Eloquent as ever," an unimpressed voice said from the gloom.

Liam jolted upright. "Who's there?"

A soft glow lit the cavern, and soon Samael and Agon appeared before him.

"Samael. Agon," Liam said, leaning his head against the rock wall behind him. "Please tell me you haven't come to take me back. I still have a wee bit of time, and you promised."

"Yes, we did," Agon said kindly, lowering his body into the ground so his face was level with Liam's. It was disconcerting to see only his torso sticking up from the rock floor, but Liam had known them a while now, and he was growing used to their odd ways. "We've just come to give you... What is that phrase again?" He glanced at Samael.

Samael arched a brow. "I believe you called it 'moral support.'"

"Yes," Agon said cheerfully. "Is it working?"

Liam crinkled his forehead. "Aye, I suppose so. Nobody likes to feel alone in the dark, do they?"

"No one ever is," Agon said. "Even in your darkest hours, you are never alone."

"Did you know about Boyd?" Liam asked suddenly, crossing his arms to keep off the chill. The angels glowed from within, but there was no warmth in that dark place.

Rather than answer with words, Samael waved a hand, and a roiling mist appeared on the cavern wall. Liam watched a scene unfold with rapt attention.

Kinsley, Ireland, 1844

Boyd lurked like a wraith in the shadowed corridor of Margaret Brady's mansion, his attention fixed on the room at the end of the hall. Her room. His ragged boots made almost no sound as he crept across the richly woven rug, past the gilt-framed paintings of Brady ancestors and heavy velvet curtains that overlooked the courtyard. With a surreptitious glance toward the far staircase to make sure he remained unnoticed, he pushed open her door.

Margaret was sitting before a mirror at her dressing table, riffling through a sparkling box of jewelry. She appeared to be choosing a necklace to go with her silk gown.

When Boyd stepped silently into her room, she saw his reflection and gasped in shock. "Who are you? What are you doing in my bedchamber?"

Boyd's smirk held dark intentions no woman ever wanted to see. He swept closer, a sharp knife glinting in his hand. When Margaret opened her mouth to scream, he rushed forward and slapped his free hand over her mouth, muffling her cries. "Make one sound, lass, and this blade finds a home in your soft, lovely breast." The tip of his knife hovered just above the fine lace of her neckline. "Do you hear me?"

Margaret nodded her head, her wide gray eyes glancing toward the wall near her bed.

His gaze followed hers, and he scoffed. "If you're thinking to use the bellpull to alert someone, know that I'll kill you and disappear before any of your lazy maids have a chance to come to your rescue. Nod if you understand."

She nodded, and after one long, assessing look in the mirror, Boyd let her go. He leaned against her dressing table, using the tip of his knife to flick the lace on her bodice. "Pretty." He yanked the comb from her hair and it tumbled loose to fall around her face. "Very pretty. It's no wonder my friend was so taken with you."

Margaret's eyes widened. She opened her mouth to speak, then seemed to think better of it.

"Good," Boyd said with a nod of approval. "A man doesn't like a woman to talk too much." He waved a hand by his ear like he was swiping at flies. "It's the incessant, never-ending nagging that makes him want to plunge his knife deep until the nagging stops. In fact..." He used the tip of his knife to sweep the lock of hair from her face, but the sharpened edge just severed the strands until they fell silently into Margaret's lap. Her breath hitched with fear. "The world would be a better place in general if pretty little mindless doves didn't speak at all. They're really only good for one thing. Don't you agree?"

Margaret made a small keening noise in the back of her throat, but she remained still, trembling on her velvet stool like a bird in the grip of a snake.

"Good. Now, I've come to make you a deal. I know you've been carrying on with Liam O'Connor. It's no secret you've been making a cuckold of your husband behind his back."

Margaret's face blanched. "We're not—"

"Ah, ah." Boyd pressed the flat blade of his knife against her lips. "Don't start squawking now, dove. Just listen." A single tear slipped from the corner of Margaret's eye as Boyd pulled his knife away and continued. "Your husband is a very wealthy man, and I happen to be in need of some wealth myself. Now, John Brady is not known for charitable acts of kindness, so I've come to give you this opportunity to rectify that. You will take that lovely box there." He pointed to the jewelry box with his knife. Several necklaces lay within velvet-lined compartments, along with a handful of sparkling combs and earrings. "And you will place the contents…" He stepped over to the bed, yanked a frilled pillowcase free, and tossed it to her. "In there. Go on, then. Be quick about it."

With frightened, jerky movements, Margaret scooped out her jewelry and tossed the pieces into the pillowcase.

"Now you and I will take a trip to your husband's study," Boyd said, grabbing the sack of jewelry. "And you can show me where he keeps his real money."

"I don't know anything," Margaret said in a tremulous voice. "John keeps all his wealth locked away. All I have is the pin money he gives me for allowance, and the jewels he drapes around my neck."

Boyd sneered and jerked her by the arm. "The pin money. Get it. Now."

Margaret stumbled to a chest of drawers and withdrew a soft purse embroidered with silk threads. She handed it to Boyd, and in a surprising burst of courage she said, "There. That's all I have. Now leave my house and don't come back."

"You will take me to your husband's study now," Boyd said, yanking her toward the door. "Or I'll kill you right where you stand."

He pushed her through the door and into the hall with the tip of his knife pressed to her lower back. "I know your husband isn't home, but if any of your servants happen to see us, you'll tell them to go away. Do you hear?" Boyd prodded her with the knife.

Margaret whimpered and stumbled forward. When they were almost to the staircase, she yanked her arm free and tried to run, but Boyd slapped a hand over her mouth, pressing the knife to her neck.

"Now, that was foolish, dove. You've made me angry, see?" Boyd was breathing heavily now, every muscle tensed in anger. "I hold all the cards here. If you don't do what I say, your husband's going to hear all about your sordid affair with Liam. How do you think your husband will punish you when he finds out you've been making a fool of him behind his back? And with a filthy peasant, no less? Everyone knows how much your fancy husband hates us street rats. He's not going to like knowing his pretty, proper little wife has been rolling in the gutter with one, will he? Now, *move*." He shook her hard, making her head loll back and forth on her slender neck.

Instead of crying out, Margaret began to laugh, low and long. It was a cracked, hollow sound that held no mirth, and it was clear she was at the breaking point. "You think I care if my husband knows the truth?" she hissed. "I don't. What Liam and I had was…" Her face began to crumple like used parchment. "It doesn't matter. Nothing does anymore."

When she started to chuckle again, Boyd pushed her against the banister, his face a mask of rage. His large hand squeezed her neck. She coughed, gasping for breath. "Go ahead and tell my husband," she rasped. "Whether by you or him, I'm dead either way. I'm tired of living in this gilded cage like one of his expensive collectibles. Wasting away and gathering dust. I'm just as much a pawn in this life as you are. So go on. Kill me, if you must. But you'll get nothing from me on the whereabouts of my husband's fortune because I'm just a mindless dove, remember? *I know nothing!*" Margaret ended on a scream that seemed to snap something inside Boyd.

He drew his hand back and slapped her. She cried out, her body spinning away, as she tripped over her skirts. Flailing at the top of the stairs, she reached frantically for the railing, but missed. With a terrified scream, she tipped backward and went tumbling down the grand staircase.

Boyd bolted down the hall, not waiting to watch Margaret land like a rag doll with limbs at odd angles on the marble floor. A servant screamed and went running toward her, unaware of the intruder who was climbing out an upstairs window. Boyd swung from the window to a balcony, then scrambled over the railing and dropped into thick bushes. With a choked curse, he sprang from the thorny shrubs and began running into the woods.

He kept running until he saw Liam up ahead. Boyd quickly told Liam about his plans to run away to France with Alice. Then he said his final goodbye and surprised Liam with a hug. As they embraced, Boyd slipped one of Margaret's necklaces into Liam's pocket. It was a fail-proof plan. They'd blame Liam for Margaret's death, and Boyd and Alice would be long gone by then. As Liam walked away, oblivious to the fate that awaited him, Boyd turned back to watch him disappear through the woods. A flicker of regret ghosted across Boyd's face, but it quickly smoothed into steely determination.

A lone magpie cried out in the branch above Boyd's head. He scowled, scooped a rock off the ground, and threw it at the harbinger of sorrow. Then he whirled and ran toward his future.

Providence Falls, present day

Liam watched the image of Boyd's retreating figure disappear in the wall of mist until even that faded into the gloom. The cave was so dark the only things visible were the angels, Agon and Samael.

"So, Boyd betrayed me," Liam said in a sad, hollow voice. He was surprised that it hurt as much as it did. In this world, he had no love for Boyd, but back in his old life, they'd grown up together. They'd been almost like brothers. "I wondered how that necklace ended up in my pocket. Funny how you think you know someone so well... I always knew Boyd was a hothead, but I never would've thought him capable of murdering poor Margaret." Liam was suddenly overcome with guilt. "She didn't deserve that."

"No, she did not," Samael said solemnly.

"Wait a minute." A sudden thought occurred to Liam. "Why is Boyd here, then? He committed murder almost two centuries ago. Shouldn't he be paying for his sins, you know...down there?" He pointed to the ground below them, reluctant to say the word *hell* out loud in the icy darkness. If ever there was a place where evil things might be lurking, it would be there.

"Boyd Thompson did not intend to kill Margaret Brady that

night. He was a thief, and a blackmailer, and he lacked many redeeming qualities, but he did not plan to commit murder. Because of that, he was given another life to make better choices—but he has proven himself unworthy. He shall be dealt with accordingly.

"Now, enough about him," Samael said. "There's someone else who needs you right now. Someone who could use a… What's that word?" He glanced at Agon.

"Boost," Agon said triumphantly.

"Yes." Samael turned back to Liam. "There is someone who could use a boost. You said you wanted to do some good in your last moments here. Go and make yourself useful." They began to fade in a shower of sparks until Liam was once again surrounded in darkness.

"Wait!" Liam jumped to his feet. "You can't just say that and then disappear. I'm trapped down here, remember?" He kicked the cave wall in aggravation. Heaven, save him from infernal angels and their cryptic messages. "Why can't you ever tell me anything straight?" he yelled, spinning in a circle. "Come back!" His shout echoed for a long time, which surprised him. The chamber he'd fallen into seemed to be much larger than he'd expected.

There was a faint sound in the distance, and for a moment, Liam thought the angels had come back to say more. But then he realized it was someone calling for help.

"Who's there?" Liam called into the gloom. He kept his hand on the wall, carefully placing each step until it occurred to him he could use his phone light. The screen had cracked during the fall, but it still worked. Straining in the silence, he listened for another sound. For a few moments, he heard nothing, until…
There. It was a faint call for help. He moved as fast as he could, following the wall of the cave until his feet splashed into water.

It appeared to be a narrow underground stream. There was a crevice in the rock wall. He stepped through it, calling, "Hello? Is someone there?"

"Here," a weak voice answered. There was a cough and sound of shoes scraping on the ground. "I'm over here."

With a start, Liam recognized the person speaking. *"Finn?"*

23

CORA KEPT HER EYES ON BEAR'S PENLIGHT, TRUDG-
ing behind him for another hundred yards until suddenly his
light blinked out. They were instantly engulfed in the thick,
cloying darkness.

She cringed. With the stale air and the scents of dust and
decay, she felt like they were entombed. "What—"

"Shh!" Bear whispered. "We're almost there. Listen."

At first, all she could hear was the whistling breeze and the
faint sound of a stream far below. Then she heard it. The distinct echo of scuffed footsteps and something scraping along the
ground. Bear inched forward, rounding a curve in the tunnel
to stop just outside a large cavern illuminated by a faint glow
of light.

The cave was massive, with a high, cathedral-like ceiling
and stalactites looming overhead like sharp teeth. Cora shivered
with apprehension. It felt like they were about to step into the
mouth of a monstrous beast. In the dim light, she could see large
crates stacked along the walls, and random chests strewn over
the floor. A scraping sound came from the left, where a shad-

owed figure was dragging a large trunk away from the wall. He propped open the lid and began digging through it with frantic, jerky movements. There was a small camping lantern on the ground near his feet, and when he straightened, Cora saw Captain Thompson's triumphant face. He was holding stacks of cash in both fists, which he began tossing into a canvas duffel bag on the ground beside him. So intent was he on his task, he didn't notice them as they began to edge closer.

Cora scanned the cavern for places to hide as she tried to come up with a plan. Between her and Bear, they could overpower him easily, but that wasn't the problem. Captain Thompson always carried a gun. There was no way he came here without a firearm for protection. She placed her hand on Bear's arm to warn him, but it was too late.

Bear lurched forward to attack. In the split second it took for him to reach the circle of light, Captain Thompson jerked his head up, withdrew a gun from a holster at his back, and shot. The sound was like an explosion in the cave, amplified by the close proximity of the stone walls.

Cora's gasp was concealed by the noise as Bear fell to one knee and roared in pain. Captain Thompson walked toward Bear, who lay writhing on the ground, holding his leg.

"You didn't actually think you could get the jump on me, did you?" Boyd sneered as he kept his gun pointed at Bear. Lifting his lantern, he pivoted in a half circle. "Who else is with you?"

Cora quickly ducked behind a pallet of boxes before Boyd could see her. She crouched low, careful not to displace the rocks scattered near her feet.

"No one," Bear ground out. "But they're coming. I was the closest, so I got here first."

"You must be dumber than you look to come here alone and

unarmed." He kicked Bear's wounded leg with the toe of his boot.

Snarling in pain, Bear said through clenched teeth, "You're going to have to run forever. We won't stop hunting you."

Boyd scoffed. "You sure as hell aren't going to stop me." He turned away and began shoving more stacks of cash into the open duffel bag on the floor. "In ten minutes, I'll be long gone. You think I haven't thought this through? Ever since that girl showed me the picture she took outside of John Brady's house that night, I knew I'd need an escape plan. Didn't want it to come to this, but that's life. You roll with the punches."

"That college girl," Bear said, breathing fast through the pain of his wounded thigh. "You killed her."

The captain waved his hand like he was brushing away an annoying gnat. "Lindsey Albright got in the way. It was unfortunate that she took those pictures and caught me in the background, but that's on her. If she hadn't come nosing around, I wouldn't have had to shut her up. The sniveling little brat swore up and down there weren't any copies after I promised to let her go."

"But you didn't let her go," Bear said. "You killed her. Just like you killed your buddy Blackwell."

Boyd shrugged and continued throwing money into the bag. It looked like he planned to fill it to the brim, only taking what he could carry. "I didn't need him anymore, and he was getting too greedy. A symbiotic relationship only works if you each benefit. When Magnus was in jail, he threatened me. *Me*. Said he'd expose all our past schemes if I didn't find a way to let him walk. That's when I knew our partnership was over." His mean hiss of laughter sounded like sharpening knives. "We had a good run, but he was a wild card, and contrary to what it may look like, I'm not much of a gambling man. Can't leave any loose ends."

Bear was lying on his side now, clutching a hand over his leg. Cora wanted to run to him and add pressure to the wound or find something to wrap around his thigh. But Bear seemed to sense this because he glanced into the dark where she was hiding and said, "Don't do it." She knew he was speaking directly to her, but Captain Thompson misunderstood.

"I'll do what I want, and don't insult my intelligence by begging for your life," he said absently, almost as if he was talking to himself. He moved on to another trunk, threw back the lid, and began yanking out more bundles of cash. "Finn had the good sense not to. Although, in fairness, he fell into the caverns, so he must've figured begging would be futile."

"Where is he?" Bear demanded. His normally deep voice was growing thready and weak.

Captain Thompson snorted. "Probably flitting around in the clouds with a golden harp by now, if you believe in all that nonsense. Finley Walsh was too righteous for his own good. Thought he could earn his way into heaven doing good deeds for the needy. But you and I know better, don't we?" He zipped the duffel bag shut and stood, hauling it over his shoulder. "One life's all we get, and nothing comes after, so we gotta game the system." He aimed his gun as Bear. "Unfortunately, the game's over for you."

Cora was crouched low, and she braced herself to spring forward. She grabbed a rock near her shoe and threw it as hard as she could against the opposite wall.

Boyd spun around and shot into the dark. Then he scooped up the lantern and ran through an opening in the far wall of the cavern.

Using her phone light to see, Cora rushed toward Bear. She crouched low and whipped off her shirt, leaving nothing but her thin tank top to stave off the chill. She gripped his power-ful leg, trying to locate the wound.

"I knew you'd warm up to me eventually, doll face," Bear joked in a strained voice. "Just a little bit higher and to the right."

Cora shook her head. "Unbelievable. You just never quit, do you?"

"That's what all the ladies say," he said on an exhaled hiss.

Finally locating the bullet wound on his upper thigh, she used her shirt to tie a makeshift tourniquet, yanking the knot tightly.

Bear made an agonized gurgle in the back of his throat. A light sheen of sweat had broken out on his forehead. As much as he was trying to appear nonchalant, Cora could tell he was in serious pain.

When she was satisfied the tourniquet would hold, she looked him square in the eye and demanded, "Give me your shirt."

Even through the pain, Bear tried to smile, but before he had a chance to comment, Cora added, "*Hurry.* We need a bandage to stanch your wound. We can't take a chance that you'll bleed out before help arrives."

That seemed to knock some sense into him. He managed to lift his arms enough for her to pull off his shirt. Then he fell onto his back with a groan. "You have to go after him," he said after a few shallow pants. "If you don't stop him now, he's going to disappear. *Go.*"

She shook her head, torn between the desire to run after the captain, and the driving need to take care of the wounded man in front of her. She hated the idea of leaving Bear alone in the dark to pass out...or worse.

He laid a huge hand on her arm and surprised her by gently saying her name. "Cora."

She glanced at his somber face, torn with indecision.

"You fixed me up right good. Thank you," he said kindly.

"I'll be okay. Now go catch that bastard like the badass cop I know you are." And because he was Bear, he added, "I promise you can continue feeling me up when you get back."

Cora rolled her eyes and jumped to her feet. "Don't go anywhere," she commanded. Then she slipped through the back tunnel and went to catch a killer.

24

"I'M HERE," FINN CALLED FROM THE OTHER SIDE
of the cave.

Liam rushed forward, splashing through the small stream until
he practically stumbled onto Finn. He was propped with his legs
outstretched, leaning against the wall of the cave.

"Finn." Liam crouched over him, gripping him by the shoulders. "It's me, Liam. I'm here."

"Thank God," Finn said hoarsely. "I thought I was going to
die down here."

"You may still," Liam quipped. "I'm trapped down here myself." He flashed his phone light over Finn's exhausted face, and
Finn squinted, lifting his hands to shield himself. There was
dirt streaked across his chin, neck, and arms, and a large bruise
on his forehead. He also sported the remnants of a fading black
eye, along with scrapes on his hands and arms.

"Are you hurt?" Liam asked. "Any broken bones?"

"No. Nothing like that. Just weak. Hungry enough to eat a
horse. I've been down here ever since I followed Magnus. What
day is it?"

"It's Wednesday. You've been missing for over a week." Liam quickly scanned the empty cavern. "How have you been getting by?"

"Water from the stream." Finn scooted to sit higher against the wall. "Wasn't sure how much longer I could last with no food, though. I kept hoping someone would realize what happened. How are you here?"

Liam quickly told him everything he'd missed, including how he'd become separated from Bear and Cora by falling into the lower cave. "What happened to you, Finn? The last we heard, you texted that you left town unexpectedly. Then today they found your car down in a ravine not far from the state park."

"I drove here that day to spy on Magnus and find out who he was meeting," Finn said with a weak cough. "When I saw it was Captain Thompson, I was shocked. At first, I thought the captain was there to apprehend Magnus for something, but then I realized they were working together. I followed them up into the woods. I thought I could get close enough to learn more. It was stupid of me, because by the time I thought to text you guys—"

"No cell service," Liam said.

"Right. I heard them talking outside the cave about stealing hidden money from the Booze Dogs. 'Every last cent' was what Captain Thompson said. Anyway, I followed them into the cave, using my phone light to see. I thought I was far enough behind them to remain unnoticed, but Magnus and Boyd must've heard me trailing them. They jumped me in the tunnel, and it was too dark to get my bearings and fight them off. I fell and got trapped down here. I must've dropped my phone up there when we fought. Couldn't even try to call for help, not that it would've mattered with no service."

"That explains the text we got from you a couple of days

ago," Liam said grimly. "It was likely Boyd pretending to be you because Cora and I had just reported you missing. He seemed unconcerned, and he even made some assumptions that you killed Magnus."

Finn jerked his chin back. "Magnus is dead?"

"We found him down in the parking lot in his car the day you went missing. Stabbed. Maybe he and Boyd had a fight over the money. We think Boyd killed him."

"Would Captain Thompson kill his own accomplice like that?" Finn sounded jaded and resigned, as if he wasn't that surprised because he'd seen and heard worse. In his line of work, he probably had.

"Boyd would sell his own mother down the river if there was enough money on the line," Liam said, sliding to the ground beside Finn. He felt suddenly soul sick and world-weary. They finally had some answers, but that didn't make the information any easier to bear. Between what was happening now, and everything he'd just learned about Boyd's past betrayal from the angels, Liam needed a hundred years just to process everything. Unfortunately, he didn't have that kind of time.

"How did Boyd find out about this place?" Finn asked. "I didn't even know it existed, and I've been working with the Booze Dogs for years."

"Magnus found out first. He was carrying on with Wally Jensen's girlfriend. Wally let it slip to her, and she passed the information on to Magnus. Eli kept an antique map of the cave location in his office, and Magnus stole it the night he robbed the Doghouse. Magnus must've told Boyd, and they hatched a plan. Maybe they were going to work together to steal everything out of the caves. Maybe Boyd got greedy after Magnus showed him all the money, so Boyd killed him and framed you. They left you up here for dead, after all. Boyd probably figured if he dumped your car in the ravine, it would look shady enough for people to suspect foul play between you and Magnus. It was no secret that you and Magnus did not see eye to eye. Even your colleagues at work would've agreed, if interrogated."

Finn swore under his breath and began to cough again.

"We have to get you out of here," Liam said, worried. "You sound like a drowning cat, and you don't look much better."

"Thanks," Finn said wryly. "But I've traced every inch of this place over the past few days. Until Bear and Cora come back with a ladder, we're stuck."

Liam dragged himself up to stand. "Perhaps not." Using his phone light to cut through the inky darkness, he walked the perimeter of the cave. Above them, he could just make out an overhanging ledge, and the floor of the main tunnel appeared about six feet above that. A plan began to take shape in Liam's mind. He glanced at Finn, shining his light on the exhausted man's face.

Finn raised a hand to shield his eyes. "I've been living like a bat down here for days, Liam. That's like sunlight to a vampire."

"Sorry." Liam swung his phone light in a different direction. "Finn, how strong are you feeling right now?"

Finn's choked laugh ended on another cough. "Right now? About as strong as a newborn foal."

"That's actually quite strong," Liam said thoughtfully. "They're able to walk almost right away, you know. Unlike humans, who need over a year to take their first step."

"Then a dying newborn foal. Why are you asking?"

Liam shone his light back to the ledge that was about twelve feet off the ground. "See that outcrop of rock? If I stood on your shoulders, I could reach it."

Finn slowly dragged himself up the wall until he was standing. He peered at the ledge above them. "And then what?"

"I brace my arms on the ledge, and you climb up to my shoulders until you reach it. Then you pull yourself over and help pull me up. Once we're both on that ledge, we do it again, until we make it to the main tunnel above it. That's assuming you're strong enough to make the climb, and assuming you'll have enough strength left to help pull me up afterward."

"Let's do it." Finn was already positioning himself underneath the ledge.

Liam hesitated. "You sure you can hold me?" He took a moment to study Finn closer in the dim light. Beads of perspiration clung to his forehead and around his hairline, his ashen complexion suggesting he was more qualified for a sickbed than a physical test of strength. "You've been starving down here for days. I could lift you up first, but I think it would be harder for you to bear my weight once I started climbing."

"We can do this. And you're right. It's better you go first, then give me a boost."

Boost. Liam squinted up at the rock ledge that looked almost too far away for them to reach. That was what the angels meant. Suddenly filled with determination, he braced himself to climb.

25

THE CAPTAIN WAS MOVING FAST, AND CORA STRUG-
gled to follow in the darkness. Her phone light was too bright
and would look like a beacon, so she had to slide it into her
pocket and keep pace by feeling along the tunnel wall. As long
as she kept her gaze pinned on his lantern up ahead, she could
manage. When he disappeared around a corner, she was forced
to hurry, which was dangerous on such uneven ground, but she
couldn't risk losing him.

As he took another turn, and yet another, Cora grew increasingly uneasy. She tried to commit their path to memory, but the
pitch-black tunnel was disorienting, and she didn't have time to
mark her passage. She had no choice now but to follow a cold-
blooded killer until he led her out of the caves. It was hard to
believe the captain, a person she'd worked alongside for years,
a person she'd trusted, was such a terrible criminal. And right
now, he was her only link to the world above. Fear shuddered
down her spine, and she picked up speed. If she lost him in the
tunnels now, she could remain lost forever.

Several yards ahead, Captain Thompson came to an abrupt stop.

Cora slammed her body flat against the wall, her heart galloping like a racehorse.

He turned in a circle, eyes narrowed into slits.

Frozen, barely allowing herself to breathe, she tried not to panic. Unlike Bear, she was armed, but it was too dark to consider shooting or even alerting him to her presence. If she waited and followed him outside where there would still be ambient light, she'd have a much better chance of stopping him. Down here, with no knowledge of the tunnels, he had the advantage.

For long moments, the captain did nothing but stare into the gloom where she was hidden. Cora started to draw her gun, her heart still racing laps around her rib cage. If he decided to backtrack, she'd be trapped and have no choice but to confront him.

Muttering, he hooked the lantern to his belt, reached above his head with both arms, and began to climb.

Cora crept forward as quietly as she could, dragging her fingertips along the cave wall, using his disappearing lantern light as a point of reference. When she came to a rickety wooden ladder, she carefully gripped the rungs and began to follow. The ladder was ancient, with some rungs too rotted to bear anyone's weight. Nimbly skipping over them, Cora continued to climb, hoping it would hold both their weights.

He was farther above her now, and she hastened to catch up. She was only about ten feet behind him when there was a screech of metal, followed by a loud clang that seemed to vibrate through her bones. She cringed, flattening against the ladder until she realized it was the sound of a round metal hatch opening on rusty hinges. Beyond the hatch, she could see a sliver of the evening sky. The roar of the waterfall nearby seemed to drown out other sounds. Captain Thompson tossed the canvas duffel through the hole, then began to climb after it.

Cora shot forward, climbing as fast as she could. It didn't matter anymore if she made noise; this was her only chance to catch him. If he slammed the hatch and somehow locked it from the outside, she'd be trapped in the tunnels and never find her way out.

Within moments, she reached the top of the ladder, grateful that he hadn't tried to close it during his escape. Peering cautiously over the edge, she didn't see him anywhere, so she pulled her gun and hauled herself out. The familiar sight of the waterfall's lookout point was just beyond the trees. There was a viewing platform with a metal railing overlooking the falls for visiting tourists, along with a small kiosk showing a map of the trails. In all the years she'd hiked to the waterfall, she'd never known there was a network of tunnels just a few yards away.

Something hard settled against the back of her skull, and she heard the chilling sound of a gun's hammer cock. Every hair on the back of her neck and arms rose.

"Don't move," Captain Thompson said in a gruff voice that was so familiar Cora had the dizzying sensation of relief quickly followed by dread. He wasn't the captain she thought he was anymore. He was a bad man who'd done terrible things to people.

"Captain," Cora said, trying to keep her voice from shaking. "You don't want to do this."

"Needs must, McLeod." He shoved the gun harder against her head. "Toss the gun. *Now.*"

She flung her gun into the trees, thinking fast about her self-defense training. She knew how to disarm an attacker, but the captain was no fool, and he was already behind her with his gun at point-blank range. She had to keep him talking and try to disarm him when he was distracted. Mouth as dry as parchment, breath scraping in and out of her throat, she asked, "Why did you kill John Brady?"

He scoffed. "A little late for interrogations, don't you think? Now, walk."

"He was a decent man," she continued, wincing as he shoved her forward with the butt of the gun. "What did John Brady ever do to you?"

"He stood in my way. I never planned to kill him. Sometimes you have to roll with the punches, McLeod, and he was an unfortunate sacrifice."

"What really happened that night?" She tried to walk as slow as she could, realizing with a jolt of alarm that he was leading her toward the lookout point. There was nothing on that viewing platform but a metal railing overlooking a two-hundred-foot drop. Even if he didn't shoot her first, the fall to the rocks below would kill her. She had to keep him talking and look for an opening. The gun would go off, no question. Her goal now was to maneuver herself out of the path in any way she could.

"I was driving home and saw his front door wide open. Went to investigate, and I found him sobbing in front of his open safe. He might've been a rich man, but he sure as hell wasn't smart. He was drunk and sloppy that night, crying to himself about some woman, instead of paying attention to his surroundings. Let's just say, it was an opportunity I couldn't pass up."

"That's it?" Cora said in disbelief. "You killed him for money?"

"*Serious* money," the captain corrected. "There was a fortune in jewels and gold in that safe, and it was scattered all over the floor at his feet like nothing. Like an afterthought. That's the problem with rich men like him. They have no concept of how the rest of us have to scrape and bleed and suffer for years just to make a fraction of what they have. John Brady was a pillar of the community," he sneered. "That's what the papers said. His poor wife, Margaret, devastated at his untimely death." He barked a curse as he pushed her up the steps onto the viewing platform. "Both of them were cheating on each other, but the media painted them like angels on their ivory pedestals."

"Alice thinks you're having an affair," Cora said, resisting as he shoved her closer to the railing. Every nerve in her body was on high alert, but she fought to keep him talking, waiting for the right moment to act. The thunderous roar of the waterfall did nothing to drown out the frantic beating of her heart. Grabbing the rail in a white-knuckle grip, she stared into the churning water below. In the twilight, the jagged rocks were softened by shadows, but Cora knew they were as deadly and unforgiving as the man standing behind her. Bracing herself, she poked the hornet's nest. "She told me you were sleeping with someone else. Are you cheating on your wife, Captain?"

With a furious curse, he clamped a hand painfully on her left arm, spinning her to face him.

Now. Cora dropped her weight and turned with him, harnessing the momentum and using it to her advantage. She struck out hard with her right fist, aiming for his solar plexus. It was a solid move, but Captain Thompson knew her too well. Jerking to the side, he avoided her strike at the last second. Then he raised the gun and backhanded her across the face. Pain exploded across her cheekbone, blinding her with agonizing pinpricks of light as she bit back a cry.

His ruddy face was a mask of fury. "I would *never* cheat on Alice," he spit. "Everything I've done over the years has been for her."

"That's not what she thinks," Cora managed, forcing the

words past the pain. "She told me you bought fancy jewelry for your mistress."

"Wrong." He jerked his head from side to side, like a wild animal harassed by bees. "Alice found one of the necklaces I was planning to sell. She believed I'd bought it for another woman, and nothing I said would convince her otherwise. But she'll understand soon enough."

"Did you tell her you'd been stealing and taking bribes for years?" Cora knew she was on borrowed time, but she had to keep the conversation going. He was clearly bothered about Alice, which Cora might be able to use to her advantage. An emotional opponent was a sloppy opponent. "Did you tell her you killed John Brady? Lindsey Albright? Magnus Blackwell?"

Captain Thompson's angry face flickered with unease. "She's flighty and impulsive, my Alice. She doesn't need to be bothered with irrelevant details. She just needs to sit tight for now. I promised her a better life when we got married, and I'm damn well going to give it to her." There was a maniacal gleam in his eye. If he actually believed he could still walk away from all this and have a normal life with his wife, then he wasn't just greedy and desperate. He was unhinged.

A cold finger of dread skated down Cora's spine. She squared her shoulders and lifted her chin, drawing on all her training in an effort to appear calm and cool. "So, what's your plan, Captain? You take the money and run? Doesn't sound like an easy life. Even if you manage to evade the law, you'll still have to flee the country."

"Shut up." He spun her around again, shoving until the railing pressed painfully against her stomach, making it hard to breathe. She squeezed her eyes shut, trying not to stare at the deadly two-hundred-foot drop into the frothing cauldron below. She had to *focus!*

"Alice doesn't strike me as the kind of woman who'd be happy living the rest of her days hiding in some backwater town on the other side of the planet." Her mouth had gone bone-dry, but she licked her cracked lips and forged on. *Keep him engaged.* "You know what I think?"

"Enough!" he roared. "I don't give a rat's ass what you think, McLeod."

She tamped down the fear that shot like wildfire through her veins. "I think Alice realizes something you don't." It wasn't easy to speak hard truths to a crazy man holding a gun on her, but every second she kept him engaged was another moment she kept breathing. "You can't win, Captain Thompson. Even if you take me out, there's nowhere you can run that the law won't find you. We know too much, and you can't cover it up this time."

"Watch me," he sneered. Cora felt the cold barrel of the gun at the nape of her neck and knew she was out of time.

26

LIAM GRIPPED THE EDGE OF THE LEDGE WITH HIS fingertips, pulling himself up until he had both arms braced over the rock's surface. It was their third try, and he prayed this time it would work because Finn was losing energy. The man was surprisingly strong considering he'd been starving for the past week with nothing but water to drink, but his energy reserves were fading fast. Liam's hands skidded over the rock, searching for indents to grip. When he'd finally found divots to brace his arms against, he called down to Finn. "Ready."

Finn took a running leap and grabbed Liam's legs, using them as leverage to climb up Liam's back.

"Hurry!" Liam managed, his muscles straining with the effort of holding Finn's added weight. Just when he felt his hands beginning to slip, Finn hauled himself up over the edge of the rock ledge and flung onto his back, gasping for breath. In the next moment he rolled to help Liam as he hooked a leg over the ledge and climbed up after him. They rested for a few minutes with nothing but the light from Liam's phone.

"We did it," Finn said with a gasp that turned into a cough.

"Almost." Liam glanced at Finn from the corner of his eye, wondering how much farther Finn could go before he collapsed from exhaustion. "The tunnel above is much closer, so it won't be as hard this time."

They lay there for a few moments to catch their breath. Then Liam dragged himself to his feet. He reached for Finn and helped him stand, shining the light of his phone at the ledge ten feet above them.

"If you brace on my shoulders again," Finn said, "you can just pull yourself up and over the edge."

"What about you? I'm not leaving you behind," Liam said before Finn could try to suggest it.

"When you get up there, lie on your stomach and reach your arms down. I'll jump up to catch your hands, and you can help pull me up."

"That's quite a leap. The ledge we're standing on is only a few feet wide. It's not like you can take a running jump."

"Just trust me," Finn said in a voice that brooked no argument. Liam almost smiled at the exhausted man's steely core of determination.

With a nod, Liam climbed onto Finn's back once again, bracing his feet on Finn's shoulders until he could stretch up and grab on to the ledge above them. This time, it was much easier to climb. When Liam reached the top, he laid his phone beside him and stretched both arms out for Finn. "Ready when you are."

Finn took a cautious step back to gain momentum, then leaped toward Liam with surprising dexterity. His hands slapped against Liam's biceps, sliding down until they locked forearms. Liam almost shouted in relief, until he felt Finn's hands begin to slip farther. He could hear the exhausted man's labored breathing, and for a moment, Liam had a terrifying glimpse of what could happen if he let go. Finn could tumble down to the narrow ledge and roll off it, or he could miss the ledge altogether and fall into the cavern below. In his condition, he wouldn't be able to sustain another fall like that.

Finn grunted with effort to hold on, but his hands continued to slip. Liam squeezed harder, but the sweat from exertion made it difficult to grip. Swearing under his breath, Liam tried to pull Finn up, urging him to hold on, but Finn had reached the end of his strength.

"Come on, man!" Liam shouted. "We need to keep going. Cora needs us."

That seemed to jolt Finn into action. With a strangled groan, he tightened his grip and jerked himself higher until they were clasping wrists.

"That's it," Liam said. "You've got this. Now, just hang on." In slow, strained increments, Liam helped pull Finn up and over the edge until they both lay panting on their backs.

"I'm getting too old for this," Finn said between raspy breaths.

"You weren't so bad," Liam said with a chuckle. "You jump like a March hare."

Finn grunted, coughed, and began to stand. "We have to keep moving. Which way did they go?"

Liam scooped his phone and stood, shining the light into the tunnel ahead of them. "This way. Stay right behind me and walk where I walk. This path we're on is narrow, and we don't want to take another tumble into the abyss."

They moved as swiftly as they could, staying close to the wall until they came to a large cavern filled with pallets of boxes and metal chests. Liam shone his light in a semicircle. "Cora! Are you here?"

"Just me," Bear said gruffly. He was lying near a wooden crate with his leg wrapped in a makeshift bandage covered in blood.

Liam rushed forward and crouched by his side. "What happened?"

"Boyd took a shot at me," he said in a low growl.

Finn knelt near his shoulder and studied the bandage. "You look worse than I feel."

"Finn." Bear blinked in surprise. "We thought you were dead."

Finn's mouth kicked up at the corner. "Almost. I followed Boyd and Magnus up here last week. They cornered me and threw me into a cavern. Left me for dead. Liam found me."

Bear glanced at Liam and gave him a begrudging fist bump to the shoulder. "Good man."

"Where's Cora?" Liam asked.

"She went after Boyd."

"Where?" Liam shot to his feet, fear stabbing like an icy blade through his guts. "Did he hurt her? Tell me!" He barely refrained from grabbing the injured man and shaking him like a rag doll.

"She's okay, last I saw," Bear said. Finn was trying to check on Bear's wound, but Bear pushed his hand away. "There's no time for that. Eli and the guys will be here soon. They'll help me." He turned to Liam. "Boyd took the money and left through the back tunnel. He didn't know Cora was here with me. She followed him out."

"Tell us where to go," Liam demanded.

"There's only one way out through the back. It leads to a ladder up to the surface." He gave them directions and reached into his pocket, withdrawing the penlight and handing it to Finn. "Take this. The more light you have, the faster you can go."

Liam was already striding toward the back of the cavern when Finn caught up with him.

"You should stay with Bear," Liam told him.

"Not a chance." Before Liam could argue, Finn continued. "Eli and his men will help him."

Liam opened his mouth to point out that it wasn't Bear's health he was concerned about. With a ghostly pallor and sweat breaking out on his forehead, Finn looked dead on his feet.

"Cora could be in trouble," Finn continued stubbornly. "I'm not going to sit back there and leave her at the mercy of a killer if there's something I can do to help."

Liam didn't answer because there wasn't anything left to say. He couldn't waste time arguing with the exhausted man trailing him, and in a way, Liam was grateful for his presence. Finley Walsh was nothing if not loyal. It humbled Liam to know the man was willing to risk himself for Cora. The angels had it right from the beginning. Finn was an exceptional man. Far better than himself. Liam saw that now, and it made his heart crack around the edges. If only it wasn't too late to make things right.

The rotting wooden ladder was exactly where Bear said it would be. Liam gripped the rungs and began to climb as fast as he could. He had to find Cora before Boyd could hurt her. Adrenaline surged in his body and his muscles screamed as he flew up the ladder. He'd failed to protect Margaret Brady from Boyd in his old life. There was no way in hell he'd let Cora fall prey to that evil bastard now.

When he reached the open hatch, he hauled himself out, surprised to find Finn right behind him. Finn's face was white as parchment and drenched with sweat. He doubled over and braced his hands on his knees, gasping for breath.

"You have to stop," Liam said, scanning the tree line. The air was foggy with mist, and he could hear the roar of the waterfall nearby. "You're going to collapse."

Finn shook his head stubbornly. Before Liam could argue, a man's guttural shout tore through the forest. *Boyd.* In the next breath, Liam was running. He didn't stop to think or plan; he just reacted. All he knew was that Cora had been following Boyd, and now she could be in danger.

27

LIAM BURST FROM THE TREES TO A SIGHT THAT stole the breath from his lungs. Time slammed to a halt. His insides crackled, icing over in brittle fear, only to explode into molten rage. Boyd was aiming a gun at Cora's head. She was backed up against the metal railing overlooking the waterfall, and though he couldn't see her face, her chin was lifted in stubborn resolve.

"Stop!" Liam roared, rushing toward them. He couldn't get to her fast enough. Every drag of his lungs to breathe felt like an eternity as he ran, drawing the gun from his holster.

Boyd jerked, then grabbed Cora around the neck with one arm and spun to face him. He held the barrel of the gun against her temple.

Liam's vision narrowed to a pinpoint. The trees disappeared. The ground under his feet vanished. Even the last vestiges of daylight were swallowed up by his unyielding focus. All Liam could see was the face of the man who threatened Cora's life. A man he'd once called a friend. A man he'd once trusted. Nothing Liam had ever experienced could prepare him for the utter fury burning him from the inside out. How *dare* Boyd? He didn't deserve to breathe the same air as Cora, let alone touch her or threaten her life.

"One more step and she's dead," Boyd shouted, jolting Liam from his rage-filled mission.

Liam forcibly locked his muscles, skidding to a stop near the railing just a few feet from them. He didn't dare glance at Cora, for he knew if he saw her face racked with fear, he wouldn't be able to hold himself back. "Let her go."

Boyd scoffed. "You don't get to make demands, O'Connor. Now, toss the gun."

Liam's arm shook, his fingers itching with the effort it took to override his instincts. Letting go of his only weapon would give Boyd even more of an advantage, but Liam had faced down formidable people before with nothing but his fists. He could still take Boyd down. Before he could change his mind, Liam flung the gun over the waterfall with a curse, then dared to glance at Cora.

She was trembling, but there was a hard set to her jaw and fire in her eyes, which only made Liam love her more. His brave, brilliant woman wasn't going to give Boyd the satisfaction of seeing her waver. "Point the gun at me, Boyd," Liam demanded. "She doesn't deserve to die, but I do."

"No," Cora choked out, glaring at Liam. "No one deserves to die today."

"I can think of one." Liam stared hard at Boyd, mentally calculating the distance between them. If he could somehow take him by surprise, create a diversion, Cora could run to safety. But Liam knew her. She wasn't the running type. *Damn it.* How could he fix this? He'd done so many things wrong in this life. All that mattered now was her. The angels had given him a reprieve because he wanted to spend his last days doing as much good as he could, yet here he was. Failing even at the end.

"That's the problem with people like you, McLeod," Boyd said in disgust. "You think if you follow all the rules, life's supposed to be fair. You believe no one deserves to die, but you are missing the whole point of living. He who holds the gold makes the rules. You should've listened to Magnus when he offered you a cut of the money. Maybe if you'd embraced the game, we could've helped each other out. Instead, look where your precious moral compass has led you." He shoved her at Liam.

She stumbled, landing hard against Liam. He caught her in his arms, then thrust her behind him to shield her.

Boyd laughed. "It's no use, O'Connor. Whether I shoot you first, or her, makes no difference. Same result." Boyd aimed the gun and started to back away. "McLeod. O'Connor. I can't say it's been a pleasure."

A blur of movement drew Liam's attention.

Finn appeared out of the shadows, running head-on toward Boyd. Liam saw everything as if in slow motion. Boyd began to turn, his outstretched arm about to fire on Finn.

It required no thought. For all Liam's scheming and machinations since the angels had dropped him into this crazy life, his sudden act came from a place far removed from anything familiar. In the split second it took Liam to jump in front of the gun, there was no fear of what came next, only the wholehearted wish to save a good man who deserved so much more than Liam ever had.

"No!" Cora screamed.

A bolt of agony slammed into Liam. The abrupt crack of the gunshot mirrored his own shock as he stumbled backward from the impact. Finn shouted something, but Liam didn't hear it over the jarring thud of his body landing on the unyielding ground.

He blinked up at the sky. Stars were just beginning to appear against the canvas of deepening twilight, and then an angel appeared. The most beautiful angel he'd ever seen, with eyes deeper than the ocean and a face dearer to him than life itself.

"Liam!" Cora leaned over him, pressing her hands against his torso. Pain spiraled out in molten waves, stealing the breath from his lungs.

Boyd let out a guttural shout. Another gunshot rent the air.

Liam's head fell to the side, and he saw Boyd pushing Finn up against the railing. They were still grappling with the gun, but Finn was losing. He was taller and broader than Boyd, but the fatigue and days of starvation made it obvious he couldn't last much longer. Boyd swung his arm in an arc, using the gun's momentum to punch Finn in the face.

"Stop," Liam tried to shout, but it came out as a hoarse whisper. He needed to help Finn. He needed to stop Boyd from hurting more people. But no matter how hard he willed his body to comply, he couldn't move.

Finn's head snapped back. His arms flailed as he began to tip backward over the railing. He reached for Boyd's shirt, yanking hard to stay upright.

Boyd lost his footing and lurched forward, slamming into Finn and propelling them both over the railing.

"No!" Cora screamed.

It all happened so fast. One moment, Finn and Boyd were standing there, and the next...

They were gone.

Cora cried Finn's name into the wind, but there was no answer. Just the terrible blank space where he'd been.

Grief exploded in Liam's chest. He wanted to shout, but he couldn't drag in enough air. He wanted to go after Finn to save him. To take the fall for him. He'd shielded Finn from the bullet so he could *live*. So he could have a chance at the happiness he deserved. It wasn't supposed to end this way. Not like this.

"Liam, stop." Cora was weeping now, hot tears streaking down her face, but the pressure of her hands on his torso never wavered. "You have to stop moving. You'll make it worse. Please. You have to remain still."

He didn't realize he'd been struggling to rise. With a defeated groan, he let his head drop back to the ground and squeezed his eyes shut. Like a weakling, he sought refuge in darkness, but it didn't help. His mind kept replaying the image of Finn going over the edge, and the shock on his face as he toppled backward to his doom.

A shout came from just beyond the trees. It wasn't far.

"Over here!" Cora cried. "We need help." She tipped her face to the sky as if she could call down heaven itself. *"Please."* She glanced at Liam with an expression so shattered he wanted to hold her and do whatever it took to put her pieces back together. "Don't move. You're going to be fine. Help is coming." She didn't understand that there was no help for him. He was beyond saving now. Maybe he always had been.

Cora was still holding her hands to his wound, but the pain was beginning to fade. In slow increments, the tension in his muscles eased, and his limbs grew heavier, as if he could sink into the ground below and become one with the earth. It wasn't bad at all this time. It felt almost restful. The last time he'd lost his life, he'd been filled with an emptiness so vast nothing felt real. But this time, he saw and felt everything. The warmth of Cora's silvery teardrop on his face. The desperate love in her eyes. Her tremulous smile as she tried fiercely to cling to hope.

"I'm sorry." His apology was barely a whisper, and so very inadequate. Two simple words to represent a maelstrom of remorse and regret. All the lost dreams for a future that would never come to pass.

"No." Cora lowered her forehead to his, clearly seeing something that alarmed her. Were their hearts so entwined that she could sense him slipping away? "No, Liam," she sobbed. "You can't go. Stay with me."

If only he could. The strength of her love humbled him. He could live a thousand lifetimes and still never deserve it, but by God, he'd take it. She'd once said love was the only thing you took with you when you died—the only thing that mattered. If that was true, then he'd grab fistfuls of this. He'd cloak himself in it. Weave it into every fiber of his soul. And he would never forget that, once, he was an unworthy thief who loved a girl with all his heart. And she loved him back. *She loved him back*. And it was everything.

28

CORA KEPT HER HANDS CLAMPED HARD ON THE wound in Liam's side, her heart tripping painfully against her ribs. Dread was an uncoiling snake in the pit of her stomach as she stared down at Liam's ashen face. He'd passed out, but she could still see the shallow rise and fall of his chest. *Thank God.* "You're not leaving me like this, Liam O'Connor. This is not how it ends for us. Do you hear me?" Every jagged, choppy breath that escaped her was a prayer as she silently begged him to hang on.

"Looks like you need rescuing, girl." Eli Shelton's casual observation scraped across her mangled nerves like asphalt on road rash. He was the last person Cora expected as a savior, but in the moment, even street thug Santa was a welcome sight. He ambled toward her out of the woods, hitching the waist of his sagging jeans higher over his substantial beer gut. Then he scratched his dingy white beard and stared down at Liam with a cold, hard assessment that could only come from someone who'd seen life-threatening situations before. Often. "Yeah. He don't look too good."

"No," Cora agreed, biting off a sarcastic retort. Many things about Eli rubbed her the wrong way, but right now she wasn't going to give in to her burning desire to tell him. "We need help." Her voice ended on a hitch of desperation as painful emotions threatened to spill over. Fighting for control, she added shakily, "He needs medical attention immediately, or—"

"I reckon he does." Eli's slow, lazy drawl made Cora want to stab her fingers into his Harley-Davidson T-shirt and shake the living daylights out of him. If she wasn't using both hands to keep pressure on Liam's wound, she would. How could he stand there acting like he had all the time in the world to sit and chat when Liam's life was waning with every passing second? She was just about to start screaming at him when Eli said something that derailed her train of thought. "Good thing I already called for a mountain rescue. A helicopter's on its way."

Cora gaped at Eli's smug face. That meant there was still hope. An air rescue was the only way Liam would have a fighting chance. Relief swept over her in cold, tingling waves. Had she not already been crouched on the ground, her knees would surely have buckled. Cora felt an unexpected surge of gratitude toward the surly Booze Dogs president, and she had to fight to keep her hands steady. "Thank you."

"Ain't no thing," Eli said dismissively. "I don't like cops, but you helped Bear when he got shot. He's one of ours, and you took care of him, so we owe you."

Cora nodded, grateful Eli saw it that way, even though she'd have stopped to help anyone in Bear's situation. Even a criminal. Only a heartless person would ignore someone with a gunshot wound. Maybe Eli was used to dealing with the kind of people who'd prioritize their own desires over someone's safety in a situation like that. Either way, she was grateful, and she told him.

Eli made a dismissive grunt in the back of his throat and

changed the subject to something he clearly felt was more important. "Your police captain scum. Which way did he go? I've got my men all over this mountain searching for him."

Cora winced at the memory of Finn and the captain toppling over the railing to their doom. She gestured to the edge of the viewing platform with her chin. "Th-that way."

Eli's bushy white eyebrows shot toward his hairline as he stared over the railing at the open abyss. "Did he now?" The roar of the waterfall hitting the rocks below seemed louder and more ominous than ever.

Cora found Eli's smile unnerving. It wasn't his obvious satisfaction that bothered her; she expected that from him. It was the unmistakable twinkle of delight in his eyes. It heightened his resemblance to the right jolly old elf who brought toys to children, which was just creepy.

"He was fighting Finn for the gun, and they both fell…" She trailed off, unable to speak past the painful lump in her throat. It was hard to believe Finn, the calm, steadfast man who'd always been there in the background of her life, was gone. She'd only just begun to understand the depths of his kindness, and he'd become a dear friend.

Eli's gleeful face suddenly fractured around the edges, and he looked stricken. He uttered Finn's name and turned away sharply. Then he walked to the edge of the platform and stared down, as if searching for him. Cora knew what he saw—the blinding white rush of the waterfall crashing toward dark, shadowy rocks. Anything or anyone unfortunate enough to tumble over the edge of Providence Falls would be long gone by now. Either sinking to the depths or carried away by the unstoppable force of the river.

Cora quickly told Eli what had happened. "I'm not even sure

how Finn got here," she added miserably. "We haven't had contact with him in days."

Eli was standing with his back to her as she recounted everything. Finally, he straightened his shoulders and turned to face her again. He spoke in halting stops and starts, as if each word had to be checked for stability in case they tumbled cracked and broken from his mouth. "Bear told us. Finn was trapped. In the tunnels." He glanced away for a few moments, then added angrily, "Your captain and Magnus threw him off a ledge and left him to die down there." Eli wasn't the type to debase himself by crying—he'd see it as an obvious display of weakness. But Cora could tell he was struggling. His gaze roamed aimlessly over the surrounding forest, and he shook his head. "He was a good man, Jack." Eli used Finn's nickname from back when he was the Jackrabbit, participating in the Booze Dogs' underground cage fights. For a while, Eli had been a type of mentor to Finn, back when Finn was young and angry and aimless. Cora felt certain there was nothing she and Eli would ever have in common, but in this exact moment, she understood and shared his pain.

The minutes ticked by with infinite slowness as they waited for the air rescue, Cora constantly checking Liam's condition with growing fear. She was no medical expert, but if help didn't arrive soon, Liam wouldn't— *No.* She refused to even entertain the thought of a world without Liam in it. He was going to be okay. To distract herself, Cora decided to focus on a conversation she'd been meaning to have with Eli. He'd grown silent and pensive after her revelation about Finn, but she imagined he wouldn't remain that way when she brought up his transgressions.

"The police are going to be crawling all over this mountain," Cora finally said. She was reluctant to bring up the ramifications of the Booze Dogs using a state park to store their secrets, but it had to be said. "I don't know what you've stashed in all those boxes in your cave down there, and right now I don't care. But it's—"

"Not your problem, girl." Eli's familiar scowl snapped back into place. "My men are moving the last of our things as we speak. Should've done it a long time ago, but the hideout's been with the Booze Dogs since the beginning. Guess none of us wanted to give up going to church." There went that creepy smile again. He really should just stick to scowling.

"And what about your illegal gambling ring?" Cora challenged. "The cage fighting out at the barn?"

Eli's expression blanked. It was the equivalent of white noise, and she wondered how long it had taken him to perfect it. "Told you I don't know anything about no fight ring."

"I saw it with my own eyes," Cora said impatiently. "The crowd, the announcer, the cage. What do you have to say about that?"

"I'd say you must've hit your head pretty hard in the scuffle just now," Eli said, tugging at his beard. "Or maybe you dreamed it. In fact, I reckon if you went to look at this barn you're talking about, you'd find nothing but a pile of hay and some dirt."

Cora mashed her lips together. Of course that was all she'd find. Eli was too shrewd to risk keeping his operation there, now that Cora had admitted she knew it existed. The Booze Dogs were probably already dismantling everything and erasing all traces of them ever having been there. But Cora knew it wouldn't be the end of it. The cage fights were far too lucrative for the motorcycle club to stop. She felt certain they'd ramp up again somewhere else in the near future. "Even if you set up shop somewhere else, I'll find it eventually."

"Do what you need to do, girl. But I always say it's best not to go looking for trouble. People who don't stay in their lanes sometimes find themselves in a head-on collision with something much bigger and more powerful than them." His ominous tone spoke volumes she never wanted to read.

Cora stared him dead in the eye. "Is that a threat, Mr. Shelton?"

He shrugged. "Just an observation. Might want to consider your priorities and focus on problems closer to home, for now." He nodded at Liam, then turned his attention to the sound of the helicopter appearing in the distance. The rhythmic *whump-whump-whump* of the blades grew louder as it approached.

After checking Liam's vitals for the umpteenth time, Cora said a silent prayer of thanks for the mountain rescue. In the grand scheme of things, Eli was right, because Liam's survival was her sole focus. Everything else that seemed so important in her life faded to background noise. Nothing mattered to Cora as much as the beloved man whose precious life she was holding in her hands.

29

LIAM BECAME AWARE OF HIS SURROUNDINGS IN small increments. The low, electronic beeping of a machine near his left ear. The crisp scratch of fabric against his skin. A faint whiff of antiseptic that tingled his nose. He tried to crack his eyes open, but the ambient light was too bright. Instead, he strained to make out the hushed voices in the room. Someone was using phrases like "vulnus sclopetarium" and "missed vital organs" and "scheduled antibiotics," which meant nothing to Liam. Everything about this place felt strange and unfamiliar. A moment of confused panic seized him until, suddenly, memories came flooding back in an onslaught of vivid, visceral images that had him gasping. Like startling pictures on a movie reel, his last day's events snapped into focus. The caves. Finn. Boyd holding Cora at gunpoint.

Cora. Liam gave an involuntary jerk, and his fingers clenched as if he could hold on to her. The last thing he remembered was staring up at her tear-streaked face as she begged him not to leave. He'd have moved heaven and earth to stay with her, but that was never part of the bargain, was it?

With effort, he tried to sit up, but he was as weak as a new-born kitten. Again, he fought to open his eyes, relieved when he could finally make out the paneled squares on the ceiling and the stark white walls surrounding him. He was in a chamber with a single chair and a large window in the corner with bare metal blinds. It wasn't the house he'd shared with Cora because it lacked all her decorative touches. There were no cheerful curtains. No splashes of bright color. No purring cat to greet him. This place seemed sterile and cold. Bleak as the future that awaited him. Was this it, then? Was he dead? He shifted on the rather comfortable bed, confused by the lack of fire and brimstone. It made no sense. As far as hellish afterlives went, this wasn't at all what he'd expected.

"Liam." Cora's soft presence enveloped him like a welcome hug, and he felt her gentle fingers squeeze his hand. No way this could be hell. Not if she was here. He still had a bit of time left, then. That was the only logical explanation.

"I'm so glad you're awake," she said in a voice thick with emotion. She ran out of the room, and within moments, Liam was surrounded by a doctor and nurses who were poking and prodding him and asking questions. It seemed to go on for ages, but through it all, Liam kept his gaze focused on Cora. She stood in the corner watching him with a tremulous smile on her face. When most of them eventually left and he finally had a moment's peace, he reached for her.

"How are you feeling?" Cora asked gently, coming to the bedside and gripping his hand.

He tried to answer, but his throat was dry, and his tongue scratched the roof of his mouth like fine grit sandpaper.

"Here, drink this." Cora helped lift his head and pressed a cup of water to his lips.

He stared up at her in wonder, drinking the cool water in

great, thirsty gulps. It soothed him almost as much as the sight of her beautiful face. When he finished, she helped him to lie down again. His hand encircled her wrist as he fell back on the pillow. He was afraid if he didn't hold on, she'd disappear and leave him to spend his eternity in this dreary room alone. In his peripheral vision, Liam was vaguely aware of two doctors who remained near the wall. They wore white coats and were discussing something on a clipboard, but all he saw was Cora. Smiling down at him with love, her golden curls framing her face, she was like a bright ray of hope when he'd thought there was no hope left.

"How do you feel?" she asked again. "You've been asleep a long time."

"I feel…" He swallowed. His throat was swollen and sore, but his heart was light as a helium balloon bouncing against his rib cage. Cora was here. *With him.* He never thought he'd see her again. Whatever happened next, he was beyond grateful for this moment. Right now, her presence was a gift, and he felt as though he could fly. "Everything."

She brushed the hair back from his heated face with cool, gentle fingers. "Is that a good thing?"

"You're here with me," he said, as if that was all the explanation he needed. "It's the best thing."

Cora leaned down and pressed a kiss to his forehead. The achingly familiar scents of lavender and warm vanilla and sunshine surrounded him, and though her kiss was sweet, he was suddenly greedy and wanted so much more. It was always this way with her. He could never get enough, especially now that this could be their last moments together. Cora was his anchor in this storm of uncertainty, and he needed her close. Tugging on her wrist, he tried to drag her onto the bed with him, but she pulled away. "You need to rest, Liam."

His surly growl made her laugh, but he was dead serious. "What I need is you in this bed with me. Where you belong."

Her face turned a lovely shade of pink as she glanced at the two medical professionals in the corner. Then she looked back at him with that trademark steely determination he recognized. Cora was about to put her foot down, and nothing under the sun was going to change her mind. "I'm afraid that will have to wait."

"Mmm." Challenge accepted. Still gripping her hand, Liam brushed his thumb lightly over the pulse of her wrist, giving her a smoldering look that deepened the pink in her cheeks. "We'll see." He could be just as stubborn as her when it came to something important. And right now, nothing was more important than having her in his arms. "Come, let me hold you, *macushla*," he coaxed. Without breaking eye contact, he lifted her hand to press an intimate kiss in the center of her palm. Cora's breath hitched, and her cerulean eyes darkened with desire. She licked her lips and seemed to be struggling with her resolve. Liam gave her a wicked smile. He loved to see her flustered like this, especially when it meant he was about to get what he wanted. "You wouldn't deny a wounded man on his sickbed, would you?"

Cora's spine snapped straight. *Bollocks!* He'd gone too far. She pulled her hand from his. "I'm afraid I would, especially when your recovery is priority one. The doctor said you'll need another week of rest before you can get up or exert yourself. In case you've forgotten, you were shot."

Liam blinked. He *had* been shot. Frowning down at himself, he noticed a needle in his hand with a tube connected to a bag of clear fluid on a pole near his bed. Someone had draped him in a shapeless blue gown, and he could feel the tightly packed bandages on his side beneath the flimsy cotton fabric. "Why aren't I in more pain?"

"That'd be the excellent drugs you're getting," Cora said. "You had to undergo an operation when you got here a week ago, but thankfully the bullet didn't hit any major organs. You were very lucky, Liam."

His head began to spin. "Did you just say...a week ago?" Surely, she was mistaken.

Cora worried her bottom lip with her teeth. Liam studied her, realizing his happiness at seeing her had eclipsed a few things he should've noticed sooner. There were dark circles under her eyes, and her mouth was taut from strain. In rumpled clothes, with her hair piled onto her head in a haphazard fashion, she looked as though she hadn't slept in days. She was downright exhausted. That was likely why she'd gotten her days mixed up.

"You had me scared to death, Liam," she said shakily. "I was so afraid you wouldn't make it to the hospital, but you somehow managed to hold on. Then, when you slipped into the coma after surgery, I thought you'd never wake up. You've been out for seven days. The doctors said it's not typical, but sometimes it happens to people who've suffered a traumatic event."

"Wait." Alarm spiked in his veins as he tried to assimilate what she was saying. When he'd made the decision to help go after Boyd, he'd gone into those caves knowing that his time was running out. He had barely any days to spare, and he'd already made peace with that when the angels gave him the grace period so he could try to do some good before he left forever. But now... If he'd truly lost a full week's worth of time in the hospital, then he shouldn't be here at all. "Cora, what day is it?"

"Thursday. Why?"

"No." He clenched her hand. "What *month* is it?"

She glanced worriedly at the doctors who were still conversing quietly in the corner. "It's September, Liam. You were shot last week at the end of August."

He gaped at her in shock, then tried to catch the attention of the doctors to verify, but they were too engrossed in his chart on their blasted clipboard. "That can't be right." He struggled to sit up again, only this time he felt a sharp stab of pain in his side, and he winced.

"Don't," Cora said in alarm, pressing firmly on his shoulder. "I'll lift the bed. Just lie still."

Liam grimaced. He hated lying still, but his weak body seemed perfectly content to play the invalid, and there was nothing he could do about it.

Cora pressed a button on the side of the hospital bed, and it rose a few inches. Then she clasped his free hand in both of hers. "A lot has happened in the last week," she said reassuringly. "It's normal for you to feel disoriented. Just give yourself some time to heal."

Before Liam could answer, Cora's friend Suzette breezed into the room, followed by Officer Rob Hopper. Suzette was holding his hand, and in her other, she held a strange bouquet of candy bars on sticks. They were arranged in colorful tissue paper in a glass vase with a big bow.

"Hallelujah! He's awake," Suzette said, strolling closer on a cloud of spicy perfume. "The scary nurse out there said you weren't supposed to have more than one visitor at a time, but Rob flashed his badge and said a bunch of police stuff, so here we are. Can you believe she thought I was a cop?" In a bright green dress with jingling silver bracelets and her red hair floating around her head, Suzette looked more like an oversized Christmas elf. "Liam, you freaked us all out. Cora's been a basket case, sitting here day after day, refusing to go home and rest. She barely ate. Barely slept. I've never seen my best friend so miserable. If you weren't already hurt, I'd punch you for that." In spite of her threatening words, her smile was bright as a sunbeam when Rob Hopper looped his arm around her shoulders. The man looked happier than Liam had ever seen him. He was clearly smitten with Suzette. If he were one of those cartoon characters Liam had seen on TV, he'd be floating after her with hearts in his eyes.

"Here." Suzette plunked the vase of candy bars on the bedside table. "Rob said to get you flowers, but I knew you'd eventually wake up, and when you did, you'd be hungry. Figured this was more your speed."

"You figured right." Liam eyed the king-sized bits of heaven in their glossy, colorful wrappers. If the world was filled with toil and strife, then chocolate, in his opinion, helped balance everything out. For some bizarre reason, the sight of that candy bouquet cemented the fact that he was still *here*, in this world. But why? How?

A young woman poked her head in the doorway. "Excuse me, Officers. The press is here again. Do you want to deal with them, or should I try sending them away? Last time they lingered outside for hours."

Cora glanced at Rob, resigned. "Let's go talk to them. Between the two of us, we should be able to appease them this time." To Liam, she said sternly, "Rest. I'll be back before you know it."

Suzette waited until they were gone before settling into the nearest chair. Crossing her arms, she pierced him with a hard look. "So."

Uh-oh. Liam recognized that look on a woman. Suzette had a bone to pick with him. He only hoped his bones would remain intact when she was finished.

Then she said the universal phrase that had men quaking in their boots since the beginning of time. "We need to talk."

He nodded dutifully, which was the only acceptable answer.

"I love Cora like a sister," she said. "And as happy as I am to see you're on the mend, I still want to wring your neck a little bit."

He couldn't blame her, especially after the conversation they'd had at the bar when he'd lied about his feelings for Cora.

"I've never seen her so broken up over someone before." Suzette rose from the chair and began pacing the room. The heels of her knee-high boots clicked loudly on the tiled floor, hammering her words home. "I told her everything you said to me. That you weren't into her, and you didn't want to be tied down because there were too many fish in the sea."

Liam barely managed to hold back a groan. He wasn't proud of that excuse. "Suzette, that was—"

"Cora was beyond upset." The irate redhead continued as if she hadn't heard him. "Even though she pretended not to care, I could see right through her. She was really broken up about it."

Liam flinched, hating that his callous words had hurt the woman he loved. "I shouldn't have—"

"How could I *not* tell her?" Suzette blurted, as if she needed to argue her point. "Even though I knew it would hurt, it's my job as her best friend to look out for her. She and I go way back, way before you came along." Still pacing, she threw Liam a fiery look, and he nodded solemnly. What she said wasn't exactly true, but he knew better than to stoke a flame into a raging inferno if he could help it. "I couldn't let her throw her heart away to some big walking cliché." She gestured wildly to him, her silver bracelets jangling. "So, I told her you weren't worth it."

"I know, but—"

"And against all better judgment," she interrupted again, throwing her hands in the air, "she went and fell for you, anyway."

Liam blew out a frustrated breath. He knew Suzette was passionate about protecting Cora, but she kept steamrolling over all his attempts to speak. Either she was blatantly ignoring him, or she was too wrapped up in her thoughts to realize it. Maybe it was a little of both.

"Cora is head over heels, one hundred percent crazy for you," Suzette admitted grudgingly. "I've never seen her like this. She's always been levelheaded and responsible when it came to guys, but not this time. I mean, yeah. I get the whole dark and sexy thing you've got going for you, but still. The stuff you told me that night at the bar? How you had other multiple women on the hook, and you wanted to keep your options open? That trumps all hotness, as far as I'm concerned."

Liam pressed the heels of his hands over his eyes, cursing himself for the stupid things he'd said back then. "All right, listen—"

"So, what does this mean, going forward? Well, I'll tell you. From now on—"

"For the love of all that is holy, woman," he bellowed. "Will you let me speak?"

Suzette looked surprised at his sudden outburst. Then she gave him a mulish look as if she was undecided on the matter. "Fine. What?"

"Here's the God's honest truth of the matter." Liam enunciated every word, so there would be no confusion. "I love her. With every fiber of my blasted heart, I love Cora McLeod, and that will never change. I will go on loving her until the oceans run dry and the sun burns out and all the stars fall from the bloody sky. And maybe that makes me sound like 'a big walking cliché,' but I don't care. It's the reality. All that shite I said at the bar? It was just my woeful attempt at creating a smoke screen so you wouldn't see the truth. I didn't feel I deserved her. Hell, I still don't." He broke off miserably, glaring down at his blunt, calloused hands. The hands of a poor farmer. A thieving peasant. Not a refined gentleman who would deserve someone like Cora.

Suzette studied him for a long moment. "What's with the Irish brogue? Yours just kicked up about a hundred notches."

Liam waved a hand. "It does that on occasion."

She cocked her head. "Why?"

Damn and blast. The woman was wrecking his head. Did she not just hear him declare his undying love for her best friend? When Suzette didn't look like she was going to let the matter of his accent go, he added, "It sometimes happens when I feel strongly about something. When I get…emotional."

She nodded and sucked her lips between her teeth. Even though she'd wrestled her expression into a no-nonsense, stern librarian look, he didn't miss the way her hazel eyes went all soft at his revelation. Maybe he'd get out of this unscathed, after all. She jerked her chin at him and said, "Go on."

Liam heaved a sigh. "I thought if Cora believed I didn't love her, then she would be free to choose a better man. I just wanted her to be happy, even if it meant without me. You were right when you said I don't deserve her. I've always known I was unworthy. Cora deserves only the best of everything in life, and I wanted that for her. But she chose to love me, anyway. So now, here I am. I don't know why, and I don't know how it's come to this, but I'm not fool enough to squander this gift. Because that's what her love is—a precious gift. And for however long this lasts, I'm going to do everything in my power to make her happy. Simple as that." Only it wasn't simple at all. He ran his fingers through his hair, utterly confused about what he was still doing in this world.

Suzette's mouth had fallen open. After a few moments of stunned silence, she said gently, "You love her so much… You

were willing to let her go." It wasn't a question; it was a revelation.

"Aye." He let his head fall back on the pillow. Granted, his recent gunshot wound didn't kill him, but this conversation surely
would if it continued much longer. He wasn't used to baring
his soul and talking about his feelings on demand, but Suzette
was important to Cora, so Liam had to be straight with her. As
annoying as it was to be interrogated while lying prone in a
hospital bed with a hole in his side, he rather admired Suzette's
warrior spirit when it came to protecting the woman he loved.

"Okay, then." Suzette nodded abruptly. "Cora loves you, and
you love her back, so that's that."

Liam gave her a dubious look. Surely it couldn't be that easy.
Two minutes ago, she'd been ready to tear into him like an
angry lioness defending her cub.

"What?" Suzette asked with a shrug. "Far be it from me to
stand in the way of true love, and I can see now that you're just
as crazy in love as she is. *But.*" She held up a finger in warning. Ah, there it was. He knew that she-cat was still lurking in
the background. Suzette was fiercely loyal to Cora, which was
a good thing. She was a worthy friend. "I've still got my eye
on you, Liam O'Connor. One false move, and you'll have to
deal with me."

He gave her the only acceptable answer a man could give
when a woman stood over his sickbed, glaring at him like a
Valkyrie sharpening her swords. "I understand."

Suzette gave a perfunctory nod. "Good talk." Then she left
the room, her heels click-clacking down the hall.

Liam blew out a breath. He was glad they'd cleared that up,
but he was far from comfortable. The dull ache in his side was
becoming more pronounced, and a headache was brewing. He
felt like a mighty plow horse was dancing a jig inside his skull.

Cora had told him to rest, but there were too many unanswered questions knocking around in his head. He let out a groan of frustration. Like hell he'd just lie there resting. He'd never been one to sit idly, and wounded or not, he wasn't going to start now. Grimacing, he tried again to pull himself to a sitting position. If he could just disconnect the needle in his hand, then swing his legs over the edge of the bed, he could go looking for clothes, and then maybe answers, instead of lying around like some inva—

"But you *are* an invalid," a stern, familiar voice said. Startled, Liam turned his attention to the doctors who'd been standing in the corner all along. How could he have forgotten they were there? Even Suzette had paid them no mind when she'd been tearing into him.

The short doctor had blond curly hair and a round, cherubic face. He was holding a clipboard. The taller, dark-haired doctor was smiling down at Liam, radiating happiness. With a start, Liam realized who they were.

"S-Samael?" he sputtered in disbelief. "Agon?" He watched as the two angels dropped their mortal disguises and appeared like they always did—in flowing robes with an ethereal, glowing light surrounding them. "I don't understand. I thought my three months were over, and I was supposed to be gone forever. What am I still doing here?"

"That is the question, Liam O'Connor. And for once, we will give you the simple answer." Samael floated forward and tapped the clipboard with his hand. Then he slipped it into a pocket of mist, and fixed his unnerving, ancient gaze on Liam. "Though it's not actually that simple. It seems there's been a strange turn of events."

"Indeed," Agon said brightly. "In all the years I've been working at the Department of Destiny, I've yet to witness something like this. It's quite extraordinary, really. So many different factors coming together in such a serendipitous way, and with such a fortuitous outcome. It's moments like this that remind me what an exquisite honor it is to witness the glorious resilience of the human spirit. Your astounding ability to persevere and learn and grow, even in the face of seemingly insurmountable odds."

Liam stared back and forth between the angels, biting his tongue before he could point out they were being as cryptic as ever. "I don't understand."

"What my colleague means," Samael said smoothly, "is that you've miraculously managed to skip over the warp and weft of your old destiny, and you've been woven into a new one. The path before you now has the same outcome that should've happened between Cora and Finn, only this time—"

"It's you!" Agon clapped his hands, unable to contain his happiness. "You can stay and live your life with Cora, as you've always wanted."

The tendril of desperate hope that had been winding around Liam's heart ever since he awoke and saw Cora's face suddenly burst into full bloom. His breath sawed in and out of his chest as he glanced back and forth between the two angels. "How can this be possible?"

"The sin you committed in your former life was based on selfishness, and your desire to steal that which did not belong to you," Samael said. "Even after you were given a chance to make things right, you struggled with your old set of values, unable to see past your own desires. But in your final moments, we witnessed a change in you so profound it caused you to sacrifice yourself—not to save Cora, a loved one whose life directly mattered to you, but to save a man you felt was worthy of the love you didn't deserve. Without stopping to think, your instinctive reaction was to jump in front of that weapon to save

Finley Walsh. Your reasons had nothing to do with your own desires or well-being. It was your heartfelt display of utter selflessness that turned the tide and helped alter the course of your destiny. Choosing to save Finn's life was a powerful statement, Liam O'Connor, though you didn't realize you were making it. What you did had no ulterior motive other than you truly wanted to save an honorable man who deserved more."

Liam was shocked down to the core. "I didn't expect—"

"Of course you didn't," Samael said. "That's why it counted."

"So, you're saying just because I committed a selfless act of kindness in my last moments, I've changed fate? That's all it took?" It seemed almost too easy. It was hard to believe that Agon had never witnessed this type of thing before in all the centuries—or however long—he'd been observing human nature. People grew and changed all the time. There was no way Liam was the only person who'd ever sacrificed themselves for someone else at the last moment.

"No, that's not all. It definitely worked in your favor, but it takes much more than that to alter fate." Samael glanced at Agon, and Liam could tell they were having a silent conversation. He wondered what could possibly have happened to shift the scales so much in his favor. Then Samael tilted his face up with a sigh. His wings stretched out, then folded shut in a decisive snap. "You had an advocate," he finally admitted. "Someone who pleaded most convincingly to spare your life."

"Who?" Liam asked helplessly. He could think of no one who cared enough to—

"Finley Walsh, of course," Samael said.

Liam stared blankly at the two angels. "He fell over the railing..."

"And died? Yes. The tumble he took from the top of Providence Falls released his soul from his mortal body."

"He didn't deserve that," Liam whispered, filled with remorse that he hadn't been able to save him. "He was a much better man than I could ever hope to be."

"Finley Walsh was indeed an exceptional human being. For this reason, he was given the rather surprising choice to move on toward his just reward, or to remain within our ranks and help us watch over humanity. He has certain personality traits that would make him ideal for such a role."

"Knowing Finn, he agreed to help," Liam said. There was no question in his mind. Even in the afterlife, Finn would jump at the chance to help others and see that justice was served. Liam was suddenly, fiercely proud of the man, and a little awestruck. He was grateful he'd had the chance to truly know Finn, even for a short while.

"You are correct," Samael said. "He did agree to join our ranks. But when he stood before us in the Chamber of Judgment, he begged a favor in return. Something that we didn't expect. When we told Finn how your and Cora's destinies had been intertwined with his, and how you'd tried and failed to right the wrongs you committed in the past, Finn pleaded for your soul. *Yours*, Liam O'Connor. Quite phenomenal, really. It was his single request that ultimately saved you. Finn was steadfast and resolute in his conviction that you and Cora belonged together. He stood testament to your love for each other and swore allegiance to serve mankind to the best of his ability if we would grant you the life he'd never have."

Grief punched Liam hard, even as an infinite well of gratitude began swelling from somewhere deep inside him. It filled up all the cold, empty places, rising so high it clogged his throat and made it difficult to speak. "I can't believe he'd do that for me."

Samael inclined his head. "As we said, Finley Walsh is an exceptional being."

"Thank you," Liam said in a choked whisper.

"Though your gratitude is noted, it wasn't up to us. The ultimate decision came from much higher up. We're just the messengers, after all. Even we don't know the mysteries involved in reweaving a person's destiny. But somehow, yours and Cora's have been realigned. Your fate is now intertwined, and because Finn pleaded so convincingly, you'll go on to carry out the original plan in his place."

"The original plan," Liam whispered. Then he remembered why it was so important. "What about the child they were supposed to have? The one who would someday help the world?"

"You needn't worry about that," Samael said with a wave of his hand. "She will come along in due time, and someday fulfill her role as expected."

"She?" Liam's eyes flew open wide, his thoughts spinning with the possibility of someday having a little girl with the woman of his dreams. He could just imagine a tiny whirlwind running around with golden ringlets and a gamine smile. Someone who looked just like her mother. He wanted that with Cora. A family. A future. He wanted it so much he practically shook with the knowledge that it was now a true possibility. "I don't... I have no words..."

Agon reached out and patted Liam fondly on the head. His touch was like a lightning bolt of pure, unfiltered joy. It radiated outward, filling every corner of Liam's soul until all he could feel were peace and happiness and an overwhelming sense that everything was right with the universe.

"I could live a thousand lifetimes and still never be able to thank you enough," Liam managed.

"Thank goodness it will not come to that," Samael exclaimed with an uncharacteristic chuckle. He and Agon began to shimmer and fade, both of them looking, for the very first time, like the benevolent, joyful messengers of light Liam had always imagined angels to be.

"Is this goodbye forever, then?" he said with sudden alarm, unwilling to let them go. He'd rather grown to like their strange presence in his life. What if he still needed their guidance? What if he messed up again? The sudden fear of failure gripped him in its steely teeth, and he trembled with the thought of ruining the beautiful life he'd been granted.

The angels paused, half-visible in the shimmering light.

"You will be just fine," Agon said kindly.

"You don't need us anymore," Samael added. "You now have the destiny you always wanted. Go, and be happy." They faded away in a shower of sparkling light until he sat alone in the empty room.

"I'll miss you," Liam whispered.

"Someday we'll meet again." Samael's voice echoed from far away until it disappeared, replaced by the occasional beep of the machine beside his bed and the faint sounds of the medical professionals going about their business.

Liam clenched fistfuls of the thin cotton blanket, overcome with mixed emotions. Loss. Elation. Sadness. Gratitude. Before he could dwell on all the angels had revealed, Cora stepped into the room. In her smiling face, Liam glimpsed their future, and suddenly he knew everything would be okay.

"Come here," he said, reaching for her.

She leaned over and kissed him, letting out a tiny squeak of protest when he pulled her onto the bed. The sharp lance of pain in his side was nothing compared to the feel of her beside him, where she belonged.

"Liam, you'll hurt yourself," she said, struggling to back away.

"Only if you keep fighting me," he said, grinning into her

neck as he breathed in the familiar scent of her. How he loved this woman. "Indulge me. Please."

"But your wound," she insisted, pushing against the pillow with both hands.

Liam refused to let her go. "It won't kill me to hold you for just a few minutes."

"It may not, but there's a drill sergeant of a nurse in the hallway out there who will. Have you seen her? Normally, I can hold my own, but she's got biceps to rival Bear's. Do you really want to get on her bad side?" Cora finally gave up and sank beside him, careful not to jostle his bandage.

"I can handle her." He nuzzled the soft skin on her neck.

"You overestimate your charm," she said primly, though her voice was tinged with humor, and she tilted her head to give Liam more access. "That nurse's sour disposition could curdle milk. I've been tiptoeing around her all week."

"I'll have her eating out of my hand like a wee lamb in no time," he said, chuckling at her dubious snort. He kissed the sensitive spot between the base of her neck and shoulder. Her soft sigh of pleasure sent a flare of heat spiraling through his body. "Let's get out of here. I need to take you home so I can do wicked things to you."

"Absolutely not." Cora squirmed and finally managed to slip off the bed. "As much as I like the sound of that, you're not going anywhere until the doctors say it's okay. You almost died."

He reached for her again. "Aye, and it will surely finish me off if I have to wait one minute longer to have you all to myself."

"Liam." Her eyes filled with sudden tears. "I thought I'd lost you."

He wanted to wrap his arms around her and tell her everything was going to be okay, but instead he settled for holding her hand. "You'll not be rid of me that easily, *macushla*. I'm afraid you're stuck with me from now on."

"For how long?" she asked in a tremulous voice.

"For as long as we both shall live." He squeezed her hand tightly to remind himself that she was really there, and this was real. "If you'll have me."

Cora's breath escaped in a whoosh, and her eyes flew wide. "What exactly—"

"Marry me," Liam said, just as a hatchet-faced nurse bustled into the room. The woman was built like a barrel with stocky arms and blunt features. Her default expression was a pinched frown as she began checking Liam's drip line along with the machine near the bedside. Cora hadn't been kidding when she said the woman was intimidating, but Liam couldn't bring himself to care. He was too intent on Cora's answer. Staring at her from underneath his lashes, he murmured, "Will you?"

Cora shifted uncomfortably, and a small fissure of alarm rippled down his spine. He couldn't lose her. Not after all they'd been through. Why was she hesitating? He swallowed hard and added, "Please?"

Shaking her head in disbelief, Cora leaned forward to whisper, "I can't believe you're asking me this *right now*." She tilted her head toward the nurse. "She can hear you."

Liam glanced at the dour-looking matron, then back at Cora. "I don't care if the entire world hears me. I'll shout my love from the rooftops. I'll tell anyone who'll listen for the rest of my life." He gave the nurse a roguish grin. "You don't mind, do you, lass?"

"Mmph," the nurse grumbled, though her razor-thin lips twitched.

"See?" Liam said to Cora, jerking his thumb in the direction of the woman. "She's overcome with happiness for us. Can't even find words to convey her joy."

With a scoff, the nurse's face cracked into something that may actually have passed for a smile, before she marched out of the room.

"She's only charmed because your Irish accent just got thicker," Cora said with a laugh. A rosy blush stained her cheeks. "You're crazy, Liam."

"For you, yes," he said with absolute sincerity, gripping her hand in his. "Please marry me, Cora. This isn't a snap decision on my part; it's not some whim based on oversentimentality or a confusion of emotion. I've loved you across time and oceans and continents. My soul was yours from the moment we met. I love you with everything that I am. So much that I ache when we're apart. I know I'll never be as good as you deserve, but I promise always to try. If you can find it in your heart to accept me, I will spend the rest of my life proving to you how very precious you are, and how grateful I am just to walk alongside you in this wild, wonderful world."

Cora was so still, the only movement was a tendril of hair that hung over her forehead. It fluttered with every exhalation as she stared at Liam in open astonishment.

"Please say yes." He watched her, waiting for her answer with his heart beating in his throat. Because there was a God, she didn't keep him waiting long.

Her lips curled into a soft smile. "Well, when you put it that way, how could I possibly refuse?"

Then they were holding each other and grinning and whispering sweet words that had the stodgy nurse rolling her eyes and the doctor chuckling to himself, but Cora and Liam were too filled with happiness to notice or care.

30

CORA SMOOTHED THE FOLDS OF HER SHIMMER-
ing white gown, marveling at the twists and turns her life had
taken over the past few months. Ever since Liam was released
from the hospital, the two of them had been inseparable. From
the Saturday afternoon when he'd knelt by the lake, held out
a ring, and gave her what was—in his words—"a right proper
proposal," to the whirlwind preparations for their intimate backyard wedding, Cora felt as though she'd tumbled head over heart
into a fairy tale.

After the ordeal at Providence Falls State Park, the town's
police officers had become a bit like local celebrities for a few
weeks. When word got out that Liam and Cora, two of the
same officers who helped bring down the corrupt police captain,
were in love and getting married, it had stirred the local media
into a frenzy. Though she could've done without the news in-
terviews, the morning show appearances, and the various other
town meet and greets, it had all been worth it because it led her
here, to this moment.

She stood before the mirror in the master bedroom of her

dream cottage, ready to marry the man she loved. It seemed almost too good to be true when the owner of the cottage turned out to be the spearhead of several community outreach programs, as well as one of the founders of the Teens in Action center. When the house went on the market and started a bidding war, the seller had chosen to let them have it at fair market value. Of course, Liam's decision to secretly donate large sums of money to the teen center over the past few months might've helped their cause. Apparently, the seller found out Liam was the anonymous donor and—paired with his and Cora's local celebrity status—it was a done deal.

"Just one more," Suzette said, pinning a delicate white flower into Cora's hair. Today she wore it loose, cascading in blond waves down her back, with the front section pulled back in soft curls to frame her face. A nature-inspired circlet of roses, leaves, and sprigs of fresh lavender sat lightly on the crown of her head.

Cora waited until Suzette put the final touches on her hair, then turned and gave her best friend an impulsive hug. "Thank you, Suze."

"No hugging!" Suzette said in alarm. "You can't touch anything or anyone until after the ceremony. We can't risk putting any of this perfection at risk." She waved both hands from the top of Cora's head to the tips of her sparkly strappy sandals.

Cora spun back toward the mirror with a laugh. Her silk wedding dress had an overlay of shimmering chiffon that swirled around her like sparkling mist.

"Wow," Suzette breathed, standing behind her in the sea green maid of honor dress they'd picked out together. "You've always been gorgeous, Cora, but today you are utterly divine." She sighed happily, her autumn-bright hair gleaming in its tasteful updo. "You look like a cross between a fairy princess and a forest nymph. Every man out there is going to lose it when they see you like this."

"Maybe not *every* man," Cora said, nudging Suzette with a knowing grin. "Rob Hopper only has eyes for you. I could ride down the aisle on the back of a woolly mammoth, naked like Lady Godiva, and Rob would still be too busy staring at you to notice."

"You might be right," Suzette said with a laugh. Her freckled cheeks grew pink in an uncharacteristic blush that Cora found so endearing she risked another hug, in spite of her friend's mumbled protests that she'd wrinkle her gown. Suzette and Rob were officially together now, and to Suzette's continual amazement, Rob was proving to be a sensitive, caring boyfriend. Cora had never seen Suzette so content in a relationship, and she was infinitely grateful that her dearest friend was finally with a man who appreciated what a wonderful person she was.

"Hey, you girls ready?" Hugh McLeod, Cora's father, knocked once on the door and poked his head in the room. His thick gray hair was combed neatly back from the stern face Cora knew and loved. "Holy smokes, hon," he exclaimed with admiration and fatherly pride. "*Look* at you. You are an absolute vision." Her father was never comfortable with emotional declarations, but Cora could tell he was overcome with emotion when he cleared his throat and added gruffly, "I wish your mother could see you now."

"Thanks, Dad." She reached up to touch the gold necklace with the rose pendant she always wore. Even though her mother had been gone from their lives for a long time, Cora felt certain she was with them in spirit right now. "I have a feeling she does."

Hugh's expression softened, and he smiled at Cora with glittering blue eyes that mirrored her own. "I think you might be right."

Cora followed Suzette and her father down the stairs to the backyard. Sweet, lilting music wafted through the air, melding with the rustle of leaves in the trees and the sound of the softly flowing brook that ran along the edge of the property. Rose petals were strewn over the grass leading toward an arched trellis bursting with a profusion of hothouse flowers and greenery. On either side of the aisle, chairs were filled with friends and loved ones who rose, beaming, when Cora appeared.

At the end of the aisle, Liam stood waiting for her. Tall and powerful, with broad shoulders and tousled dark hair, he was wickedly handsome in an exquisitely tailored suit and an open-collared shirt with no tie to hide the strong column of his neck. Cora gave him a tremulous smile when their gazes caught and held. He took one look at her, and his face momentarily blanked. Then a stunned smile played at the corners of his mouth, as if he couldn't believe his luck. Cora knew exactly how he felt.

When she came to stand beside him, he reached for her hand and whispered, "Tell me this is real, *macushla*, and you're truly mine." His grip was firm and almost too strong, as if he was afraid she'd disappear if he let her go.

"It's real. I'm yours," she answered, smiling. "And you're *mine.*"

Impulsively, Liam pulled her close and sealed the declaration with a kiss. Neither of them noticed the whispered laughter of their friends and family, or the gentle throat clearing of the wedding officiator, who stood nervously by as the groom broke protocol and kissed the bride *before* the wedding vows. Everything faded into the background because Cora and Liam were too caught up in the mysterious thrumming sensation that seemed to ricochet between them, tugging at their heartstrings and twining around their souls. Later, neither of them would be able to explain the momentous feeling in exact detail, only that they were overcome with the sheer *rightness* of it—the glorious, bone-deep certainty that they were together now, where they belonged, with their lives stretching out before them, shiny and new and glowing with possibilities.

Far above in a celestial chamber, two angels stood watching through a wall of mist. One held a clipboard, and the other was holding a white cat. With reverence and joyful anticipation, they bore witness to the precise moment when the threads of Cora's and Liam's destinies snapped together, weaving into a single strand that glowed so brightly its light would shine for centuries.

The cat began to purr.

The angels began to smile.

And time marched on, proving once again that even in the face of all odds, love would prevail.

EPILOGUE

===

Fifteen years later…

"CAPTAIN CORA, WE'RE GOING TO BE LATE." LIAM dropped a kiss on his beautiful wife's head as she tried to wrestle her curls into a tight bun at the nape of her neck.

Cora was seated at the large vanity table in the master bedroom of their home. They'd done some remodeling over the years, expanding one of the bedrooms into a nursery when their daughter was born—and later adding a playroom when their son came along. As the children grew, so did the floor plan, but Cora and Liam chose to keep the master bedroom exactly as it had been on the day they got married. With Cora's promotion to police captain, and Liam's successful launch of a nonprofit organization to help the poor, they'd had more than enough money to move into a bigger, newer house if they'd preferred. But the cottage on the edge of town had become a haven that defined them all, a place where love and happy traditions had seeped into the walls so deep none of them could imagine living anywhere else.

"It's just so messy and wild," Cora said, hastily dragging a comb through her mass of curls. Her golden hair was streaked with a few strands of silver now, and the corners of her blue eyes had faint smile lines from years filled with sunshine and laughter. To Liam O'Connor, she had never looked more beautiful.

"Mmm, I like it messy and wild." He lowered his head to nuzzle the crook of her neck, breathing in the sweet scent of her skin with a sound of pure masculine appreciation that ended on a rumble like a great jungle cat, ready to pounce.

"Oh, no," Cora said with a laugh, waving him away. "Don't start with me, Mr. O'Connor, or we'll never get out the door." Liam didn't see a problem with that, and opened his mouth to tell her so, when a holler came from downstairs.

"Mom, Dad! We're going to be late for the science fair." Their daughter's voice was filled with preteen angst.

"Is your brother ready?" Liam called.

"Yes, he's already outside." She let out an exaggerated groan and added, "And now he's climbing a tree."

Liam grinned. He could just imagine their daughter pacing back and forth near the front door in her denim overalls and red Converse high-tops. Her tawny blond hair was probably swept into its usual messy bun, complete with the pencil she always stuck there "just in case." At only twelve, she was already exhibiting an aptitude for complex math and physics, often stopping to scribble random notes whenever inspiration struck. She also had a deep love of nature and earth science and could usually be found outside teaching her little brother about the things she was learning.

"We'll be right down," Cora called. Leaving her hair loose, she stood from the vanity and threw Liam an exasperated smile. "I don't know why she gets so nervous. She wins first place at the science fair every year."

Cora swept from the room, and Liam began to follow when he heard a familiar scratching sound behind him. He glanced back and saw their old white cat, Angel, perched on the ledge outside, pawing at the window. Liam walked over and slid the window up to let him in.

The cat gingerly stepped over the sill, yawning and stretching like he had all the time in the world. And maybe he did, Liam mused. He often reminded himself that cats had nine lives, preferring not to dwell on the fact that Angel no longer jumped to the top of the bookcases in the family room like he used to. He also moved a lot slower and slept a lot longer. Liam didn't know exactly how old Angel was, but it was clear the cat was in the twilight of his life.

"Where've you been, old friend?" Liam gently scratched him between the ears. Lately, Angel had been disappearing for longer stretches of time. The family had begun leaving food and water outside on the back porch every day, since Angel didn't always come home for dinner. Neither Cora nor Liam had the heart to keep him locked inside the house, both accepting that Angel was a free spirit and always happiest when he could roam where he pleased.

Angel began to purr, nudging Liam with his cold, wet nose.

Liam smoothed his hand down the cat's back. A soft, downy feather came loose from Angel's fur. It floated to the floor, sparkling in a beam of sunlight. This wasn't the first time Liam had pulled downy bits of fluff from his coat. It seemed to be happening more often in the past year, and Liam suspected he knew exactly where Angel was spending more of his time. One of these days, Liam was afraid the cat would straddle the line between this world and the next and choose to stay on the other side.

"Don't leave us yet, old man," Liam pleaded softly, giving the cat an affectionate pat. A pang of sadness filled him at the thought of Angel moving on. It seemed the universe—in all its perfection and glory—had made a vast mistake when it granted beloved pets much shorter life spans than humans. From the very first day Liam had come to Providence Falls, Cora's cat had been a loyal friend to him. Over the years, Liam had grown so fond of the feisty feline he couldn't imagine life without him. Angel had given him unconditional acceptance even back when Liam had been a self-serving rogue who didn't deserve it. Not only that, the cat had seen and interacted with the angels. Liam felt as if they were connected on an even deeper level because of that shared experience. Losing his beloved friend would feel like losing a piece of himself.

Angel meowed in understanding, which drew Liam from his melancholy thoughts. Lifting him from the windowsill, Liam gently placed him on the edge of the bed. The cat sank into the homespun quilt like a dollop of marshmallow fluff.

"You tell those meddling angels you're still doing good work down here, and we need you," Liam said. "*I* need you."

Angel's whiskers twitched. Then, in perfectly aloof cat fashion, he began grooming himself. Liam recognized when he was being dismissed, but he didn't take it personally. He'd long ago accepted the fact that cats existed on a higher plane than humans, and he was fairly certain Angel had loftier things to worry about.

Downstairs, the front door flew open and a younger child's high-pitched voice shouted excitedly, "Mom! Dad! I found a kitten stuck in the tree outside, and I rescued him. Look!" Liam could hear his son's excited chatter rising in crescendo with his daughter's squeals of delight. Cora and the kids began talking over each other in a jumble of exclamations.

"Oh, how sweet."

"He looks just like a miniature Angel."

"Please, can we keep him?"

"He's all alone and needs us!"

Liam glanced suspiciously at Angel, who was calmly licking a paw as if everything was going according to some grand plan. Not liking the direction this was heading, Liam crouched down until he was nose to nose with the scheming feline. "I see what's going on here, cat. And I want you to know, *I object*. Do you hear me? No other mangy beast can take your place. So, if you're thinking of leaving us with a wee, mewling ball of fluff to help soften the blow? It won't work."

Angel settled on the king-sized quilt, tucking his paws and staring at Liam through half-closed eyes like a wise sphinx. A soft purr began rumbling in his chest. It was the feline equivalent of a benevolent pat on the head, and Liam felt like he was being placated by an elderly mentor. He didn't like it one bit.

"Now, you listen here—" Liam began.

"Dad," his son interrupted from the bottom of the stairs. "Mom says we have to put up Lost Kitten ads in the neighborhood, but if no one answers, we get to keep him!"

Liam narrowed his eyes at the still purring cat. "No one's going to answer those ads, are they?"

Angel glanced away, ignoring him, which was answer enough.

Liam opened his mouth to argue further, but Cora called up the stairs, reminding him it was time to leave. He stood and lifted his chin, stubbornly pointing a finger at the cat. "This conversation is not over."

Then he hurried downstairs to join his family, his own voice melding with theirs in a chorus of boisterous exclamations and good-natured teasing as they all walked into the sunshine together.

Many years into the future...

"Look at her go," Agon said proudly as he sank into the cushioned lounge chair. "Liam and Cora's daughter has exceeded all our expectations."

"Did you ever doubt it?" Samael asked from the matching recliner beside him. They were sitting in the Chamber of Judgment, now a rather inviting place awash in colorful works of art, brightly patterned rugs, and even an elevated cushion in the corner for their four-legged friend. Over the years, Samael had begrudgingly agreed there was no harm in adding a few creature comforts to the place, and Agon had proceeded with joyful abandon. It was such an improvement to the original stark chamber that others who worked in their division had begun to follow suit. Though Agon knew Samael would never admit it, he suspected it gave his colleague no small amount of satisfaction to know they'd started a trend at the Department of Destiny.

Now they watched through a wall of mist as a lovely woman with tawny curls and dark, soulful eyes received a prestigious award for her contribution to the discovery of cold fusion.

"I always had faith in our rogue," Agon said with a satisfied sigh. "And now there will be more peace and less strife in the world. A happily-ever-after, if ever there was one."

Samael gave him the side-eye. "You've been reading those fanciful books again, haven't you?"

"I've grown quite fond of them," Agon admitted. "Every story is a window into the beauty of the human spirit. I do believe mankind would be a lot better off if every person would slow down once in a while and embrace the power of a good book. Especially the ones that prove love conquers all."

Samael pursed his lips and shook his head. He feigned disinterest, but Agon just smiled, knowing it was only a matter of time before he won his stoic colleague over.

When the image on the wall faded away, Samael rose from his chair and pulled his clipboard from a pocket of mist. As always with the small blond angel, it was time to get back to business. "Hmm," he said, glancing at the next person on the list. "This should be interesting." With a wave of his hand, a new scene unfolded on the misty wall.

Against a backdrop of silvery stars, a warrior angel hovered above a city at night. Gold-tipped black wings sprang from his broad, muscular shoulders, and across his back, inked in scrolling Latin font, was the phrase FIAT JUSTITIA RUAT CAELUM.

"Such a fine warrior, our Finley Walsh," Agon said with admiration. "He's been an outstanding addition to the Department of Justice. I heard they were bestowing the highest honor on him for all the good work he's done. Of course," he added with a chuckle, "he might not see it that way."

"Perhaps not at first," Samael agreed.

Together, they watched as Finn swooped into an alley under the cover of night. He appeared to be tracking someone inside an art gallery on one of the darkened city streets.

"When is he scheduled to meet his true love?" Agon asked.

Samael glanced at his clipboard just as an earsplitting burglar alarm wailed from inside the gallery walls. "Right now."

Suddenly, an old woman with wobbling jowls and graying hair burst through the doors, hollering that they'd just been robbed.

Agon cocked his head. "She seems a bit old for Finn, but I suppose love works in—"

"Not her," Samael said. *"Her."* He pointed to the lithe, curvy figure of a woman in black leather springing over a chain-link fence behind the gallery. She paused to adjust a stolen canvas in a satchel strapped to her back, then disappeared into the night.

"The *thief*?" Agon blinked in surprise, then murmured, "Our fine, upstanding Finley Walsh and...a cat burglar." He was both mystified and charmed.

Through the wall of mist, they watched as Finn floated silently onto a rooftop, folding his impressive wings. They snapped